About the Author

Sonia Day spent twenty years as a gardening columnist for the *Toronto Star*. She is the author of eight previous books including the best seller, *Incredible Edibles: 43 Fun Things to Grow in the City.* She lives in a small town in Ontario, Canada but visits Mexico frequently. This is her second novel. Visit soniaday.com

The Mexico Lunch Party
A Sisters of the Soil Novel. With Recipes

Sonia Day

The Mexico Lunch Party
A Sisters of the Soil Novel. With Recipes

Olympia Publishers
London

www.olympiapublishers.com
OLYMPIA PAPERBACK EDITION

A CIP catalogue record for this title is
available from the British Library.

ISBN: 978-1-80074-161-4

This is a work of fiction.
Names, characters, places and incidents originate from the writer's
imagination. Any resemblance to actual persons, living or dead, is
purely coincidental.

First Published in 2022

Olympia Publishers
Tallis House
2 Tallis Street
London
EC4Y 0AB
Printed in Great Britain

For all the wonderful women I know, with thanks for the lovely lunches

"Ask not what you can do for your country. Ask what's for lunch."

— *Orson Welles*

Beginnings
New York, 26th August, 2006

Something amazing is happening in a tropical greenhouse at Brooklyn Botanical Garden. No one who works there can quite believe it. A peculiar plant called the Corpse Flower has suddenly, for reasons known only to itself, started to send up a flower stalk.

Huge excitement engulfs the Garden, because this promises to be no ordinary flower. The salaciously-named *Amorphophallus Titanum* (which means 'Misshapen Penis of Titanic Proportions' in Latin) produces the largest flower ever seen on this planet — wrapped around a stalk that will soar skywards, as high as ten feet, in only forty-eight hours. Then monstrous, skirt-like petals will unfurl, followed by a nose-clogging stench like rotting flesh (hence its nickname) that aims to attract pollinating flies. Finally, having made a death-defying thrust at perpetuating the *A. Titanum* species, this extraordinary erection will collapse in a messy heap, spent, never to rise again.

Worthy of a horror movie, for sure. But also, big news in the botanical world because Corpse Flowers rarely, if ever, bloom in captivity. Indeed, this is the first time that a specimen has deigned to put on a penile performance in New York for over seventy years.

Thus, the Garden's PR department, with an eye to the

publicity value of their 'Baby' (the plant's incongruous nickname), hastily sends out a news release inviting media to come and witness this once-in-a-lifetime event. And somewhat to their surprise, dozens of eager gawkers drop everything to rush to New York.

They come from all over: botanists, horticultural experts, plant nerds, writers on gardening for newspapers, magazines, social media and blogs, TV and radio talk show hosts. Baby's burgeoning stalk even stirs international interest. A few curious folks show up from Canada, the U.K., France, the Netherlands, even China.

These observers sit, fascinated, glued to folding chairs set up around the Corpse Flower for hours at a stretch, not wanting to miss one moment of a phenomenon that's widely regarded as the Holy Grail of Horticulture. And out of this intense, shared experience, a particular kind of friendship blossoms. Eight of the attendees — all older women from different backgrounds, yet united by an enthusiastic, uncompetitive and genuine passion for plants — are so delighted to discover like-minded souls that they agree to stay in touch and meet again.

And they do.

The women begin by exchanging emails about everything from spotting the first snowdrops of spring in their gardens, to tracking down a new, rare species of tree peony. As the bond deepens, they hold their first 'Titan Reunion' at the Connecticut home of Abby Holt, who writes a gardening column for her local newspaper. Three years later they gather again in Houston, Texas, following an invitation by Lola Honeybone, editor of *Our Southern Gardens*. Then Nathalie Delannoux, author of several books on flowers, caps that with a call to meet up again at her home in a town on the river Seine, outside Paris. On each occasion, the women share a spectacular lunch, to which they all contribute something. They devote the entire day to drinking wine, eating far too much, laughing a lot, reminiscing about the unforgettable time in New York when they formed this bond and updating each other on their lives, their gardens and their new plant discoveries. The ritual of a Titan Reunion becomes, in all their minds, a welcome break from the pressures of an increasingly chaotic world. They pledge to carry on meeting every three or four years, if they can.

The members of the group are Abby, Tensie, Rhodo, Hannah, Lola, Mieke, Nathalie and Jing-Jing.

They call themselves the Sisters of the Soil.

The Invitation

Chapter 1

Darien, Connecticut, USA, 14th January, 2017

ABBY

"Who'd have thought? Who'd have thought that — at my age — I'd be doing this?"

Then, after a pause: "Am I nuts?"

Abby Holt, age sixty: status: just retired librarian and freelance writer, enthusiastic amateur cook, lover of gardening, asked the questions out loud. Hesitantly, with a hint of defiance, as if she hoped someone out there would affirm that she was doing the right thing. Then she chuckled and chided herself for being foolish, because there was no one around to hear her. Not a soul. The room — indeed the entire house — was empty. All that remained of the life she was about to abandon was the old leather armchair, horsehair stuffing leaking out, that she sat on, and three big, black, plastic garbage bags leaning against the back door of the kitchen. The bags she had filled to the brim with her winter clothes — coats, gloves, scarves, hats, boots, a slew of practical pants, skirts and tops she wore to work in the library. She'd even stuffed in her treasured hand-knitted Irish wool sweater, bought during a vacation in County Kerry decades ago. But no matter. Parting isn't simply sweet sorrow. It also calls for a measure of ruthlessness. She wouldn't need that thick sweater at her destination. The decision made, she was impatient to see it go.

She checked her watch. Just after two-thirty. She sighed and fidgeted in the chair. A guy from the thrift store in Darien was supposed to be on his way in a minivan to pick up the bags — and the chair — but he hadn't shown up yet. She would call the place on her cellphone if nothing happened soon. Better not miss getting a cab to the commuter train into Grand Central, the one that left Darien at twenty to six on the dot. She'd sold her car. And she was spending just one more night in the Lower East Side digs of daughter Hollis and her partner, Jaz, where her two lightweight travel bags — containing only summer clothes — were already standing in their cramped hallway. She had debated staying longer, treating them both to a farewell lunch at a high-end restaurant in Manhattan, perhaps Daniel on East 65th, where she and Larry used to celebrate their anniversary. But Hollis, with the aversion to risk of her generation, didn't approve of what Abby was doing and things between them had become strained ever since she broke the news of her decision to leave. Abby wasn't wild about Jaz, either. A fashion consultant, Jaz had once told Abby, with a condescending laugh and a toss of her self-important long, straight black hair, to stop 'dressing like a librarian'. Besides, the pair had become vegans. If she were to order her fave dessert at Daniel, their *Iles Flottante*, a caramel-soaked confection sitting atop a sea of vanilla custard, the girls would promptly roll their eyes at each other and start going on about the evils of sugar and dairy in the Western diet. She'd have wound up feeling fat, self-indulgent and awkward with every spoonful, while they sat watching, amused disdain on their young faces. So forget it. Tomorrow, after pretending to like almond milk in her coffee and the unappetising, green smoothie made with kale and God-knows-what, that Hollis would undoubtedly grind up in their blender for her breakfast, she intended heading out early to JFK. Her flight departed at noon. And if she waited too long for the minivan, all her plans, those plans carefully formulated over the past few months, would go awry.

While she listened for the sound of the minivan, what she said out loud startled her. Her voice sounded uncomfortably loud and unnatural, kind of eerie, bouncing off the bare walls of the house — this rambling three-storey house (four bedrooms, one in the attic, two baths, a big kitchen, a study each for her and Larry, and a sprawling living/dining room) built from ochre brick, back in the 1930s in Arts and Crafts style, with a sloping, slate roof which mostly faced north and sprouted bright green moss in between the tile cracks, and where the mullioned windows always leaked and where she could quite never banish the smell of sweaty gym socks from the basement. This imposing residence in an upscale neighbourhood of Darien that had been her home for some thirty years, but no longer was.

She gazed through the living room picture window into the garden. Felt a shiver run down her back. Yesterday was sunny and warm, so she turned the heating down low, in preparation for the new owners who will arrive tomorrow, having picked up the keys from the realtor in Darien. But it turned unexpectedly colder in the night, and now — although she checked a few minutes ago that the thermometer on the kitchen door was creeping back up again — it was gusty, grey and damp outside. The shrubs she planted over the years had gone back into winter mode, resembling lifeless, brown humps poking up from the bare earth. The puddles of snow left on the lawn looked like spilled milk. After the storm blew in a few days ago — the squalls hitting this area of Connecticut intermittently, wreaking havoc with removal of the last pieces of furniture from the house — most of the snow had melted, but the puddles lingered. They always did. So did a smattering of white down the north-facing trunk of the black walnut, whose closely-packed branches had started thrashing about in the wind like the tangled tresses of some stoned, teenage girl at a rave, trying to impress a boy beside her. Yet the black walnut never impressed Abby. On the contrary. Although she loved trees, she felt no sadness, no regret about leaving this particular specimen behind. Just huge relief. What a release it would be to excise this dark shadow from her life.

She recalled how she'd once screamed at the majestic black walnut in frustration, then hit its gnarled trunk with a garden spade so hard, marks stayed on the bark which never truly faded away and always made her feel guilty every time she looked at them. She called the tree one of Mother Nature's mean little tricks, with no purpose other than to make unsuspecting would-be gardeners like her miserable. For it wasn't until after she and Larry had moved in, after she'd started trying to make some sense of the neglected backyard, that the neighbour across the street had dropped her bombshell. She'd revealed that black walnut roots are impregnated with a poisonous chemical called juglone.

"That means it will be impossible for you... er... Mrs. Holt to grow many kinds of flowers and vegetables within fifty feet of the trunk of your black walnut," the woman said, with what seemed like a smile of triumph.

Abby had wanted to get rid of the tree right there and then.

Let's find a tree removal company in the Yellow Pages, she told Larry eagerly. But he balked. No, no, no, he said. I know you're keen to start gardening out here, Ab, after being cooped up in that walk-up in Queens, but you can't chop down a beautiful, old tree just to put in your flowers. You'll get us into trouble if you do.

And the neighbour, Mrs. Petrie, an interfering, old dame who had a sunny backyard which contained no trees at all, had backed up Larry.

"Black walnuts are native to North America and yours is an outstanding example of the species," she'd announced, the gleam in her eyes suggesting that she'd be the one making trouble if Abby so much as picked up the phone. "It would be criminal to do what you're suggesting, Mrs. Holt."

So that was that. She had unwittingly acquired a cantankerous garden companion which would make growing things difficult for her. Forever.

She didn't give up, of course. Gardening books revealed that plenty of plants could and did survive under the high leaf canopy of a *Juglans nigra*. She put in hostas, *campanulas, Monarda*, a Rose of Sharon and snowdrops which, once established, twirled prettily like maypole ribbons around the base of the trunk after the snow melted. Yet the backyard always proved something of a disappointment after that discovery. She'd been aching to create a dramatic vista out there — a landscape to rival the garden of her horticulturist dad, James Bannerman, who had travelled the world, seeking out interesting new species for the Chicago Botanical Garden, teaching himself several foreign languages in the process. Then when he came back home, had worked miracles with the uninspiring backyard behind their ordinary suburban bungalow in Chicago. But she couldn't. The tree prevented her.

And over the years, the detested black walnut became one of the things that she and Larry would snipe at each other about. A regular little injection of poison administered into their marriage, as persistent as the lethal juglone that never stopped seeping into the soil around the tree. For it always seemed that whatever they did, he — not she — had the final say. Decisions were rarely, if ever, made jointly, so that ultimately, his insistence on being right — about everything from the black walnut to the choice of schools for Hollis to the kind of popcorn popper to buy — hardened inside her, like a knot in a shoelace pulled so taut, it becomes impossible to untie. And it had brought them to this. The house was sold. They were splitting up. By mutual agreement.

A branch of the walnut fell suddenly to the ground in a violent gust as she looked out. It made Abby laugh. That darn tree. No more backbreaking routine of picking up its messy branches, no more raking up the leaves, no more crawling around, scrabbling for the big, round walnuts themselves, so disgusting with their squishy, green covering that stained her palms and ruined her gardening gloves. And they were useless nuts anyway. You could drive a Mac truck over them and the tough shells still wouldn't crack open. Larry had always contrived to be away working at the bank when it was time to clean up the mess they made. Those jobs became hers. Every fall.

She wondered if black walnuts grew where she was headed. A frisson of happiness ran through her entire body, right down to her toes, when she remembered that they didn't. She'd already checked. *Juglans nigra* is primarily found in the

Eastern US and southern Canada and its range extends only as far south as Georgia.

She looked at her watch again and out of the window. No sign of the minivan. So she leaned over and picked up her shoulder bag that was resting beside the armchair. She unzipped the bag, pulled out a slim metal tablet on to her lap. Took a deep breath. Decided it was time.

Time to email the Sisters of the Soil. Time to spill the beans at last. She'd debated doing this before, but wanted to wait until the split was final. Now it was. She would tell her gardener buddies about the life-changing step that she'd decided to take. Her fingers wobbled a little — from both excitement and nervousness — as she opened the lid of her tablet and placed them on the keyboard. She began to write. Confidently, smoothly, with no hesitation, as a sense of the rightness of this decision took over. She felt her heart soaring higher and higher with every key stroke.

Hola Sisters:

Guess what? I'm moving to Mexico. Yes, Mexico. You'll be shocked, I know, but Larry and I haven't been getting along, and we've decided to part. Our daughter Hollis is settled with her own life in New York. She has a partner called Jaz and a wild assortment of friends and doesn't need us around any more. So, we've sold the house in Darien and Larry has retired from the bank and bought a condo near Hollis. But I'm leaving the country for good.

Why? I'm tired of life in the US — and of long, boring winters in Connecticut. My library career is over, the local paper axed my column last year and I have this dream. I want to spend the years I have left surrounded by plants. All kinds of plants which I can grow year-round, not in just three seasons of the year, like I always have in Darien.

I can do that in a place with a funny name called Ajijic. It's in the mountains near Guadalajara. Someone told me it has the second-best climate in the world (I've no idea what the best one is) and that gardening there is fantastic. So, I've done some sleuthing on the web and it does seem to be true. Lots of Americans are retiring to this town. It sounds perfect for me too.

I aim to stay healthy, learn Spanish and perhaps buy myself a little house and garden, although I plan to rent first. I also hope to find a few things that thrill me and make me feel passionately alive again.

Don't get the wrong idea. I'm not talking about meeting some new guy and having great sex for the first time in years. I know there's a slim chance of that, ha, ha, at my age and in any case, I don't want the hassle of having a man around any more. Who does?

Abby looked up and gazed out of the window, smiling to herself. She pictured the last two words striking a chord with at least two of the Sisters, probably Tensie and Rhodo. The topic of men — husbands, ex-husbands, lovers, friends — sometimes entered into the conversation during their reunion lunches, not always favourably, especially after a few glasses of vino. There might even be gales of cynical laughter as they read. She bent over the keyboard again.

But is everything in life really behind us now? Is it not possible to be frivolous and silly and to get excited about something, the way we did when we were young?

I'm just not ready to be old. So Sisters, here's the deal.

Let's plan on holding our next Titan Reunion in Ajijic! As soon as I'm settled, I'll be in touch — but I'm thinking that April will probably be a good time for you to visit.

'Til then, start thinking about sun, tropical flowers and warmth, plus something delicious to eat, preferably with a story, that you could prepare for us all down there.

I can buy all the ingredients before you arrive. Ajijic is apparently quite a big town, with supermarkets and outdoor markets to shop in. As for me, the moment I get there, I'll be looking for some interesting dish, native to Mexico, that I could prepare for you all.

I can't wait, can you? 'Til soon, Sisters!

Yours in plants, Abby

She thought she heard the sound of the minivan. Got up. In the front hall, standing on the bare, parquet floors with the diamond pattern, she peered out of the narrow, oblong window that faced the street. A pretty window, topped with a panel of stained glass, a copycat William Morris, she'd always liked it. But the street revealed no one. It was as silent as the house. Most of her neighbours were at work, their kids in school, and the older retired ones had stayed indoors, out of the biting wind on this inhospitable day.

She returned to the chair. Kicked it. Twice. *Bam. Bam.* It felt good. The chair stirred memories of the day she and Larry splurged on a matching pair of these armchairs in shiny, brown leather at a high-end furnishings store in nearby Stamford. It was raining when the boxes were delivered, they both had the day off, and they'd felt so happy, so excited, so in tune with one another, staying indoors out of the rain and peeling the cardboard wrappings off, then pushing their purchases this way and that, seeking exactly the right place to position them in the living room. The perfect spot — either side of the fireplace — finally selected (by him), they'd impulsively ripped off their clothes and rolled naked all over the arms and seats, revelling in the feel of soft, supple leather against their skin. Then, laughing their heads off, they'd fallen on to the rug in an undignified heap and made love. Hollis was conceived that day, she always thought.

But so long ago. Both chairs have become ancient relics now, the leather torn, seats sagging. Yet when the house was being emptied, Larry wanted to keep his. "It's the only truly comfortable thing I've ever sat on," he'd griped. "No way mine is going into the dumpster." He took the battered chair with him to New York. Abby wondered now, sitting down again, if he ever felt nostalgic about the day when the chairs arrived, as she just did. But she banished the thought quickly. There is no point in wandering down the perilous path of memory when what's done is done. Dredging up happy times, glossing over the unhappy ones, ruminating on how things might have worked out differently if only you'd done such-and-such just means spinning round and round in circles, like a top, until you think you'll go mad. So stop, she told herself. To heck with the armchair. To heck with Larry. He'd insisted on tobacco-brown leather, she'd wanted forest-green. But none of that mattered any more. Time to throw away the past — and the chair — with two hands.

She hit 'Send'. Heard a knock at the front door. Ah, the thrift shop guy at last. He must have driven the mini-van up the driveway while she was engrossed in writing the email, for she didn't hear a sound. Heading down the hall to let him in, Abby caught sight of herself in the long, antique mirror that the new owners had asked to keep. She felt pleasantly surprised. Hey, kiddo, she thought, not bad. Not bad at all. Belly and backside bigger than I'd like, but my face is okay, fresh and bright and relatively unlined, no bags underneath the eyes yet, and the new round glasses with pale-blue rims look kind of hip. But the best part? The new curly bob with an auburn tint — splurged on two days ago at a pricey salon in Manhattan. Wow, it's taken ten years off my age.

Yet the grey sweater and pants? No, no. Jaz was right. They're bookish, boring, so befitting a librarian. Time to embrace colour. Hot, tropical colour. She pictured the new white linen jacket and pants she'd just bought, plus the half dozen tops in wild hues — canary-yellow, orange, lime-green, peppermint-pink — that she intended to pair with them. They were all waiting for her, crisp and new, in the two bags at Hollis's. What fun it would be to transform herself, transform her life, with this new wardrobe.

She'd only been to Mexico once before, to a resort in Cancun to celebrate Hollis's graduation from university. The three of them went. And it wasn't exactly a successful trip, she recalled. A good-looking young guy kept flirting in a gentle way with Hollis at the beach, clearly annoying her. Larry wondered why she rebuffed him, asked later why she never had boyfriends. Then on their last night, after too much wine, Hollis, red-faced and nervous, had come out to them, revealing that she'd known for years that she was sexually attracted to girls, not boys. Larry had looked stunned. He'd sat up 'til the early hours fuming, sipping Scotch, agonising over what he'd done wrong as a parent. Abby had just listened. Made soothing noises. Tried to placate his disappointment in his daughter. Yet Hollis seemed so happy and settled with Jaz now. And Larry had finally accepted the fact. He wanted to stay close to her, had bought the condo a few blocks away from her place so he could. But how ironical, now here she was, embarking on a brand-new adventure a long way from both of them. Heading to this little town called Ajijic. Undoubtedly different from Cancun — vastly different — because it wasn't in a tourist area of Mexico. Weird how things could turn out. Such an unexpected finale to their story as a family. Sad, too. But there it was.

The prospect of what lay ahead filled her with excitement one minute. The next, she felt scared as hell. She had no idea what awaited her where she was going. But she did know one thing for sure.

She wanted to give Mexico a try.

Chapter 2
Outside Bogotá, Colombia, 15th January, 2017

TENSIE

Hortensia Antonella Rojas de Hernandez Castro, age sixty-one, occupation: flower farm owner outside Bogotá, Colombia, proud promoter of her country's cuisine, known as Tensie by her English-speaking friends, was not only shocked by Abby's email. She felt devastated. Abby and Larry had always struck her as a solid, settled kind of couple, heading into the last chapter of their lives without misgivings, destined for cosy evenings in those comfy, old leather armchairs they kept either side of their fireplace.

Sitting at her desk in the cluttered office of *Flores Rojas Hernandez* — or Rojas Hernandez Flowers as it was known abroad — she stared in disbelief at the computer screen, shaking her head.

She re-read the email. Tapped her fingers on the keyboard — scrupulously clean fingers, the nails clipped and unpainted, scrubbed with a bristle brush that morning, before driving out to the farm from her condo in downtown Bogota. Tensie began observing a daily ritual of vigorous scrubbing— she avoided nail varnish, rings or bracelets too — after discovering that delicate hothouse flowers will pick up bacterial and viral diseases from a multitude of sources, but in particular, hands that aren't properly cleaned between the fingers and also under the nails. So she'd become obsessive about her own digits — rewashing them with soap and hot water several times a day. She also insisted that every worker on the farm, irrespective of whether they went into the greenhouses or not, followed her example. And everyone did, although not always gladly.

Tensie knew that a big order of carnations, every bud furled tight as an umbrella and not yet open, was waiting in ventilated cardboard boxes in the humidity-controlled *Flores Rojas Hernandez* warehouse. The building stood at the far end of the long swoop of plastic-roofed greenhouses she could see from her office window. Over 20,000 of these greenhouses, looking from the air like some huge game of checkers on a green board, spread out across the lush, green Savannah outside Colombia's capital. For a telling reason. The plateau's cool climate, 8,600 feet above sea level, coupled with rich soil, had been proven to be one of the best places in the world to grow flowers. And although *Flores Rojas Hernandez* was a minor player in the huge cut-flower market, Tensie took maternal pride in every specimen they produced. She went over to the warehouse to personally check the latest shipment herself yesterday, running her graceful fingers along the stems, examining every bud, like a gardener looking for leaks in a garden hose. And yes, they were perfect. The buyer in Miami, a picky Cuban émigré called Pedro Gonzales, drove a hard bargain, but he would be satisfied.

Yet staring at the screen, thrown off-balance by Abby's startling announcement, she was allowing vital minutes to slip by, with the result that the flowers were in danger of missing their flight to Miami.

"We need their phytosanitary certificates sent to customs,

señora," her assistant Luis reminded her gently a few minutes ago, standing in the doorway of her office, worry creasing his smooth young forehead. "The truck is ready to take the flowers to the airport."

"*Lo sé, lo sé.* I know, I know," she'd replied, irritated. Time is always of the essence with cut flower shipments. The buds may droop or open prematurely if they aren't dispatched promptly after their stems have been cut. And without the crucial documents accompanying them, certifying that the plants are free from disease and pest infestations, customs at Miami airport would not permit them to enter the US. Luis didn't need to remind her of that.

"But just give me a few moments, will you, Luis?" she asked. "And close my door, please."

"*Entiendo, señora,*" he said. I understand.

Luis shut the door, not really understanding at all. He wondered if he had done something to offend the boss. She was normally so efficient, so timely with the shipments, so easy to get along with. All the staff felt a huge weight fall off their shoulders when she decided to come back home to Colombia from New York to help her brother-in-law Alejandro run the farm. *Flores Rojas Hernandez* had been struggling. Alejandro knew all about the complex techniques of hybridisation but turned out to be no businessman, after taking over from Tensie's father, who'd died suddenly of a heart attack. And Alejandro twice dithered while the scourge of late blight, *Phytophthora infestans* rampaged through the greenhouses, wiping out every single plant. But now they were making a modest profit again, shipping potted hydrangeas, cut carnations, Peruvian lilies, chrysanthemums and exquisite long-stemmed roses with romantic names like Heart of Gold to countries all over the world. Luis was hopeful of a bright future with *Flores Rojas Hernandez*, and recognised that the turnaround was largely due to the señora's management skills. Her fussiness about clean hands was also, he had to admit, a contributing factor.

He involuntarily checked his own hands — he always did, before going into and after coming out of her office — — and returned to his own cubbyhole. He concluded that a new email has unsettled her. She'd looked preoccupied, peering at the screen, her mind not on the job, while he stood in the doorway. Perhaps the email came from her estranged husband in New York, Juan Diego, he thought. The señora was sometimes tense, with a tendency to snap, after hearing from that *hijo de puta*, that son of a bitch. Luis shrugged. He realised that whatever the problem, she wouldn't be long. Tensie never wasted time and she didn't tolerate anyone else doing so, either. The boss ran a tight ship. He didn't mind.

Yet today, closeted in her office, reading Abby's email yet again, Tensie sat in an uncharacteristic daze, concluding that no one ever really knew what went on in other people's marriages. How extraordinary that her friend had wound up in the same situation as she was — on her own, separated from her husband, just as she was starting to get old. It seemed unthinkable.

Tensie and Abby had met for the first time at the Brooklyn Botanical Garden — on the momentous day when scores of people showed up to watch the Corpse Flower come into bloom. Tensie, married to a Colombian diplomat based in New York, was a volunteer at the garden, helping out in the tropical greenhouses. Abby was on the media list of invitees. They'd sat next to one another on the folding chairs, taking in the spectacle, and bonded immediately after discovering that they were both named after plants.

"People hear 'Abby' and think my name is Abigail, but it's not. It's Abelia," Abby had said with a laugh. "My dad was a horticulturist, you see, at the Chicago Botanical Garden, and he named me after his favourite shrub."

"*Ay*, what a coincidence," Tensie exclaimed, chuckling too. "My papa was the same. I am called Hortensia, which means hydrangea in Spanish."

After that revelation, they'd spontaneously leapt up, hugged each other, and become firm friends. Then when Abby suggested holding a Titan Reunion at her home in Connecticut, inviting the other women they got to know over the three-day event, Tensie had been more than happy to help organise it. The Sisters of the Soil, as they'd started to call themselves, proved to be a fun crowd. At that first reunion they had cooked up a storm together, with Abby serving up heavenly, hot lobster rolls, a specialty of Connecticut. Then Hannah, from England, made some pastries called Bakewell tarts, which were the hit of the day. And Rhodo, the Canadian writer who joined them from Toronto, prepared pancakes with real maple syrup from a friend's farm for breakfast the next morning.

But what had drawn her closer to Abby than the others, was the lifeline that this particular Sister of the Soil threw out after Juan Diego announced that he was leaving her to live with Cecilia, the sly little *puta* who worked for him at the Colombian consulate in Manhattan. Because Cecilia was pregnant.

"You can't. You can't do this to me," Tensie had wailed. "It's not right. We've been together for so long, our families have been linked together at the farm for generations, your papa and mine are cousins, my sister is married to your brother and…"

"But be reasonable, Tensia. Look at how it's worked out for us," he'd said. "We've never been able to have kids because…"

"Oh stop!" she'd screamed. They had been standing in the kitchen of their upper East Side apartment about to eat dinner, and she hurled her wine glass at him. It missed, smashing on the tiled floor, liquid bouncing everywhere. Rivers of red dripped down the white cabinets like blood. Then she clamped her hands over her ears, sobbing, "Stop it, stop it… don't keep telling me that…"

"All right, I won't," he'd shot back, infuriatingly calm, ignoring the mess. "But I'm leaving you Tensia. I have to. Because I want this child."

Tensie knew he meant it, too. For Cecilia would be bound to produce the son that Juan Diego — indeed all Latin men — always yearned for, even if they didn't admit it, the son that she'd never been able to give birth to herself, although it hadn't been for want of trying. *Ay*, those discouraging rounds of visits to doctors and fertility clinics — in both Colombia and New York. The recollection made her wince. What a hateful waste of time. For no offspring, male or female, ever resulted from their union. She presumed she was cursed, that God had turned his back on her, because of something shameful that had happened when she was young and innocent and didn't know any better.

And the day Juan Diego had moved out, she'd been so grateful to Abby. She called Darien in hysterical tears and Abby calmly ordered Tensie to drop everything and take the train out there immediately. Then on her arrival, she was told to carry on crying on the sofa for as long as she liked. "And scream, Tensie, scream, if you want. Let it all out. It will help."

In the succeeding days, Abby had even plied her with *copelias cocadas*, the coconut candy she loved from Colombia (where did she manage to find them?) Then later, after Tensie decided to move back home, Abby stayed in touch, asking often how she was adjusting to being single again, in her mid-fifties.

"It's hard," she'd admitted, "but it's good to have a routine to my days. Alejandro leaves me to handle the business, and I've discovered I'm good at it. I guess my problem is…" she hesitated, "…I'm a woman who likes to feel loved. And needed. I miss having a man around."

Tensie felt sheepish admitting to such a thing. It might sound weak and silly to Abby. But her friend had just replied briskly, "Yes, of course you do, nothing wrong with that."

And now… Was Abby enduring a similar stranded feeling because her own long marriage had ended? Perhaps yes. Yet perhaps no. Tensie felt confused by the email, especially the comment about '…not wanting a man in her life any more'. Did she really mean that? Larry seemed like a nice enough guy, although she'd barely exchanged more than a few words with him during her visits to Connecticut. He was always at work or just arriving home in the evening. Then he would disappear into his study straight away with a vodka tonic after taking his coat off and not come out all evening. Tensie read the sentence again, thinking that American women have always been something of a puzzle to her. So independent, so strong, so intent on pursuing their own goals. So unlike her. Juan Diego was a trial — always leaving his socks and underpants lying around the bedroom for her to pick up, never letting her know what time he'd be home, going out drinking many nights with his buddies at the embassy, flirting with every pretty women he met and, she surmised, sleeping with them if he got the chance. Yet she still missed him. Acutely. An aching emptiness invaded her life after he left. She felt cut adrift, unanchored. And she knew, with a sinking heart, that she would always feel that way.

How different American culture is from ours, Tensie concluded, not for the first time. It doesn't revolve around the family like it does in Colombia. During her years in New York, the gulf in attitudes had always been glaringly apparent. She regularly met women there who didn't stay in touch with their families, and didn't seem to miss the connection either. They lived alone and liked it. She recalled, with surprising sharpness, the young woman she once sat next to at an awards dinner the Colombian Embassy hosted. Stunningly beautiful, with long, pale, straight hair like cornsilk and an immaculate row of white teeth, this intimidating creature had arrived at the embassy without an escort and flirted outrageously with Juan Diego (who drooled in an embarrassing way over her, his usual habit with blondes). Then she told Tensie candidly during a trip to the ladies' room that she was thirty-four, estranged from her parents, hadn't seen them for years, was marketing manager for one of the States' biggest coffee importers — and that she was seeing three men at once, but made it a rule not to allow any of them stay in her apartment overnight. "I cherish my freedom," she concluded with a self-satisfied smile, pouting her Marilyn Monroe lips to touch them up with scarlet in the washroom mirror. "I don't want to see two toothbrushes in my bathroom when I get up in the morning."

How very odd, Tensie still thought. She fingered her own hair — once almost black and shoulder length, but now shorter and more practical, framing her face, and rinsed with a reddish tint every two weeks to hide the grey. She'd been a stunner like that girl once, a Miss Colombia runner-up, tanned legs up to her armpits in a swimsuit, teasing brown eyes, and a toothpaste ad smile, with a posse of admirers at her beck and call. But she hadn't wanted to wind up alone like the coffee marketer from Texas. She'd wanted to spend her life with Juan Diego. It was all she ever wanted, and she'd thought he'd wanted that too. They'd been together ever since they could climb trees at the farm, and how chivalrously he always behaved in those days, helping her to reach the highest branches, where they sat side by side and stared out at the Savannah, while she giggled and he didn't say much. He'd seemed so content to simply be with her back then. She shut off the memory, softly cursing him, and looked out of the window. The sky was unusually cloudless, the blue almost as bright as the hue of some of the potted hydrangeas the farm sold, with great success, to gardeners abroad. And down past the greenhouses where they raised the shrubs, she could spot the red roof of the *Flores Rojas Hernandez* warehouse standing out like a beacon. The low-slung, cottony cloud-cover that perpetually drifted in from the surrounding mountain range at around noon every day, hadn't yet cloaked the roof in a fine, damp fog. And standing there in front of the warehouse was a big, white truck, with a red rose and the logo FRH painted in large letters on its side.

The sight jerked her back to reality.

"*Dios mio*, the carnations," she murmured, putting her hand to her mouth, annoyed with herself. She leaped up from the computer and hurried out of her office, over to Luis' cubbyhole.

"*Disculpe*, Luis. I'm sorry. I'm sorry" she said, out of breath. "Silly and careless of me. I got sidetracked by an email from a friend."

Luis smiled and said, "Not a problem."

He secretly hoped the email which had so preoccupied her was from a new man in her life. The *señora* seemed so lonely.

She hurried over to her office, sat down again, found the crucial phytosanitary certificates stored on her hard drive — she had already filled them out — and dispatched the documents to both the Colombian and U.S. customs authorities. The task only took minutes. Then duly informed, Luis texted the warehouse that the flowers were ready to go. Tensie watched from her window as the humidity-controlled vehicle backed inside the building to load the cardboard boxes. She heaved a huge sigh of relief as it drove away, across the rolling Savannah, which was dusty and dry as a bone in some places, but lush paint box green where irrigation made its presence felt. It turned in the direction of Bogotá airport.

Settling down in her office chair once more, she switched back to email and re-examined the one from Abby. She wished fervently that her friend wasn't moving to Mexico.

Tensie was a seasoned traveller — to many countries on diplomatic missions with Juan Diego and, more recently, on her own, finding buyers for the farm's flowers. But she had never been to Mexico and wasn't keen to go now. Painfully, she cast her mind back to the reason why.

Back when she was a teenager, an upsetting incident occurred with some Mexican workers at the farm. Her poor grandpapa. The strain of what happened killed him. Yet he was not to blame. The memory made her shudder now. Awful.

Horrible. So much sadness for everyone involved. She'd tried to blot it all out for years, but had never really succeeded. And if she went to Mexico, would she be forced to re-live that humiliating episode? *Claro que si.* Yes, of course.

Yet there was good, kind Abby, her loyal, supportive friend, so jubilant about embarking on a new life there. She couldn't let her down, could she?

Tensie tapped her unvarnished fingers again, on the desk this time, pondering the situation. After a minute or two, she sat up, brightening, like a languishing rose in one of the greenhouses, revived by a long drink of water.

Why not go to Mexico and make *Ajiaco*?

Yes, *Ajiaco*. This reunion would be the perfect opportunity to introduce the Sisters of the Soil to *Ajiaco*. It was THE celebrated dish of Bogotá, served in restaurants all over the city and Tensie felt intensely proud of it. She often made *Ajiaco* herself — and she could easily do the same in Abby's kitchen. It would be a novelty for everyone because *Ajiaco* was unique — a thick soupy stew simmered with *guascas*, a special herb that wasn't used in cooking anywhere in the world but Colombia.

Tensie's heart swelled, thinking what a clever idea she'd come up with. She'd often wondered why *Ajiaco* was not better known. When she and Juan Diego used to entertain in New York, American guests always looked blank when she announced that they'd be tasting Bogotá's pride and joy for the first time. Hardly any of them had ever heard of the dish. *Ajiaco* deserved a better image. She'd always thought that. By now, with globalisation, it should be as commonly recognised and consumed around the world as pizza, sushi and Pad Thai.

Why hadn't that happened? The more she mulled over the idea of serving *Ajiaco,* the more she liked it. After all, in Abby's email, she asked the Sisters to think of something 'interesting' to prepare, with a story attached. And *Ajiaco* did have a fascinating history which she could reveal at the lunch.

So yes, she would visit Abby in Mexico, even though it would be nerve-wracking travelling to that country. Those old, difficult memories would inevitably surface — memories that she'd never discussed with anyone outside the family because she'd been so determined to bury them. And dredging them up again would undoubtedly make her sad. But she'd do it for the sake of Abby, friendship with the Sisters — and for *Ajiaco.*

She stared out of the window once more, at the clouds. They were descending over the warehouse now, a bit later than in the day than usual, pouring like waterfalls over the mountains, cloaking the building's roof in a vapour that made it seem to miraculously disappear. She told herself that she must do that with the past. Make it disappear. Forget what happened, if only for a brief time. Go to Mexico. Have some fun with the Sisters.

Gritting her teeth with resolve, she clicked on reply.

Chapter 3
Toronto, Canada, 15th January, 2017

RHODO

Roslyn Chaffey, age fifty-four, status: full-time writer about gardening for magazines, blogger, author of five books, host of a springtime TV show called Grow For It; nicknamed 'Rhodo' by her gardening buddies because of her passion for rhododendrons, was stunned by Abby's email too. But not in the same way as Tensie. The revelation that Abby and Larry were splitting up left her completely unfazed. Single all her life, not always happily, Rhodo had acquired a cynical view of the matrimonial state over the years and presumed that Abby, to her credit, had belatedly woken up to the realisation that the male species were more trouble than they were worth. Well, good for you, girl, she snorted. Join the club.

But Abby's choice of Mexico as a destination did shock her. MEXICO? Rhodo was floored, thunderstruck. She was a perpetual worrier — the kind of person who hears a garbage truck crashing about on the street at night, emptying bins, and immediately thinks that terrorists in suicide vests have blown up the subway station around the corner. And Mexico sounded so... so worrying. An all-out horror show, in fact. Drug cartels, politicians getting shot, tourists murdered at resorts, bodies left in ditches with their heads missing. Holy moly. Nothing positive ever hit the headlines about Mexico.

What on earth had possessed Abby to move there?

If she wanted warmth, why not Arizona? Or Florida?

The invitation was perplexing.

Rhodo was a medium tall, strong-jawed woman with thin lips often clamped together in a straight line, mousy hair on the reddish side and piercing blue eyes the colour of cornflowers, her best feature. They matched the jean shirts she perpetually wore, winter and summer. She was sitting on a stool at her kitchen counter when Abby's email came in, ping, ping, on her cellphone. The clock on the wall said nearly nine p.m. and it had proven to be a drippy, dreary night. Freezing rain was falling. With northern winters getting warmer, this kind of rain — hard, sharp, stinging cheeks like splinters of glass — made life in Toronto a misery from the beginning of November through April. Rhodo hated it. She never minded the big dumps of snow the city used to get. The white stuff was prettier, more user-friendly, a reminder of home far away in Newfoundland, tobogganing down hills with her little brother, Jeffy. But this drizzle, this recent phenomenon, made driving hell, complicated everything and turned sidewalks into skating rinks. Her cosy little downtown semi — which she'd finally scraped up enough money to buy three years ago — had become her personal bulwark against climate change. She had hardly bothered to leave the place this winter. The parlous state of the planet sent her into hibernation mode back in November, like a curled-up squirrel in a drey, high in some tree, unwilling to venture outdoors to look for nuts except on fine days.

Her buddy from school days, Monica, who was also from Newfoundland and looked rather like Rhodo due to their shared Irish ancestry, had come over for supper and squatted on another stool opposite her. The love of her life, a long-haired, calico cat called Azalea, waited under the counter, mewing piteously now and then, commanding attention, even though she'd cajoled treats out of her mistress twice already that evening.

Rhodo read Abby's email out loud to Monica. They were about to share a pizza which Rhodo ordered online at six p.m. It arrived late on account of the weather. The pizza deliveryman, who had a big bushy beard and swarthy face, was profusely apologetic about the delay. She said "Not to worry" and gave him a big tip. Poor guy, she thought, closing the door on his retreating form, holding the big white plastic insulated bag against his chest as a defence against the horrible night. He didn't seem to have a proper coat. He was probably a brain surgeon or something back home in the Middle East. Now he's reduced to slithering around our icy streets in a little car with a vulgar yellow and red illuminated sign on the roof, bringing nightly rations to lazy slobs like me. Life is unfair.

The pizza was cold. It seemed too late to turn the oven on to warm it up. In any case, Rhodo felt not so much hungry by now as half-drunk, her head starting to spin, after anticipating the deliveryman's knock for so long. They'd opened a bottle of cheap Merlot from somewhere in Eastern Europe during the wait. Now it was almost empty and Monica had started to get on her nerves because, tongue loosened by the wine, she wouldn't stop yapping about Mexico. As they bothed chewed doggedly through the leathery crust, pondering Abby's email, she launched into a graphic tale about her 'brush with Senor Montezuma; as she called it, during her latest all-inclusive package week in Puerto Vallarta.

"Two days emptying my guts — from both ends — in the

hotel bathroom. Couldn't stop pooping and vomiting," Monica said with relish. "I tell you, I wanted to die."

"What caused it?" asked Rhodo, aghast, feeling bile in her throat, ready to vomit herself.

"Oh, street food, for sure. A quesadilla thing with a sauce that I ate at a stall in the market on my second day. Silly of me. It tasted yummy but was obviously off."

"Did you see a doctor?"

"Nah. I just kept crawling back to bed between bouts on the can. You have to wait it out, you know. It does go away eventually, although your insides feel like they've been scoured with a toilet brush afterwards.

"But then…" she added happily, "I did recover and had a blast. Oh boy, those margaritas. They…"

"Well, no way I'm going," Rhodo interrupted, shuddering. Her insides gurgled at the thought of quesadillas.

Mexican food gave her the burps at the best of times, anyway. She wasn't a fan like Monica. She thought of Graham Greene, his non-fiction memoir *The Lawless Roads* about Mexico, in which he derided the 'shrivelled bits of this and that, all delivered to the table at once'. Well, nowadays Graham, she wanted to tell him with a laugh, it's more likely to be suspicious-looking combo plates and soggy nachos, drowning in sour cream. But it's still as revolting as the stuff they served you.

So no, Rhodo thought, only half-listening to Monica rattling on. While she loved Abby, loved the Sisters of the Soil, loved the chatty emails that winged back and forth among them about anything and everything to do with plants, she'd pass on the next Titan Reunion. Staying home in the rain sounded like a better — and much safer — proposition.

Yet Monica, her cheeks glowing from the wine and her recently acquired suntan, wouldn't drop the topic of Mexico. She moved on from Montezuma's Revenge to rave about an 'awesome' place she'd stumbled on by chance during the trip.

"It was full of tropical rhododendrons," she said, with a sly, expectant smile, as if trying to wind Rhodo up.

And her buddy took the bait. Rhodo perked up, immediately interested. She put her glass down on the counter and tipped her head on one side, listening.

"They were part of the Vallarta Botanical Garden," Monica continued. "I took a bus ride out there from the hotel on a cloudy day, when going to the beach was out. A woman I met in the hotel gift shop told me about the place. And it's awesome, Rhodo, totally awesome. Believe it or not...." her tone turned mischievous now, "...it was started by an American guy who is as nuts about rhododendrons as you are."

"You're kidding."

"No, I'm not."

Rhododendrons. Rhodo was all ears now. It had become a long-standing joke among her gardening pals, this passion she had for the woody plants, which she saw — and loved — for the first time, years ago, in Newfoundland's Botanical Garden. It was how she wound up with her nickname, which she kind of liked. It was catchy. People remembered Rhodo — a plus when you were in the business of getting writing assignments from gardening magazines. Over the years, she'd acquired an encyclopaedic knowledge of many of the two hundred species of rhodos and was gradually building her own little collection of them in the long, skinny, shady backyard behind her house. But she'd never seen the tropical kind, except in greenhouses at botanical gardens. This revelation of Monica's excited her.

She was eager to know more.

Yet Monica took her time. Pleased to have finally caught Rhodo's attention, she picked up the bottle. Tipped the last of the wine into her glass. Took a sip. Swilled the liquid tantalisingly slowly around her mouth, letting a dribble escape and trickle down her chin, as she spun the story out like a fisherman reeling in a big one.

"The rhodos I saw down there are amazing," she said at length, wiping the wine off her chin with a knuckle. "Absolutely amazing."

She leaned forward on the counter, enjoying herself. She and Rhodo had been buddies, almost like sisters, since school days and Monica, who was single too, quite liked gardening, in a modest way, on her apartment balcony in downtown Toronto. But she wasn't in the same league as Rhodo, who often irritated her, playing the big expert, always telling her what to do with her geraniums every spring. As if she hadn't learned a thing or two about growing flowers by now. Gardeners are such know-it-alls, she often thought, forever rattling off those baffling Latin names, making the rest of us feel hopelessly inadequate. And Rhodo knew so much about botanical gardens too. She'd visited them everywhere from the Netherlands to San Diego, invited on what she laughingly referred to as the four Fs (Fabulous Freebies For Freelancers) by publicists, hoping she would write a story about whatever it was they were promoting. Monica, who did conveyancing for a legal firm, never got invited anywhere. She was envious about the four Fs. But she also felt in awe of Rhodo, who'd become the leading writer about gardening in Canada after starting out with a column for the local newspaper back home in Bay Roberts, Newfoundland. She'd even found some fame in the US too. Monica felt flattered to have stayed her friend, to still be included in her circle. Yet here, finally, was her chance for a bit of one-upmanship. Because Rhodo had clearly never heard of the Vallarta Botanical Garden.

Monica paused deliberately once more and took another swig.

"I can see why rhodos fascinate you now, Rhodo. Truly I can," she said. "The ones down there are so beautiful, with such delicate shapes and amazing colours. And did you know..." her tone turned teasing, "...did you know that this garden has amassed the largest collection of Vireyas, the tropical kind, in the world?"

Rhodo shook her head, impressed. It wasn't like Monica to show this level of knowledge about species of plants, nor to use their Latin names.

"Well, they have. And they're *es... es... tupendo*, as they say down there." Monica laughed as she mangled the Spanish word. "The whole place is *estupendo*. You just HAVE to go."

She leaned forward on the counter, drained her glass and smiled encouragingly.

"You should. Truly," she urged. "Don't you need a break? I mean, look at it out there. Aargh."

Monica waved at the uncurtained kitchen window above the sink and pulled a face. The sky beyond the glass had the sickly, blackish-yellow hue of a stagnant pond. Freezing rain kept hitting the panes like someone fooling around with a drum. Rat-tat-tat. Rat-tat-tat. Then, after a pause, ratta-tatta-tatta-tatta, quicker and harder, more like machine gun fire, as the rain beat down louder. Yet indoors, on a ledge above the sink, as if in defiance of the bleakness outside, stood two potted amaryllis, their huge blooms flaring like angels' trumpets. One was classic scarlet, the other, the aptly-named Dancing Queen, sporting a froth of frilly white petals tipped with orange which did indeed resemble a can-can performer's petticoats.

"You always say you couldn't get through the winter without having some of those indoors," Monica declared, waving a hand again at the flowers. "And yes, they're lovely, but wouldn't you like to see the real thing growing in people's gardens? You can, you know, in Puerto Vallarta. Amaryllis are quite common, especially the red and white ones."

Rhodo didn't answer. Uncertain how to respond, she got off the stool, busied herself with clearing away the discarded pizza bits and pieces. She carried their plates over to the sink, bent down to offer a crust to Azalea en route, who took a cursory lick and stalked away. The cat hated anything with tomato in it.

"And please don't take offence," Monica continued, determined not to let the topic rest, as Rhodo dumped the debris in the garbage can under the sink, "but you've become such a stick-in-the-mud, Rhodo. You hardly ever go out. You worry about everything. But life's a risk, isn't it? So's Mexico. You should accept your friend's invitation. Because..." she grinned, "... I think you'll love it down there."

Rhodo sighed. A deep, long, drawn-out sigh, as she stared at the Dancing Queen. She wished Monica would shut up and go home, because she hadn't exactly been loafing around all winter. A new book, *Native Rhododendrons of North America*, was in the works, and she was busy putting together the final chapters. She'd also already wrapped up her springtime garden show, filmed in a Toronto studio late last fall. Yet part of her — a sneaky, nagging, annoying part— conceded that her friend might have a point about her unwillingness to abandon the comforts of home. It was true that she'd hardly left the house for weeks.

Thus, a few mornings later, rain still slicking the sidewalks, Rhodo found herself venturing out to a store in her Portuguese neighbourhood. In worrying mode again, this time about fish. Specifically, cod. Having pretty well decided to accept Abby's invitation when it arrived in April, she had already emailed her saying yes, she'd love to come. The possibility of a side trip to see those Vireyas was too exciting to miss. In fact, she'd stayed awake until the small hours the night after Monica came by, doing mental calculations of the money she could earn, writing about these tropical species for magazines and websites. Maybe there would be even a book in it, a sequel to *Native Rhododendrons of North America*.

But then another little worm of worry wiggled its way into her head this morning, while she was making toast. What on earth could she cook for this Titan Reunion?

Abby said she was expecting the Sisters each to contribute something 'interesting' to the lunch. Her email made that clear. Yet Rhodo wasn't exactly a dab hand in the kitchen. Never had been, truth be told. She'd only pretended to like cooking on their previous get-togethers, because she enjoyed the camaraderie and swapping of information about plants. The reality was, though, cooking bored her. Totally. All that peeling and chopping. The ridiculous instructions in recipe books to MINCE garlic and SWEAT onions. Who owned a mincer nowadays? She barely even had a sharp knife. And what exactly did 'sweat' mean? Roll up your sleeves and start perspiring, girl, if you embark on this next step in the recipe? No, she had no interest in learning how to cook. Cookbooks were incomprehensible and exasperating. She had none on her kitchen shelf, just a row of gardening books, some of them written by her and all much more helpful with instructions than cookbooks. Sure, she could manage French toast, even pancakes and maple syrup or a baked potato with a slab of cheddar if she was in the mood. But they were about the limit of her culinary expertise.

What to do? She recalled Hannah, sweet, soft-spoken Hannah, the Brit who came all the way from the English countryside to Connecticut for Abby's Titan Reunion and thrilled the Sisters with those amazing pastry things called Bakewell tarts that they all scarfed down in minutes. She couldn't possibly compete with Hannah.

Yet like Tensie, Rhodo was struck by a unique idea: Newfoundland cod cakes. They'd probably be a snap to make — basically just fish and mashed potato — and such a novelty for the Sisters, because she could talk, when she served them, about dear old Gramma Mercer, family matriarch, proud fisherman's wife, who took her and Jeffy in after their mom and dad split up, and who spent her entire life making imaginative meals out of cod out there on the edge of the cold, grey Atlantic, back in the good old days when the big, ugly fish was plentiful and cost nothing. And how as a kid, she and Jeffy had hated having to eat 'fish' — what cod was invariably called, to the exclusion of other species — yet they still loved those simple, fried patties.

The night after Monica left, Rhodo dug out Gramma's recipe book. With some difficulty. The collection of thin pages, grease-smeared and torn, ingredients scribbled mostly in faded pencil, was hidden away in the bottom of a drawer in her office upstairs. She hadn't opened the book since Gramma passed, many years ago.

What a surprise to find recipes scribbled inside the pages. Gramma, after all, knew every one of her recipes by heart. She didn't need to consult a book. Perhaps she just felt compelled to write things down for future generations. Because holy moly, along with what was needed to make Newfoundland specialties like figgy duff and blueberry grunt and seal flipper pie, there she found it. The cod cakes recipe.

Salt cod is essential, Gramma insisted in her spidery writing. So now Rhodo stood outside the fish shop, debating whether to go inside. A trial run of the cod cakes, prepared at home, had been on her mind ever since supper with Monica. She'd committed to go to Mexico, the idea excited her, but she couldn't run the risk of screwing up down there, not around all those frighteningly competent cooks. And she could invite Monica over for supper to try the cakes in advance because Monica was, after all, the one person in the world who would tell her what she honestly thought.

Yet Rhodo hesitated. She peered in through the steamed-up window, fingering a strand of hair poking out from under her wool hat. It felt unpleasantly wet. She'd walked by this store with the Mediterranean blue sign many times but never really paid any attention to it. The place didn't look very busy — or friendly. It was mostly patronised by grim-faced Portuguese housewives, always dressed in black and hauling bundle buggies. They doubtless knew everything there was to know about cooking fish, especially cod and they were always jabbering away in Portuguese when she saw them around the neighbourhood or on the subway. There was only one in the shop at that moment, a stout matron in a shabby coat and cheap plastic boots with zips up the sides, making the fat around her knees bulge over the top. She had her back to Rhodo and was talking to the serving woman behind the counter, who wore a white apron that was smeared on the chest with fish blood. Would they think she was a jerk if she went in and asked for advice? Or not even understand what she was saying, because they didn't speak English? Although Rhodo had spent her early years in Newfoundland, where life revolved around cod, she knew absolutely nothing about how to cook it. The only kind of fish she ever ate now — and not that often, either — came in a frozen package with a grinning fisherman in an oilskin on the front — and it was ready battered. All she had to do was throw one of the slabs on a cookie sheet and bake it in the oven.

Yet she thought of the Vireyas. And of warm, sunny days. And of flowers — loads and loads of tropical flowers, whose names she didn't know yet and would love to learn. They'd be snaking up the trunks of giant trees, tumbling over whitewashed walls, resplendent in gardens year-round, a rainbow of colour that was positively dazzling and heart-stopping to a gardener like her. She'd seen the proof: some photos Monica showed off on her cellphone after her last trip to Puerto Vallarta. And Rhodo's hands at that moment had gone numb in her thin, wool gloves. The non-stop rain was trickling off her soaked hair and making its way down her back and…

She pushed open the door of the fish shop and stepped nervously inside.

Chapter 4
Dorset, England, 15th January, 2017

HANNAH

Hannah Luxcombe, age sixty-four, status: gardening columnist for a major British newspaper, author of three books on herbs, superb pastry cook, reacted quite differently from both Tensie and Rhodo to Abby's idea for a Titan Reunion in Mexico. She was — in a word — ecstatic.

Not quite believing the words displayed on her computer screen, not even waiting to get to the end of Abby's email, she leaped up from her big, old-fashioned, wooden desk in a flurry of excitement and promptly smashed her left knee against one of the desk's carved, oak legs.

"Ouch," she yelped, rubbing the knee (which was increasingly stiff nowadays, on account of arthritis). "Bloody hell, that hurts. Ouch. Oooo…"

Yet hopping about on her good leg, she still managed to execute a clumsy jig of joy around her office.

Mexico! How brilliant. How absolutely bloody marvellous. The place sounded so exotic, so colourful, so unlike anywhere she'd ever been before. She'd always wondered what Mexico was like. And what an adventure it would be, meeting up with the Sisters there.

"Charles," she called out breathlessly, leaning against the

desk in mid-jig, as bouncy as a balloon filled with helium, in spite of the knife of pain shooting down her left calf. "Charles, wonderful news! I've been invited to Mexico!"

Charles didn't answer.

Hannah sank back, gasping, still rubbing the knee, into her ergonomically designed chair (she had recently developed a dodgy back too) presuming that her husband, who was in the early stages of deafness, couldn't hear her. Then the realisation dawned — a little sadly — that even if he could hear, he wouldn't be the slightest bit interested in the news about Abby's invitation. For Charles, ensconced in an armchair downstairs in the living room, was transfixed by a slim, grey device balanced on his lap.

This device, an iPad, had been a present from his engineering firm at his retirement party a year ago. He'd felt quite taken aback at the time, made polite thank you noises to his co-workers who stood clapping while he opened the foil-wrapped box, but inwardly, he'd cursed them for giving him yet another baffling piece of technology to master in his old age. Since then, however, he had taken to the iPad with the zeal of an app-mad teenager. It was as if the device has become some strange new part of his anatomy, sprouting from the ends of his long, bony fingers. For he was never separated from it.

Mornings, afternoons, evenings, even often into the small hours, long after Hannah had gone upstairs to bed, he sat with the iPad, reading, listening to or watching something on the little screen. In fact, what he found there engrossed him so totally, he rarely spoke to his wife of thirty-nine years any more, except to impart some snippet of news — usually depressing — that he'd just clicked on.

"Awful floods in Bangladesh," he'd announced this

morning at the breakfast table in the conservatory, without looking up. (Charles never looked up when the lid of the iPad was open.) "They say the entire rice crop will be a write-off this year."

Then, a minute later.

"Another ISIS bombing in the Philippines. They don't yet know how many people are dead. Could be hundreds, thousands."

And after another pause.

"The U.N. says female strawberry pickers are being sexually abused in Spain."

"How awful," Hannah murmured in response to the last one, dipping a silver-plated teaspoon inherited from her grandmother into her soft-boiled egg. But she didn't care. Not really. She was sick of the news. Sick of reports that were always negative, always exposing the dark side of humanity, always trying to somehow make her feel guilty about her comfortable, middle-class existence, especially if they were written by some po-faced lefty in the *Guardian*. For what could she personally do about these problems? Nothing. She'd got beyond the age of wanting to write angry letters to the editor, or of posting some pithy comment on Facebook or Twitter (not that she'd ever mastered the art of doing either) or of marching in street protests, brandishing a placard about the latest issue that had captured the attention of the media.

No, she'd had enough. So last November, on her sixty-fourth birthday, Hannah made a silent pledge to herself that she wasn't going to spend the years she had left getting worked up about all the appalling things going on in the world over which she had no control. She just didn't want to know about them any more. She would assume the role of the proverbial ostrich, and bury her head in the sandy soil of her beloved garden. This decision, announced to her family over turkey with chestnut stuffing on Christmas Day didn't really register with Charles (who, persuaded by Hannah to at least put the iPad aside for the duration of the meal, then sat at the table with the fidgety, anxious look of a chain smoker who's dying to go outside for a puff). Yet the declaration had appalled their three grown up children. The youngest, thirty-one-year-old Alice, who was always active in some cause or other, looked particularly put out.

"You're awful, Mum," Alice said in a horrified voice, practically choking on her roast potato. "That's so elitist, so smug, so typical of Conservatives like you and Dad. You SHOULD care."

Hannah had simply smiled, calmly cut herself another morsel of turkey thigh and said, "I'm getting old, darling. When you're my age, you probably won't care either."

And if Charles wouldn't stop bombarding her with the gloom and doom he discovered daily on the internet — and he wouldn't, she knew that — well, she'd simply tune out.

As she did this morning.

Up in her office hideaway, tucked under the eaves of their old farmhouse, Hannah felt a twinge of annoyance that she couldn't rush downstairs and interrupt Charles with the news about Abby's email, because he probably wouldn't even look up from the iPad. But being a tranquil kind of person — the peacemaker of the family, everyone agreed — who disliked confrontation, she concluded that it was best to leave him be.

In any case, Charles hated travelling. Although they'd honeymooned on the Amalfi coast, once took weekend trips together to Paris, and he'd even accompanied her to the

Keukenhof Gardens in the Netherlands, after she received an invitation to write about their spectacular displays of spring bulbs, that was ancient history now. Since his retirement, Charles had barely left Dorset. And he kept saying that he couldn't understand why people took tiring flights to strange countries and ate strange food there that promptly made them violently ill. Undoubtedly, if she did start enthusing about Mexico, Charles would immediately read out something terrifying about that country from his iPad.

So Hannah did what she always did when she had some thrilling news to impart. She called her sister, Ada.

Hannah and Ada were identical twins. Though they didn't see each other often — Hannah and Charles occupying their renovated farmhouse on just one acre outside the town of Dorchester, while Ada and husband Tom struggled to raise sheep on a real farm of one hundred acres in Herefordshire, near the Welsh border — they were still thick as thieves and confided to each other about everything. This closeness had its origins back in their schooldays when an English teacher called Mrs. Burrell pointed out, with a chuckle, that both Hannah's and Ada's names were palindromes — that is, they could be spelled the same way, forward or backwards. The other girls in their class found this enormously funny and started calling Hannah and Ada the Palindrome Pair — or the Pee Pees for short — a nickname which they found embarrassing and grew to detest. Thus, feeling isolated and different, they'd always found solidarity in each other's company.

The quirky aspect of their names had been no coincidence either. Their father, a failed writer who went off by tube every day to some mysterious job in Whitehall, was obsessed with palindromes. He would come home at night, pour himself a Scotch and wander about their bungalow in Ealing shouting things like, "Listen to this one, girls. 'Madam in Eden, I'm Adam'. Isn't that clever?" Then, "'Do geese see God?'" They assumed he did this to annoy their mother, Polly, who'd grown tired of her husband's literary pretensions. Polly would sometimes shout back, from her sewing room at the end of the bungalow. "Oh, shut up, Duncan. Can't you see the girls are trying to do their homework?" Yet although they thought their dad was a bit barmy, they adored him — because he made them laugh and, after Polly's outbursts, he would sneak with a guilty smile into the kitchen and help them with their English composition.

Decades later, the sisters still looked remarkably alike: both tall and slim with the high cheekbones and ruddy complexions of a class of Englishwomen who spend most of their time in the country. They wore their blonde-grey hair the same way too: long and flowing down their backs (but for special occasions, hoisted up into messy top knots and fastened with identical tortoiseshells clips, given to them as children one Christmas by their maternal grandmother). Old corduroy trousers and baggy sweaters constituted their standard wardrobe.

The twins didn't at all resemble — in looks or personality — their much younger unmarried sister, whose name was also a palindrome. Dark-haired, devilish Eve was forty-three, lived in Rome and was rather wild. She worked for a caterer, blogged in English about Italian culinary traditions, wore black miniskirts no bigger than postage stamps, and kept changing lovers. Indeed, she was so different from her older siblings, Hannah and Ada had often speculated that Polly must have had a fling in midlife with Roger, their one-time, good-looking rogue of a neighbour, because Eve vaguely resembled him. And that morning, the sisters' first topic of conversation was Eve — their usual practice — because her life always sounded so much more interesting than theirs.

"Did you know that Eve and Fabio are splitting up?" Ada asked.

"No! Oh, what a shame," said Hannah. "He's so good for her. Calms her down. And quite a hunk, isn't he, in those cellphone photos?"

"Yes, lucky Eve."

Neither of them had ever met Fabio.

"What's the reason, do you know?"

"No idea. She's tired of him, I guess."

"Is there someone else in the picture?"

"Don't think so. She didn't mention anybody. Just sounded upset and said something about coming to England to see us."

"Well, she'd better not show up in April," Hannah said triumphantly. "Because guess what? You won't believe it, Ade, but I've been invited to Mexico that month."

"Mexico? How fabulous. Lucky you, Han," said Ada, genuinely pleased for her sister, but also envious. That morning she'd noticed a worm crawling out of a sheep's anus down in the south pasture of the farm. It would mean a big vet bill for treating the whole herd. So no trips to exotic places in the offing for her and Tom.

"Why are you going?" Ada asked. "Is this something to do with your column?"

"Yes, sort of. You know how I became friends with a group of women when I went to New York to see the Titan

Arum? And then we met up again later in Connecticut and Texas and more recently in Paris?"

"Yes, of course." Ada had been secretly jealous of those jaunts too.

"Well, the woman from Connecticut — the one called Abby — has split up with her husband and is moving to a Mexican village in the mountains. And she's invited us all there."

"Sounds splendid," said Ada. "So I take it this won't be your usual beach holiday?"

"Doesn't seem likely. This town is a long way from the sea on a lake. But it's a great climate for gardening, so I might be able to pick up some ideas for the column."

Hannah was always looking for material for *Dirty Fingernails*, a column that she felt proud to have written —not missing one deadline — for nearly thirty years. The plum freelance assignment landed in her lap by accident, when, at an art gallery opening in Dorchester, an editor from one of the UK's biggest newspapers took a shine to her. His name was Christopher Couillard, he had a weekend retreat nearby, and after she'd told him, emboldened by two glasses of wine, that she loved gardening and wanted to write articles about it, he'd leaned his equally flushed face into hers and said, "Well, you lovely English rose, send me a few sample columns and I'll consider it." To her surprise, she got the job. Then Christopher, who was separated from his second wife, invited her over to his cottage, plied her with wine and they'd shared a passionate kiss amid a tangle of *Clematis tangutica*. But that was all, just a kiss, and only once, she'd confided to Ada afterwards, blushing. Guilt about Charles and the children had set in. Yet the mutual attraction remained, she advised Christopher on plants to buy for his garden and helped him find the right spots for them, and when her writing mentor died suddenly of an aneurysm eight years later, she'd been so shattered, she hid herself away in her office and — unknown to Charles — wept her heart out.

As for the column, that proved to be an even bigger surprise to Hannah than landing the assignment in the first place. With no prior writing experience, she took to the task of finding subjects of interest to gardeners like a butterfly to a buddleia bush, quickly becoming one of the newspaper's most loved columnists. *Dirty Fingernails* was now eagerly awaited in the Saturday edition by thousands of gardening enthusiasts all over the U.K. Daddy's early lessons in English composition undoubtedly helped, she'd once surmised to Ada.

She told her twin about Abby's idea that each of the Sisters think of something interesting to prepare for their lunch in Mexico.

"Ah, so what are you going to cook?" Ada asked.

"Don't know yet. I did Bakewell tarts when we met up in Connecticut and everyone loved those. Especially when I told them that the name has nothing to do with how to cook them, but had actually originated in a town called Bakewell. But…"

Hannah sighed.

"… I've no idea what to make in Mexico, or what kind of ingredients she'll be able to find for me there."

"You'll come up with something," Ada said, secretly envious too of Hannah's acknowledged prowess with pastry. Her own Bakewell tarts never turned out as well as her sister's.

They rang off. Hannah crept quietly down the uncarpeted, wood stairs, avoiding the living room where Charles was still bent over his iPad, because she didn't want him to dampen her enthusiasm for the trip. Besides, her head was already buzzing with an idea. She slipped on her old, waxed raincoat that was hanging from a peg on the kitchen wall and her black wellies, kept by the Aga. She went outside. The sky was as usual flat grey — the same hue as her son Edward's minimalist living room in Surbiton —a fine drizzle was falling and the plants look matted and miserable. She even detected a new greenish tinge developing over the brick paths — hardly surprising, she thought, because it hadn't stopped raining in Dorset for weeks. The whole place smelled unpleasantly of mould.

Hannah headed straight to her herb beds. In summer they were a symphony — juicy glorious greens of every possible hue spilling over the pathway dividers, punctuated by purple spires of *Perilla frutescens*, whose piquant leaves she sneaked into salads when Charles wasn't looking. She often wrote about herbs in *Dirty Fingernails* and gave recipes for their use. They were consistently her most popular topic with readers. Today though, everything was a discouraging mess of mud and sodden stalks, a few floppy, grey sage leaves providing the only evidence that life still somehow managed to cling on in her waterlogged soil.

At the end of one bed, she crouched down grimacing — the banged-up knee still hurt — in order to examine one clump closely. She pulled at a couple of dead, brown stalks. Peered into the plant's centre. Felt pleased. Yes, there was a smidgen of bright green fuzz already developing down there.

Good," she murmured, straightening up again, rubbing the knee. Looked up at the sullen sky. "Loads of leaves by April, right, God?"

The herb was lovage, a big, bossy plant that every summer she had to whack back with garden shears or dig up and divide.

Even so, Hannah loved lovage. She added the young, celery-like leaves to soups and salads (again when Charles wasn't looking) and had been thinking, since Abby's email arrived, about a gardening columnist named Beverley Nichols — and his praise of this neglected herb.

Nichols was around many decades ago, but he had nonetheless become her idol because of the way he wrote. She admired intensely his wit and wisdom about gardening (realising she could never possibly match his style) and recalled how he had promoted an unusual recipe for a lovage-laden salad dressing in one of his books.

So why not introduce that dressing to the Sisters at their lunch? It would be easy enough for Abby to lay on some mixed greens — perhaps a few avocados, too, as they'd be in Mexico — and she could tuck a few fresh, green lovage leaves, wrapped in damp paper towel, into her luggage before she headed off to Heathrow. Then she could just whip up the dressing after she arrived.

As she turned towards the house again, settling on lovage as her contribution to the Titan Reunion, Charles emerged slowly through the kitchen door. He'd put on his old moth-eaten, green wool cardigan and was carrying a shiny, metal bucket.

"Thought I'd give the compost a turn and add these slops," he said, holding up the bucket which they kept under the kitchen sink. "Might be getting smelly with all this rain, don't you think?"

He smiled warmly at her, droplets of drizzle glinting on his wire-rimmed glasses and white dome of a forehead. She smiled back, and called out, "You should have put your raincoat on, dear. You'll catch cold."

"I know," he muttered. "Couldn't find the bloody thing. Must've left it in the car."

She watched his stooped figure shuffling slowly over to their two compost bins — which he'd built himself, with inordinate pride, behind the raspberry canes — and felt a sudden surge of affection for her husband, for their long life together in this old farmhouse, for the three children they'd raised successfully and for their two grandchilden, and for the simple satisfaction of shared projects like compost heaps as they headed into their old age. Fighting her feelings for Christopher Couillard had been hard. She'd longed for him with an intensity that had frightened her. But it was all for the best in the long run.

'You're not a bad old stick really,' she thought, watching Charles empty the bucket and turn the heap with a garden fork. 'You're just boring. But then I probably bore you silly too, always nattering about my plants. Boredom will be a fact of life for us in the years ahead, like root canals, incontinence pads and strange coarse new hairs sprouting from our noses. We'd better get used to it, because there's no escaping any of them.'

Even so, she couldn't picture she and Charles going their separate ways as Abby and Larry just had. She shook her head. What a surprise. How very brave. Such an option would be unthinkable for her, like being thrown off the pier at Weymouth and left to drift out to sea. Besides, how would she manage financially, without Charles? In spite of her relative fame as a gardening columnist and author of three herb books, she'd never been paid much. He handled virtually all the expenses of keeping the creaky, old farmhouse going. He'd also treated her to that impromptu trip to New York to see the

Titan Arum, and then to the reunions in Connecticut, Texas and Paris — insisting that he had no interest in going himself.

All the same, she reflected, heading back in to the warmth of the Aga to heat up some tomato soup for their lunch, it would be wonderful to escape from Charles — and that tiresome little device of his — for a week.

This break in Mexico did sound bloody marvellous.

The Preparations

Chapter 5

ABBY

"*Rico*," a barrel-shaped woman swathed in tight red satin called out. "*Muy rico, señora. Es mi propria receta.*"

She waved a wooden spoon proudly and beamed. Her creamy white teeth, caught by a shaft of sunlight, shone like a row of pearls.

She repeated the words and added, "Joo try?"

Long, gold, hoop earrings jangled as she kept leaning forward eagerly with the spoon.

In front of the woman, on a table covered in a red checked, plastic cloth, sat an enormous metal bowl containing a pudding. She tapped the bowl's side with the spoon. Held out a paper cup towards Abby. Then she said something else, very fast.

Abby smiled back, nonplussed. She was familiar with '*rico*'. She'd heard waiters in Ajijic use the word, with an accompanying smacking of lips and persuasive grins. She knew it meant 'delicious'. But '*propria receta*' and the stuff that came after? Puzzling. Was this friendly female explaining that the pudding was her own recipe, made that morning by her and her daughter? Abby thought so. Yet understanding Spanish — let alone speaking it — was proving a headache, much more difficult than she had imagined when she left New York. So she simply nodded enthusiastically and mumbled, "*Si, gracias*" because what the woman was offering did indeed smell as *rico* as she claimed. Wafting out of the bowl she caught the unmistakeable aroma of cinnamon intermingling with *piloncillo,* the Mexican raw cane sugar that's sold in a lump shaped like an ice-cream cone, then grated and turned into a syrup. Maybe more spices too. Cloves, perhaps? Or nutmeg? And there were sultana, raisins and bits of cheese stippling the crispy, golden top. Yum. Her mouth watered.

The concoction was *Capitorada* or Mexican bread pudding. Cobbled together from leftovers and consumed by families on Good Friday as a sweet release from the deprivations of Lent, it was an old tradition, but dying out. Yet here in her new home, in the town with the unpronounceable name, Abby had been delighted to discover a push to bring it back. That morning, when she dropped by her local *abarrotes* or corner store for her 'usual' (two *bolillos,* or breakfast rolls, still warm, handed over in a brown, paper bag) Herminio, the mustachioed owner revealed that some *señoras* of his acquaintance were reviving the ritual of *Capitorada.* Thus, if she wanted, she could try several different versions of the treat in the park bordering the *Malecón*, or boardwalk. And all the samples were free.

"When?" she asked eagerly.

"*Hoy.* Today," he said, surprised by the question. "Today is Good Friday, *Señora* Abbee."

"Yes, I know it is, but what time should I go?"

"Oh, um, *ahorita.* This morning, I think. But maybe later. Perhaps this afternoon."

Herminio's vagueness was, she had learned already,

typical in Mexico, where time is a fluid concept, which no one adheres to with any rigidity. Thus when someone tells you '*ahorita*' it can mean anything from '…in a couple of minutes' to 'tomorrow or the day after'.

Yet in complete contrast to this casual approach to timeliness, it had been an agreeable surprise to discover, too, that Mexicans adhered to customs of social etiquette that have long since vanished from the US. Back home, she'd grown accustomed to being addressed by everyone from bank clerks to teenage gas station attendants as 'Abby', no matter if the familiarity rankled (and it often did). Yet Herminio, even after a dozen visits to his store, refused to use her first name only. She would always be '*Señora* Abbee' in his eyes, because she was a customer, and thus of a different rank from him, and no amount of cajoling on her part that he drop the honorific would change that gulf between them.

"There's no charge for the *Capitorada*. It is free. But, *disculpe,* sorry, I do have to charge you for my *bolillos,*" Herminio added, flashing his Groucho Marx grin. "*Dos pesos por favor, Señora Abbee.*"

"*Claro*," she said, smiling. "Of course."

Stowing the bargain *bolillos* in her shoulder bag, savouring the scent of fresh dough baked barely an hour ago, she headed home for breakfast feeling ridiculously happy.

Making this bold move, splitting from Larry, quitting the US, seeking a completely new life for herself was working out just fine, she reflected. The recognition of that reality brought an involuntary smile to her lips, a proud smile, as she walked along her narrow, cobbled street. It may have seemed kind of crazy to her family, Hollis probably wasn't wrong to be concerned for her welfare, heading to a country with a violent reputation, where she didn't speak the language. But, my darling daughter, she wanted to say, stop reading those horror stories in the media, because there's another side to Mexico and it's proving to be right for me. So right, she couldn't quite believe it.

Ajijic was about an hour's drive from the airport at Guadalajara, the second largest city in Mexico, and on the afternoon that she'd exited with her meagre belongings from a cab in the centre of the little town, her nostrils had immediately picked up a powerful perfume— she learned later that it came from a huge frangipani tree, flourishing in the Plaza —and felt a transformation stirring inside her. Spirits lifting, she sensed she was going to fall in love with Ajijic.

She remembered what a Mexican neighbour back in Darien — a charming woman married to an American- had told her. This woman had been a regular at the library where Abby worked — she borrowed lots of contemporary novels, explaining with a rueful laugh that she needed to improve her command of English slang, and when Abby revealed, also laughing, that she dreamed of doing exactly the opposite — going to live in Mexico and learning to speak Spanish well — the woman had smiled and turned serious.

"Well, then, you must go, Abby," she said. "Do it. Act on your dream. *Peligro en la demora*. There is danger in delay. It's a Mexican saying and you can interpret it any way you like. But I take it to mean…" she looked away, sad for a moment, out of the window above Abby's head, as if recalling some personal decision to delay that she'd later regretted, "…that we must all do what we want in life, or else…" a wistful smile, "…we may wake up one day and realise that it is too late for us, no?"

Thus, after endless dithering and debating — wondering if she should tell Larry that she wanted a divorce, wondering if she should stay and endure what well-meaning friends always referred to as 'a rough patch' in their marriage, even though they hadn't been getting along well for years — she HAD done it. She'd followed her dream. Not impulsively by any means, but certainly with a boldness that wasn't characteristic of her. And standing there in the plaza, feeling transformed, she'd been grateful to that Mexican neighbour. She even felt mildly angry with herself for postponing the decision for so long. Had she waited any longer, she might indeed have left it too late. She'd have grown too old to embark on such a radical step. And, as a result, she'd have missed out on discovering Ajijic, which seemed so exactly what she was looking for.

For a start, there was clearly so much history to explore, about the Aztecs and the Spanish who came after them, and the two cultures mingled together in this town in colourful ways. Walking through the Plaza, feeling the welcome warmth of sun on her skin, she'd been at once captivated by an imposing, old, colonial, mission church, still in use and beside it, two indigenous, dark-skinned women in traditional dress, who sat on the sidewalk, long, silky, black hair flowing down their backs, weaving with hand looms. But what had struck her the most was the physical beauty. Over the next few days, on walks around Ajijic, her keen gardener's eye took it all in: the blossoms of jacaranda trees falling like soft, violet snowflakes on the sidewalks; the bossy bougainvillea, billowing over walls everywhere in clouds of magenta, tangerine and shocking pink; the shiny-leafed ficus trees, pruned to within an inch of their lives, yet still somehow thriving in boxy containers on narrow, cobbled streets; the tomatoes and peppers and lemon and orange trees cultivated in old, metal cans on rooftops of cheek-by-jowl houses that seemed to be painted every colour of the rainbow, often in outrageous combinations like purple and traffic light orange. A cornucopia of colour, the whole town seemed to be. And quite magical, to her way of thinking.

There was also Lake Chapala, the largest lake in Mexico. It bordered the town and had a *Malecón*, a boardwalk, running all along its northern shoreline, punctuated by tall, frothy-leafed palms with whitewashed trunks. In truth, this body of water was no match for the pristine, clear lakes back home in New York State and Vermont — being shallow, clogged with weeds, the colour of mud, and so polluted, no one, even Mexican kids, dared to swim in it. Yet a walk along the *Malecón* never failed to provide uplifting vistas of the *Cerro de Garcia*, the brooding volcano shaped like a reclining woman on the other side of the lake, which sometimes smoked and sometimes didn't, depending upon its mood, plus the opportunity to savour spectacular sunsets. And at weekends and on fiesta days (there seemed to be so many of them) she quickly discovered the fun of people-watching, as entire Mexican families descended on the boardwalk to picnic and meander through makeshift stalls hawking candy floss, potato chips, stuffed animals, trinkets and bunches of shiny balloons. Amid this general mayhem one regular— a thin, frail man sporting a Dodgers baseball cap — always appeared, slowly wheeling a bicycle cart up and down the *Malecón*, calling out, "*Cacahuetes, cacahuetes*", 'peanuts, peanuts', in an odd mournful falsetto. And he never gave up, this poor old guy, even though he found few takers for his little packets of snacks. Periodically, swarthy muscular men in indigenous, red and black costumes would show up too, bringing with them a wooden contraption which they unfolded and fitted together like a maypole. Then they shinned up the pole, and as one of their number played a wooden flute, flung themselves terrifyingly backwards from the top, twirling down to earth, legs splayed wide, on long ropes tied around their waists.

But the best part was perhaps the weather. Sunny skies. Little humidity. Temperatures reaching 24° C most days, then dropping a few degrees at night. Perfect for sleeping. It sure beat Connecticut.

It wasn't hard to figure out why so many of her fellow citizens had headed, lemming-like, to the place whose name was a bizarre conglomeration of the letters i and j, and which derived from an Aztec word meaning 'The Place Where The Water Springs From'. Abby wished she'd discovered the water-edged charms of Ajijic (pronounced Ah-hee-HEEK) sooner herself, that she'd taken 'Peligro en la demora' to heart back when real estate was still a bargain.

Stopping at a high, long, yellow wall two blocks from Herminio's, she inserted her key into a solid, black, metal door and went through the wall to her little rented house on the other side. Although she hated to attribute finding this perfect place to serendipity, a word tossed around so freely now, its true meaning had been lost (with a librarian's love of sleuthing, she'd once found out that it originated with an obscure fairy tale about four monks in Serendip, the old name for Sri Lanka), her life here had indeed fallen into place so smoothly, it must have been a case of some kind of confluences coming together. She'd departed for Mexico in a bitchy mood, drained, bitter about the break-up with Larry (yet relieved that it had finally happened), upset about Hollis's attitude to her decision, wanting to cry all the time, but stopping herself from doing so. And by the time she got on the plane, she'd become half-convinced that her Mexican neighbour was wrong, that leaving the US and her marriage was cowardly — the running-away strategy of a deluded fool. Her first three weeks in Ajiic certainly didn't give her cause to doubt that sentiment either. The 'delightful roomy studio with private bath' that she had booked through Airbnb turned out to be nothing more than a greedy American couple's converted carport, with a barred window facing a brick wall, a showerhead that dripped, a clogged coffee maker and a river of ants across the perpetually damp, concrete floor. She'd also weathered the disappointment of missing out on nearly half a dozen pricey house rentals advertised by realtors. Competition for someplace to hang her hat in this little piece of paradise was clearly fierce. Others kept beating her to the punch.

Yet then the tide started to turn.

She joined the Lake Chapala Society, the local hang-out for expats, and started borrowing books from their library, gratified to find that it contained a well-thumbed collection of British classics. During her retirement, she'd resolved to read many of her favourites again, now that she had time on her hands. And on the day that she returned a copy of Thomas Hardy's *Tess of the d'Urbervilles* to a jovial, grey-haired American manning the library's front desk, she'd spotted a small, hand-written ad pinned to the Society's noticeboard. It said, 'Careful tenant wanted for small house on Emiliano Zapata. Long term'.

The bottom of the ad showed a number to call. That was all. She left a message. Thus the MacDonalds entered her life.

They were an ancient Canadian couple who had been coming to Ajijic every winter for nearly three decades. Their response was an equally brief return message left on her own phone asking her to 'please join us for lunch at eleven thirty a.m. at the *Nueva Posada*."

The place was a surprise. Far from being new, this Spanish colonial hostelry proved to be one of the oldest in town. Historic, crammed with dusty, dark antiques and still in operation, it gave off an air of shabby, genteel decline, with a fusty smell to match, when Abby went through its heavy wooden front door. The *Nueva Posada* also had a noon hour clientele that fitted its ambiance, for the patrons appeared to consist entirely of retired Americans and Canadians who, like the MacDonalds, depended on walking sticks and mobility devices to get around. Hunched over their lunch in the dining room, many of them looked as geriatic and worn out by life as the tired, old *posada* itself.

The couple were already seated at a table facing the lake when she arrived, promptly at eleven thirty.

They exchanged greetings and she sat down.

"We first came to Ajijic when it was quieter," said Bruce MacDonald gravely, shaking his whiskery, white jowls in a tut-tutting way, after a girl in a green uniform brought them coffee. "All you saw on the street back then were the *charros*, the cowboys. They rode down to the lake to wash their horses. We liked watching them. There were hardly any cars."

"The noise is terrible now," chimed in his wife, a frail, bird-like creature with a voice as thin as tissue paper. "All the bars, the cafes, the traffic… We love the climate here, we never go back to Canada any more, the kids come to see us when they can, but …"

She picked up the menu, scanned it in a disconsolate way, then put the plastic folder back on the table as if it contained nothing of interest.

Bruce explained that they'd loved the town right from the start, so their second winter, they'd bought a 'cheap little place downtown' not far from the hotel. But they had just moved to one of the modern subdivisions that were springing up around Ajijic. This revelation made Abby momentarily wonder why. She'd glimpsed some of these new developments on exploratory walks and been unimpressed. Charmless ghettos for gringos, she thought, reminiscent of gated suburban communities in California and Arizona, all new, all bland, all exactly the same, like collections of white cupcakes tacked awkwardly on the steep mountainsides. They possessed none of the quirky charm of Ajijic proper, closer to the lake. Yet she kept her mouth shut. Over lunch, she listened patiently to a litany of complaints about how the place had changed and nodded politely, until — hallelujah — Bruce eventually got around to saying that they were keeping the downtown house for their son John, who would be retiring himself in a couple of years. But in the meantime, they were looking for someone 'reliable' to sign a long lease.

Her heart leapt. She sat up straight in her chair, on high alert. She'd been in danger of dozing off over *Buena Posada's* dishwater coffee.

"I'd be happy to sign on for two years," she broke in. "I don't have any plans to buy myself."

Did her face look suitably eager? She hoped so, crossed her fingers under the tablecloth.

Yet Bruce took his time, asking probing questions about her background. Myra Macdonald sat silently facing the lake with rheumy eyes, saying nothing.

Then abruptly, as if some wordless connection had passed between the old pair, Myra looked back at her husband and gave the briefest of nods, barely noticeable even to Abby, who'd been holding her breath and glancing anxiously from one to the other. She exhaled with relief. It was the signal. Her explanation of why she had come to live in Ajijic clearly passed the test.

"Would you like to go and see the house?" Bruce asked, smiling, appearing to fully relax for the first time.

"I'd love to," Abby said.

"It's on the north side of the Carretera, you know," said Myra, sounding doubtful, as the couple eased themselves upright with obvious difficulty and retrieved matching carved walking sticks hooked over the back of a dining chair. Bruce led the way shakily to an SUV parked outside.

"Very crowded. Narrow, cobbled streets. Difficult to walk. Dogs. Kids," Myra went on in breathless bursts as if getting words out took a tremendous effort. Bruce, sprightlier than his wife, started the engine and they drove slowly up a steep, narrow street in the opposite direction to the lake.

"A lot of expats don't like it up here, you know," he said, looking from side to side of the street as the SUV crossed the Carretera and continued up the mountainside.

But Abby did like it. Right away. When Bruce finally slowed down, turned a corner and said, "Our street," waving a hand knobbly with veins, Calle Emiliano Zapata struck her as a taste of the real Mexico she'd been hoping to find. An old, wrinkled woman in black sat on a wooden chair outside a front door. A fat, ugly dog sprawled on its back beside her, legs in the air, pink and black spotted belly catching the breeze. Two dark-skinned little boys jumped up and down on the sidewalk playing some kind of hopscotch game and shouting at each other. The kids stopped playing when the SUV drew up and stopped. They came closer and stood in respectful silence, smiling shyly. Abby felt conspicuous getting out of a huge, ostentatious vehicle like the SUV and wished the MacDonalds drove one of the beat-up old Volkswagen Beetles that she often saw around town.

"*Buenos dias señor Mac*," the boys chirped in unison, as Bruce got out.

"*Hola, Carlos y Santiago. Como estais?*" he said and patted the smaller one on the head.

"Nice family," he murmured to Abby after she and Myra exited the SUV. "They live next door. Their dad is in construction. He did a beautiful job with our kitchen tiles even though he doesn't normally do that kind of work. But ask a Mexican to do anything and he'll find a way."

And while the MacDonalds' house was unprepossessing from the outside — the high, yellow wall punctuated by one, small barred window and the black entrance door, and squeezed in between two other equally high walls, one sugar pink, the other a lurid turquoise — the interior told a different story, as Mexican homes usually do. Abby was gratified to discover a small but adequate living room, with double doors that dissolved into a long, deep courtyard containing a colossal collection of plants: succulents, amaryllis in red and white, *Spathiphyllum*, *Dracaena*, an enormous blooming *Datura*, its upside-down blooms hanging over the sides of a decorative pot, and even a mango tree with a few tear-shaped fruit in the early stages of ripeness. One bedroom with ensuite occupied the left side of the living area, two small bedrooms shared a bathroom on the other side.

Yet the best part was the modern kitchen, which the MacDonalds had added on to the back. Airy, bright, it featured an unusual curved ceiling made of red brick (a local specialty, known as a *boveda*, Bruce explained), plenty of counter space, a built-in chopping board and the ceramic tiles laid by their neighbour in swirling patterns of orange, yellow and forest green, both on the floor and reaching half way up the kitchen walls. A professional-sized gas range, plus top-quality pots and pans hanging from hooks in the ceiling completed the picture. Abby's heart leapt again. She immediately pictured the Sisters gathered in the kitchen, sipping wine, cooking convivially for their Titan Reunion lunch. There was even an earthenware wine cooler sitting on a shelf. That would come in handy for sure.

She praised the house in effusive terms, particularly the kitchen. Myra looked gratified but exhausted. Then as they sat in the courtyard on *equipales*, the traditional leather and wood armchairs that are ubiquitous throughout Mexico, while Bruce filled out a lease form, Myra said that she was ninety-four and suffered from angina. To Abby's astonishment, she also revealed that she had been a master chef.

"I.... cooked for... er... some of the best restaurants in Vancouver, you know... and... er I wrote a cooking column..." she said, gasping for breath, her thin, high voice almost fading away.

She patted Abby's hand with her own wrinkled one, the joints knotted with arthritis, and smiled sadly.

"You'll... make good use of... my... my pots, won't you, dear?"

"I'll be sure to," Abby assured her.

"And will you want a maid and gardener?" asked Bruce. "Those aren't included in the rent, but we can give you some names."

"Um, not initially, thanks. There's just going to be me, and occasional guests."

"You realise, of course, that you'll be helping Mexicans find badly needed jobs if you do hire someone. Most people take on help here for that reason, you know," he said, his tone mildly reproving.

"Um…yes, I'm aware of that," Abby replied, feeling guilty, but at the same time thinking how much she was looking forward to total solitude. "But I'd like to settle down here first, if that's okay with you."

"Oh sure. It's your decision."

"Yes… a nice little house. Easy… easy enough to maintain for one person. I… er… I miss it," his wife broke in with her bird-like voice, looking around the courtyard sadly.

Hunched over in the *equipal* she looked like a little mouse cowering in a corner, making Abby feel wretched for Myra MacDonald. How demeaning, how humiliating, it must be to wind up like this, no longer probably even capable of cooking scrambled eggs, after what had obviously been a thriving career in the restaurant industry. She hoped some good years were ahead of her in Ajijic, before she too faced the crushing inevitability of what happens to the human body when it's nearly a century old.

Yet at the same time, she wanted to whoop with joy.

"You can count on me to take care of everything, Myra," she said, signing the lease with a flourish. "And I love to cook. I'll certainly use your lovely pots."

Myra smiled thinly again.

"Good."

***

The woman in red satin, and her equally colourful compatriots, chattered like a row of exotic parrots as they stood behind their bowls of *Capitorada*, beaming at passers-by, doling out portions to anyone who looked interested. Abby accepted her paper cupful with another, *"Gracias"* and, anxious not to spill the contents, headed over to the lake's edge, feeling guilty again. In spite of that pledge made over two months ago, she'd hardly cooked a thing in Myra MacDonald's state-of-the-art kitchen. The realisation had hit her belatedly that there was no point when you lived alone. Not when you could pick up a bundle of fresh tortillas for only a few cents from a picnic cooler at Herminio's, then wrap them around spicy barbecued chicken, pinto beans and salsa, sold at a take-out joint on the Carretera. And, as an Easter bonus, taste a Mexican specialty for free.

This freedom felt new. Strange. Liberating. After thirty-six years of cohabitation, it amazed her that every day, late in the afternoon, she no longer had to stop what she was doing and think about making dinner.

Yet once the Sisters arrived, it would be different. After some two months on her own, she'd be playing host to a houseful of guests. And that would mean reverting to her organised librarian self, being practical about matters like meals, clean towels and fresh sheets on the beds. It was an exciting prospect yet she felt strangely nervous.

Reaching the *Malecón,* the cup cradled in both hands like a chalice, she sank down on a bench and looked out at the lake, anticipating this upcoming reunion with her gardening buddies. It had been a while since she did anything like it. Back home, Larry had never liked socialising, so she maintained a circle of women friends in Connecticut — mostly from the library world- with whom she met up sometimes when he was away at work. They usually saw each other over lunch in restaurants. But they rarely prepared a meal together — as the Sisters like to do. She hoped nothing would happen to spoil her fantasy of an indolent, all-day feast in the glorious setting of her flower-filled courtyard.

Three of the Sisters were coming — Tensie, Rhodo and Hannah. They'd all confirmed by email and would arrive, on separate flights into Guadalajara, after Easter. Herminio had introduced her to an accommodating cabbie, name of Juan, who said he would be happy to drive back and forth with her to the airport three times, so she could meet them all one by one. That Lola Honeybone couldn't join the group from Texas was something of a disappointment, for Lola could have got here more easily than the others. All she had to do was hop on a direct flight from Houston to Guadalajara and she'd have been in Ajijic within a few hours. But busy-as-a-bee Lola seemed to be perpetually on deadline with issues of *Our Southern Gardens* and perhaps, Abby reflected, put off by Mexico's bad press, she didn't really want to come anyway. From Amsterdam, Mieke sent regrets that she couldn't make it either. She was holed up in her apartment, writing a biography on Carolus Clusius, the Dutch botanist who introduced tulips to Europe from Turkey. Nathalie was busy on a book too — about Josephine Bonaparte's roses at Malmaison. And as for dear little Jing-Jing so far away in China... she emailed that she was rushed off her feet, filming episodes of her TV show.

Yet Abby hardly expected to see Jing-Jing anyway. A mountain town in the middle of Mexico was, after all, she reflected, a very long haul from a giant metropolis like Guangzhou.

Still, three guests were plenty for a lunch party, and she had enough beds in the house to accommodate them all. No one would have to resort to the unregulated risks of Airbnb, as she did on her arrival.

She settled on the bench, dipped a plastic spoon into the *Capitorada*, brought it to her lips. Good. Overly sweet to her taste, she concluded, like many Mexican desserts, but full of flavour. Must be the cinnamon, she thought. It tasted so fresh here. She wondered if the bushy tree, a member of the Laurel family, whose bark produced her favourite spice, was cultivated in Mexico.

Capitorada. Cah-pee-tor-rah-dah. She liked the way the word rolled off her tongue. It was catchy.

She tapped her teeth with the plastic spoon. Yes, Mexican bread pudding as a dessert at the Titan Reunion. That would be perfect. The Sisters would all get a kick out of hearing about its origins.

And it was indeed *rico*. She ate the whole cupful.

***

Abby stopped in at Aguacate, a health food store on the Carretera, the main drag through Ajijic, before walking home.

She liked shopping there. It was spotless, and the middle-aged owner, Conchita, a cheery woman with beefy arms and enormous feet crammed into men's sandals, never failed to encourage her to speak in Spanish. Conchita chortled delightedly when Abby tried to explain, shakily, that she had just tasted, "*Capitorada… um… por la primera vez*" — for the first time.

"*Bueno, señora. Muy bueno. Es una tradicion muy vieja aqui para nosotros. Y muy rico*," she replied rapidly, clapping her hands together, before switching to English in response to Abby's bafflement. "It's an old tradition. I know those ladies who are trying to revive it. They're good cooks. But…" she chortled again. ".. you should make *Capitorada* yourself. *Es muy facil*. It's very easy."

"*Si. Yo…yo…* um… I intend to," said Abby. "Some friends are coming on a visit. We're going to cook a big lunch together and I want to serve *Capitorada* for dessert. So I need some… um… *canela*. That's the word, right?"

"*Si, claro*, we call cinnamon *canela*," said Conchita, pulling down a glass jar from a shelf behind the counter.

"And Mexican *canela* is the best," she added with pride. "It's the true cinnamon, grown in Sri Lanka and much better than the cheaper cassia kind that comes from China. Mexico is the biggest importer in the world of Sri Lankan cinnamon, because we use it so often in cooking. And of course, our hot chocolate. You'll need the powdered kind for *Capitorada*. But would you like to try some of these sticks too?"

She unscrewed the lid and pulled out a handful of brown twigs. They looked nondescript, but had a strong, cinnamon-y aroma.

"Yes, please," she said. "I might make some hot chocolate for my friends one night. And can you recommend a Mexican-style jam? I'm sure they'd like to try something other than the jars of Smuckers I see in supermarkets here." Conchita proffered a small jar containing a thick, yellowy-orange concoction that looked like marmalade.

"Pineapple jam. Made by a woman right here in Ajijic. No preservatives. And very sweet, but good on a *bolillo* for breakfast," she explained.

"Great."

On her way out of the store, Abby almost collided with a young, white woman wearing a man's straw sombrero that looked way too big for her. She also had on threadbare jeans, the kneecaps poking through, and big, black boots covered in red dust. She jubilantly barged in through the open door, holding close to her chest a red milk crate crammed with bunches of a tall plant with large, floppy leaves.

"Whoops, sorry love," she said, lowering the milk crate and flashing a broad grin at Abby. "Didn't see you there. Blame me amaranth." She nodded at the leaves which obscured her chin and mouth. "Bally stuff grows so tall. I'm just delivering some to Conchita here."

"That's okay," said Abby, smiling back, thinking that the woman sounded British. "No harm done."

"*Hola*, Gillian," Conchita called out to her from the counter. "Say hello to Abby, one of my favourite customers."

"Well, pleased to meetcha, Abby. *Mucho gusto* as they say here," said Gillian, beaming, putting the milk crate down on the floor store and thrusting out a grimy, sunburned hand with dirt under the fingernails. "You're new, aren't you, love? I've seen you walking around town."

"Yes, I arrived a couple of months ago," said Abby, shaking the girl's hand.

"Like it?"

Abby nodded and said, "Very much."

"Well, love, you should come and see me at the organic market. Shouldn't she Conchita? And then you might like funny old Ajijic even more."

The new arrival cackled with laughter, throwing her head back. The outsized sombrero almost fell off her head but she thumped her crown to clamp it down again.

"Gillian is one of our local characters," Conchita called out, in response to Abby's amused look. "And you should go see her at the market. She sells lots of unusual herbs, like this amaranth she's just brought me. And she grows them all herself, organically, out in Joco."

Conchita smiled, shaking her head in wonderment.

"I don't know how you do it, Gillian."

"Gawd, I don't know either," said Gillian, laughing once more, bringing the milk crate over to the counter. "I'm a nutter, I guess. Me back aches every bloody day. But there it is. That's me life."

She shrugged and turned back to Abby.

"Come and see me sometime, love," she added, still a picture of merriment. "I'll show you what you can do with amaranth."

"Yes, okay," Abby replied, thinking that the market might make a good outing for the Sisters after their party.

And she liked this Gillian. She was fun.

Chapter 6
Dorset, England, 15th April, 2017

HANNAH

Hannah's carry-on bag sat waiting in the hall like an obedient dog. Although her flight to Mexico City was still two days away, she'd been packing — and repacking — for a week. She couldn't decide what kind of clothes to take along. Her favourite blue cotton shirt with long sleeves? Or would T-shirts be better? Did she need a jacket? And a dress? She felt a flutter of excitement every time she unzipped the bag and started over.

But now an obstacle loomed. A very big obstacle. In the shape of her younger sister, Eve.

Eve showed up on the doorstep of the Dorset farmhouse an hour ago, sobbing her heart out. Eyes red and puffy from crying, streams of black mascara running down her cheeks, she looked like an abandoned orphan, not a forty-three-year-old sophisticated woman of the world, with an apartment in Rome, minor celebrity status as an expert on Italian traditional foods, and regular culinary assignments from one of the city's top caterers. She kept babbling about flights being full, of having to endure a 'terrible' overnight train journey to Calais and of managing to get the last ticket on the Eurostar.

"Then I had to sit for hours in Waterloo station, waiting

for a train down to Dorchester. An awful yobbo in an Arsenal shirt kept pestering me. Honestly, Hannah, why don't you live closer to London?"

Hannah sighed, said nothing. She carried in her sibling's two soaked gym bags — the rain still hadn't stopped — from the porch steps. She put them on the carpet in the hall beside her own dry bag. Helped Eve peel off an expensive-looking sodden raincoat. Underneath, the silly creature was wearing nothing more than a mini skirt, a long-sleeved cotton top and black high heels. Her bare legs felt as wet and clammy as a dead fish.

She asked in a resigned way, "What happened?" even though she didn't really want to know.

Eve shivered.

"Fabio left me," she blurted out between sobs. "I hate him. The fucking bastard. And I'm freezing. That train was so COLD. I'm going to complain. I want my money back."

Her teeth started chattering, a tad too theatrically in Hannah's view. But she didn't comment. She murmured soothing noises, found her sister a towel and some dry clothes, told her to sit on a stool in the kitchen beside the Aga. Then she made a pot of hot coffee and scrambled eggs.

After barely touching her eggs, Eve sprawled on the sofa, pulling at the tassels on a pale green, velvet cushion — and spilling out the whole story.

"He went off with Silvana, my best friend. The bitch. And he took my Toscanas with him and gave them to her. Can you imagine that? I could kill him. Kill her."

She tossed the cushion at the wall in a rage, and broke into sobs again.

"How am I going to work without those copper

saucepans? They cost me a fortune. I'm finished. I can't go back to Italy…"

"But I heard that you were thinking of leaving Fabio yourself. Ada told me…"

"I know, I know. But I changed my mind. I decided to stay. Thought he'd be pleased. But all the time he was carrying on with Silvana. I just didn't know. How dare he do that to me? I hate men."

She carried on sobbing.

Hence the obstacle in front of Hannah. She hadn't told Eve about her impending trip and it would be useless to ask Charles to babysit her neurotic sister. He always ducked what he called 'family matters'. Hannah concluded long ago that it was a biological thing with men, this reluctance to get involved, and she didn't intend to press the issue now. In any case, he'd gone out. He slammed the lid of his iPad shut the moment he heard Eve's voice, rushed out of the back door like a cat being pursued by a mad dog and sped off to Dorchester, mumbling something about getting the oil changed in the Toyota, even though it was in the garage only last week.

Yet nor did Hannah want to pack Eve off to Ada in Herefordshire. Poor Ada and Tom were up to their armpits in disinfectant and lord-knows-what, trying to put an end to all the worms coming out of their sheeps' bottoms. In reality, she had no idea what the procedure was for banishing such worms, nor what they looked like, but it all sounded perfectly ghastly and she didn't really want to know about them either. One thing was glaringly apparent though: Ada and Tom didn't need a weeping, wailing woman descending on them and getting in the way.

So she said, "Sorry, darling, but you'll have to make some

other arrangements because I'm going away. Can't you stay with friends?"

"Friends?" Eve croaked, her voice cracking. "I don't have any friends. My only friend was Silvana. The fucking whore." More sobs.

"Well, you can't stay here," Hannah said firmly. "Because I'm flying to Mexico in two days."

Like a light switch being flicked off, Eve stopped crying and looked up.

"Mexico? *Dio mio*, lucky you, Hannah. How *meraviglioso*. I've always wanted to see what Mexico is like," she said, suddenly calmer, envy in her voice, eyes opening wide.

"Yes, I'm looking forward to it."

A pause.

"Well…" Eve smiled for the first time since arriving, "I have a brilliant idea."

Another pause. "Why don't I come with you?"

Hannah had been expecting this. She shook her head.

"Sorry, no."

"But why not?" Eve persisted, her tone turning petulant. "I can pay. Honestly, I can. I have money saved from three big catering jobs for Giuseppe…"

"No, it's not possible. I'm staying at a friend's. She won't have room for you."

"But they have hotels where you're going, don't they? Mexico has loads of hotels. Why can't your friend find me one? I'm sure she will if you ask her. PLEASE." Eve's voice turned pleading. "I don't see what the problem is. How many times do I have to keep telling you, Hannah? I have the money. Honestly, I do. I'll die…" she broke into sobs again, "… if I don't do something to change my life."

She rolled over, buried her face in the back of the sofa and with great heaving gulps, began blubbering again, all over Hannah's new chintz covers.

Hannah rolled her eyes, resigned herself to the inevitable, left Eve to cry. She went upstairs to her office and dashed off a quick email to Abby. Explaining the situation briefly, she wrote that she couldn't come unless she brought Eve along. So would Abby mind very much…?

A tense evening unfolded while she waited for Abby's reply. They talked about the weather over dinner, the perpetual fall-back position of the English when seeking to avoid what's really on their mind. The non-stop rain was awful, they agreed. Eve blamed it on global warming, Charles looked circumspect and shrugged, insisting that changing weather patterns had happened in cycles throughout history. Hannah, sensing an argument in the offing, dodged saying anything at all and concentrated on doling out the lamb chops. They drank an Oddbins special red with the meal. Charles got miffed when Eve helped herself to most of it. He grumped off to bed right afterwards. Eve spent the night in Alice's old room.

To Hannah's surprise, she went into her office next morning and found an email from Abby already. And it was in the affirmative.

"Yes, your sister can come, but she'll have to stay in a B&B. There's a nice one, Casa Tosca, just a few doors away. Will go see later if they have a room. And can she cook something for our lunch party?"

Eve slept late. She grumbled when Hannah brought her tea at eleven a.m., and looked as filthy as a chimney sweep, because the mascara she neglected to remove before going to bed had smeared all over her cheeks and nightdress during the night. The thick black guck had also, Hannah noticed with irritation, found its way on to her white, linen sheets.

"This bed is too hard. You should get a softer one," Eve complained, slapping the duvet with a peeved expression then propping herself up on the pillows. "I couldn't sleep. And now my head hurts like someone's hitting it with a hammer."

She pressed her finger tips against her temples and groaned.

Hannah swallowed hard. She refrained from pointing out that overindulging in the Oddbins sell-off, not the bed, was probably responsible for the hammering. She told Eve about Abby's email.

Eve blinked and rubbed her eyes. She sat bolt upright against the pillows, as alert as a rabbit sniffing the air in a farmer's field.

"She wants me to cook something? Of course I can," she said, clapping her hands together joyously. "I'm a caterer, aren't I? One of the best in Rome. I will bake you all the most *meraviglioso* cake you've ever tasted. I picked up the recipe when I was in Capri last summer with Fab…"

At the mention of her former inamorata, she dissolved into tears again.

"Oh, stop it Eve," Hannah said crossly, losing patience at last. "No more crying, for heaven's sake. Get up. I'm going to see if I can get you a ticket."

She could. On line, she discovered — with mixed feelings — that there were still a few seats left on her British Airways flight to Mexico City. Using her own credit card, she bought one for Eve, then slipped quietly downstairs, without returning to the bedroom to break the news. Dealing with Eve's reaction could wait.

Hannah hurriedly pulled on her waxed jacket and went outside in the rain. The fresh moisture-laden air acted like a balm on her brain. She took several deep breaths, revelling at being out in the garden, her treasured garden, always her refuge in tense times and, at that moment, she couldn't have cared less if she got soaked to the skin. What a relief it was to escape from her impossible sister for even a few minutes. Her sheepskin slippers squelched on the muddy pathways (she'd been in too much of a hurry to pull on her wellies) but did she care? Not a bit. The slippers could dry by the Aga, and the feeling of her own head being ready to explode into a million tiny fragments started to dissolve miraculously in the drizzle. She headed over to the herbs. Poor things, she thought, they're like a bunch of bedraggled, forlorn toddlers sitting there together in the dark, wet earth. She located the lovage — already three feet high despite the sogginess. Pulled scissors out of her pocket. Carefully snipped a handful of the new, tender interior leaves, clasping them gently in her fingers as she returned to the kitchen. Mud tracked into the house on her soles, but she didn't care about the mess she was making either. She'd whip a cloth over the floor before Charles came in, noticed and complained.

With maternal care, she wrapped the little bundle of greenery in a piece of paper towel and stowed it in a plastic bag in the fridge. She'd already decided to conceal the bundle in a pair of pants at the bottom of her carry-on bag — a dishonesty that bothered her, but not unduly. She reasoned that the Mexican authorities, always on the lookout for drugs, would surely have bigger fish to fry than her. Feeling more relaxed now, she pictured herself serving salad to the Sisters tossed with the lovage-laden dressing that tasted so good. She was sure they'd love it.

Yet Eve WAS a worry. Hannah bit her lower lip, wishing that her younger sister — so wild, so unpredictable, so wrapped up in herself— wasn't coming. But how could she say no? She and Ada were stuck with the legacy of Eve being the baby of the family, born twenty-one years after they came on the scene. Both Polly and Duncan were so bowled over by this new unexpected gift — cute as a doll, smiling up at them with toothless gums from her cot — that they spoiled Eve rotten, and left the twins to fend for themselves during their entry into adulthood. Ada still felt bitter about the way their baby sister took over, but Hannah didn't. Family is family, she decided long ago, and stressful members came with the territory. Her second child, Toby, was, at thirty-three, a handful too — incapable of holding a proper job for long, always begging her and Charles for a loan — yet she still loved him. She also loved Eve, although at that moment she could cheerfully have throttled her.

But would Eve's incessant craving for male attention somehow get in the way of the Sisters' lunch party? And as a consequence, would Abby never speak to her again?

Be optimistic, she told herself. It's an all-female gathering. Eve won't have the opportunity to misbehave.

***

In truth, Abby did mind. A bit. She was a precise person, hated plans going awry and often attributed her lack of patience with last minute changes to her library background. Checking books in and out, cataloguing them methodically, always knowing what was what. She'd followed that kind of routine for years — and it suited her. It was the same with her gardening column. Deadlines were cast in stone by the newspaper in Stamford. Six hundred words once a week, filed on Thursday without fail, her editor had told her when she got hired. And she'd said, 'Yes, sure, no problem,' and had consistently given them what they wanted. In twenty-six years, she'd never missed a deadline.

Abby also felt oddly protective of the Sisters. They'd bonded together because of a shared love of plants and gardening, and that had never changed. Every member of the group would happily sit and talk for hours about the differences between big leaf, oakleaf, mop top, and panicle hydrangeas or the respective merits of peat moss versus coir as a potting medium, or the way the *Oenothera* species all opened their flowers at sunset. This kind of talk would surely bore Eve. She'd be intrusive, annoying. And from Hannah's email, she sounded like an airhead, anyway.

Abby also regretted suggesting that Eve cook something. A flourless cake made from chocolate and almonds? A second email from Hannah indicated that's what Eve planned, but it'd be way too rich, for sure, served for dessert at the same time as her *Capitorada*. And no way she was not going to take that off the menu for anybody. Yet she loved Hannah dearly —the British Bakewell tarts she'd produced with apparent ease were the justifiable hit of their Titan Reunion back in Connecticut — so she decided to play along. Like Hannah, she told herself to look on the bright side. Perhaps Eve would turn out to be a gardener too, a fancier of those flowers everyone called geraniums, but which were really *pelargoniums*, living as she did in an apartment in Rome. Balconies overflowing with scarlet and pink *pelargoniums*… she had such fond memories of them lighting up the Italian capital's side streets during a trip there with Larry years ago, back when they still liked each other.

In late afternoon, the hottest time of day in Ajijic, with no breeze off the lake and the setting sun a ball of gold behind the mango tree, Abby went out. She stepped carefully over the fat, ugly dog that was sprawled on his back outside, belly worshipping the sky. Her young neighbours, Carlos and Santiago had indicated to her a while ago, with shy giggles, that the dog's name was Campeon and that where he'd taken to lying, right outside her front door, had become his favourite snoozing spot. So reluctant to upset the boys, she wasn't going to insist that it moved someplace else, even though Campeon was kind of smelly and farted far too often. She turned northward into the street where Casa Tosca was located to see about a room for Eve. The B & B had a reputation of being one of the best in town, a classy establishment, hidden away behind a ten-foot-high white wall further up the mountainside, with razored glass set in cement along its top. Inset at intervals into the wall were curlicued black wrought iron grilles, fronted by shocking pink geraniums planted in stylish terra cotta urns. The owner was an American opera singer who lived in Atlanta and only visited between bookings at opera houses around the world. It was beautiful — but expensive.

A svelte young Mexican wearing black leggings and heavy, black eyeliner which curled up like wings at the corners of her eyes opened the front door.

"Fortunately for your friend we have one room left," she said imperiously in English, in response to Abby's inquiry. "And it is our best room. The owner uses it when she comes here. It has a king-sized bed and a private bathroom."

The spacious room was indeed exquisitely furnished, with antiques, a handwoven bedspread in orange and blue and paintings by contemporary Mexican artists on the walls. Abby was thankful not to see Frida Kahlo in evidence anywhere, an artist she had grown to dislike. Frida's grisly images, the blood, the meeting-in-the-middle eyebrows, the *'china poblana'* peasant costumes, had become a tiresome cliché, showing up on everything from throw cushions to fridge magnets. So she'd been pleased to learn that, in the country of her birth, the tortured painter — worshipped as such a feminist icon in the US — was regarded as strictly fodder for the tourists. Mexicans tend not to like Frida much, an American art gallery owner in Ajijic confided recently, even if they rarely say so, not wanting to offend the sensibilities of her many gringo fans. Yet Frida's fat husband, Diego Rivera, his womanising dismissed with a shrug, was generally lauded as a much better painter. Well, good. She agreed.

After examining the gleaming tiled bathroom, Abby noticed, on a table by the bed, a framed signed photo of the tenor Javier Camarena — a touch that she did thoroughly approve of. Before leaving New York, she'd watched Camarena hitting the high Cs in a mesmerising online performance of Donizetti's *La Fille du Regiment* from the Met and had been bowled over by the incredible vocal range and stamina of the young Mexican.

There were other charming little touches at Casa Tosca. The room's window faced on to a courtyard resplendent with pink and red *mandevilla* vines, where she spied a fountain, tiled in aquamarine, with water tinkling at a gentle pitch, so the effect was calming, but not intrusive. And beyond the fountain, through an ornately carved door in dark wood framed by an artistic archway of shocking pink bougainvillea, there was a dining room furnished with antiques and wooden tables covered in multicoloured, checked cloths. From somewhere, the Song of the Moon from Dvorak's *Rusalka* played softly, although there was clearly nobody around listening to the haunting melody.

The imperious girl explained that breakfast was served in the dining room 'between seven and ten a.m. No later'. Then she quoted a price per night that made Abby blanch. Yet she put a fifty percent deposit for a seven-day stay on her own credit card, figuring that would be okay with Eve, who could pay her back after she arrived.

Next, she headed to Aguacate again to pick up the 'half a kilo of organic almonds, whole and unblanched' that Eve had stipulated were necessary for her cake. Hannah's sister had also requested some of the 'marvellous dark chocolate they make in Oaxaca' if she could find it.

Conchita was pleased to see her so soon after her last visit.

"What you want is some *Al-MEN-dras*," she instructed slowly. "That's almonds, *señora. Digalo*. Say it."

Abby did, was gratified by a nod of approval, then added, "*Y también, yo quiero choco…*"

"*Cacao*," corrected Conchita, taking down from a shelf behind her a heavy jar containing chunks of dark chocolate. "This is what you mean, I think?"

"*Si, por favor. Cacao*," Abby said.

Finally, there was vanilla.

"*Vie-NEE-a*," instructed Conchita.

"*Vie-NEE-a*," echoed Abby.

She thought how pretty the Spanish word sounded, like

the call of a tropical bird. And how happy she'd be when the Sisters arrived.

As for Eve… she did at least seem to be quite knowledgeable about Mexico, asking for chocolate from Oaxaca.

And perhaps her cake would be good.

Chapter 7
Toronto, Canada, 17th April, 2017

RHODO

Rhodo was back in the fish shop. The Portuguese woman who ran the place didn't scare her any more. She'd introduced herself as Matilde the last time and was a cheerful, friendly soul, who spoke perfect English. She also dispensed valuable advice. On her previous visit, she'd told Rhodo to soak salt cod in cold water for a couple of hours not once, but three times. If she neglected to do that, whatever she cooked would taste too salty.

Rhodo had followed her instructions to the letter on yet another miserable day back in February. And it was a chore, finding a bowl big enough to accommodate the ugly, grey piece of dried-up cod, then filling it with water, then emptying the bowl, then repeating the procedure twice. She spilt some water on the floor during the second round of soaking and the kitchen still stank of fish after she got the mop out. Azalea kept sniffing the air and looking hopeful. But when that step was over, she'd made Gramma Mercer's Newfoundland cod cakes for Monica. As she'd hoped, it wasn't difficult. Just fiddly. Then her best friend, who wouldn't lie, had gone into raptures about them.

"Rhodo, they're awesome. Never tasted any as good as

this," Monica said, smacking her lips, helping herself to another of the patties. "Much better made with salt cod than fresh fish. More flavour. And I like the texture, don't you?"

Rhodo did. Salt cod felt substantial in her mouth, kind of chewy. The flesh didn't go all mushy and fall apart after cooking, like regular cod. So that had settled it. She would take some salt cod with her to Mexico. Make Gramma's classic cod cakes for the Sisters. Then, when she served them up at their lunch, she would relate a colourful story about her childhood spent beside the grey cold Atlantic Ocean, and in doing so, give a shout-out to her beloved Newfoundland, the sparsely inhabited island that's virtually unknown around the world and even ignored by most Canadians.

Yet in spite of her prior success with the cod cakes, she was still fretting, positioned in front of the long, refrigerated counter, making other customers wait, on the day before she had to to fly to Mexico City.

"You're sure it will be okay for me to put it in the overhead bins?" she asked Matilde, frowning. "I'm just taking a carry-on bag with me. It won't melt and stink up the plane?"

"Salt cod doesn't melt, ma'am," Matilde assured her, leaning on the counter. "It's dried. That's the whole point of salting. You can keep it for months and it won't spoil. I wouldn't leave it in a warm place for weeks, but it will be okay during your flight."

She smiled expectantly.

"You're sure?"

"Yes I am."

The response was clipped, a little less warm this time, because two of the fish shop's regulars, the usual stout, grim-jawed ladies in black, were waiting behind Rhodo, tapping their feet on the cold concrete floor.

"But if you're at all concerned, I can wrap it in several layers of that..." Matilde motioned towards a roll of waxed brown paper standing on top of the counter, "...and then put it in two plastic bags instead of one."

Rhodo thought for a few moments. Someone made a sound behind her like a tongue being clicked against front teeth. An impatient sound. The foot tapping grew more agitated.

"All right then. If you can wrap it like you say, I'll take a piece that weighs about a kilo, thank you, Matilde."

The slab duly wrapped, she left the store. The pavement was soggy and slippery. "Freezing-rain-mixed-with-wet-snow... Freezing-rain-mixed-with-wet-snow..." the weather woman kept saying on the radio, a monotonous mantra that hardly varied from day to day. They should save themselves some money, Rhodo often thought, make a tape of those five words, then just flick a switch every morning and play it over and over, because the message is always the same. For the entire winter Toronto had hardly seen the sun. The freezing rain mixed with wet snow seemed endless.

Arriving home, she shook rain off her coat, then hung it on a hook. Azalea sidled up, purring and rubbing against her legs for food, but she jumped away in horror when a cascade of raindrops fell on to her fur. Leaky boots and wet socks peeled off, Rhodo held one bare, white foot, then the other, over a heating vent in the living room to warm her toes. She thought once again what a sanctuary her little semi-detached house in the Portuguese neighbourhood had proven to be. So warm, so snug — for months on end. And now part of her didn't want to leave for Mexico, because that morning, while hauling her green bin out for the recycling truck, she'd spotted the first signs of spring — pale-yellow fingernail tips of daffodils poking up in her front yard. And what a glory they would be after the brutal, non-stop winter, a hallelujah chorus she wanted to shout out to the world. Hey folks, we've survived again! Come see my flowers! Here we go! Spring's coming at last!

But now she was going to miss the debut of those first delectable little daffodils.

Yet she'd promised Abby. She'd found the right dish to cook. Had bought the salt cod. Told Sara, the editor in Oregon working with her on *Native Rhododendrons of North America*, that she'd be away for a week. All that remained was to pack. Down in the basement, she dug out the lightweight sports bag that always accompanied her on trips. Up in her bedroom, she zipped open the bag. Azalea followed her and jumped into the bag, sniffing along the seams, looking anxiously up at her mistress. She always did this before a trip, a signal that she wasn't happy about the prospect of being left alone and it had been a while since they were parted. Rhodo stroked her head, an attempt at reassurance, but the cat wasn't fooled. She jumped away in a huff and ran off downstairs, flicking her tail with annoyance.

Rhodo pulled clothes out of her closet. Casual, comfortable gear mostly, some of it quite old, with worn collars and hems starting to fray. Yet she was never bothered by how she looked. Although virtually everything else in her world was a source of worry to Rhodo, she had no interest in the ebbs and flows of fashion, and privately decried it as an exploitative industry that manipulated and took advantage of silly women who should know better. It was one reason why she liked being a writer about gardening: she could wear the same kind of wardrobe year round: jeans and jeans shirts coupled with cotton T-shirts in summer, then she simply piled on wool sweaters and thicker jackets when the weather cooled off. She hadn't struggled into a pair of pantyhose — such hateful things, surely designed by a man — or a dress, for decades.

After packing, she wrote a reminder to herself to remember the cod. She went downstairs and stuck it on the fridge door.

She ate her usual — leftover pizza — for supper. She checked in online for her flight to Mexico City. Looked at the Environment Canada weather forecast on her cellphone before going to bed.

There was a bit of meteorological bafflegab called a 'Special Weather Statement' posted on the site.

'Due to periods of freezing rain, travellers taking flights from Pearson Airport should anticipate delays', it concluded.

Hmm. A bit ominous, this. She set the alarm on the phone for four a.m., figuring there were bound to be problems and turned in. But she hardly slept. It was dark, her eyelids still heavy and barely open as she wrapped an arm around a cold, metal pole in the packed public bus that jerked its way out to the airport. Bright lights bouncing off the wet roads made her squint. She worried, as she always did, about missing the stop for her terminal. Yet there it was, just in time. She clambered out in a rush, elbowing her way past two chattering, dark-skinned women wearing saris under their winter coats. They both were accompanied by such enormous bags, she wondered how they could possibly haul them through the terminal. Check-in proceeded normally — a pleasant surprise. So far, so good. She headed to the departure lounge, her flight was called on time. Another pleasant surprise. She boarded, settled into her window seat. Then waited.

And waited. The passengers were told to fasten their seatbelts in preparation for take-off. Flight attendants went through the rigmarole of demonstrating what to do in an emergency, even though no one paid attention. A perky female voice asked them to please not get up in the aisles or to go to the washrooms. Then absolutely nothing happened.

The minutes ticked by. No further announcements. Rhodo could see two female attendants sitting on their pull-down seats halfway down the aircraft, murmuring to each other. Another attendant, a man, was talking on the phone at the far end. The sight made her jittery. Was something wrong? What was going on? She pulled out the in-flight magazine from the pocket of the seat in front of her to calm her nerves. The face of the male celebrity on the cover was practically obliterated by greasy fingermarks. All she could really discern was his white, capped teeth, big and threatening, like a gorilla's. She had never heard of him anyway. The inside pages felt horrible. Sticky as jam. She flung the magazine on the floor. Scrubbed at her fingers with a Kleenex. Felt irritated that she was not allowed to get up to go and wash them off.

Still no announcements. The minutes lengthened into an hour. Then, unbelievably, another hour. The passengers fidgeted in their seats, there were periodic bursts of chatter, they looked at cellphone screens and iPads open on the pull-down tables. Then gradually the entire aircraft became as silent as a morgue.

The cabin got too warm. A middle-aged businessman sitting beside Rhodo, peering at spreadsheets on his laptop, wrestled his way out of his suit jacket without getting up, exclaiming, "Phew. Getting hot in here, eh?" to no one in particular. Forehead shiny with sweat, he turned his head away from her, shut the laptop with a bang, leaned back. Then he fell into a doze, jaw sagging. She started to worry about the fish in the overhead bin. Hoped she could trust Matilde. Pushed away panicky visions of smelly cod juice dripping out of the bin, right into the man's open mouth.

Then abruptly, without any warning, the plane lurched forward, fuselage creaking like an old boat. The cabin came abruptly to life again. Someone at the front cheered. A few people clapped. A man's voice behind her shouted, "About time guys!" The flight attendants got up, avoiding the gaze of their captive passengers, and trooped one by one, to the serving station at the end of the plane.

Rhodo peered out of the window. They were inching close to an odd-looking crane.

The crane was orange, mounted on the top of a big, black truck. It brought to mind some enormous stick insect, indulging in a weird mating ritual, for a lime green liquid kept spewing out of the end of one of its long legs. Perched on the top of the crane, in a glassed-in cabin, she spotted a little figure wearing a bright orange safety suit. He was directing this jet of brilliant green at the plane's wings.

The sight looked surreal. The black sky, the orange, the green, the winking red lights on the truck, all reflected in the changing patterns of light on the wet tarmac. And crowning it all, the anonymous figure up there in the heavens, playing God.

She pressed her face to the window for a closer look. De-icing is routine at Canadian airports in winter, but she'd never witnessed it before. It fascinated her. She felt sympathy for the figure stuck in his little glass box, out there enduring the cold, making it safe for her to fly. She hoped the box was heated. She worried more, though, about what he was squirting so liberally all over the plane's wings. Some ghastly chemical? For sure. She pictured thousands of gallons of the green stuff pouring off the runways, gurgling into the sewers, finding their way down the Humber River, endlessly contaminating Lake Ontario, source of the water that came out of her tap.

For dozens of other aircraft had already undergone their own custom session of vigorous squirting that morning. From the window, she could see them in the distance, lumbering up to the runway like a long line-up of clumsy Canada geese, impatient to get back into the air, where they belonged. One took off. Then another. And another. An unending procession skywards.

So many people flying. So much pollution. And here she was, contributing to the problem. The nagging environmentalists were right. If we truly want to halt climate change and save the planet, we should stay home, she thought, feeling immensely guilty about going now. She wished she hadn't said yes to Abby. Looked, frowning, at the little, blue, plastic water bottles the flight attendants were handing out, pushing their narrow carts up the aisles, beaming at all the passengers, saying in placating voices that they'd be leaving soon. She wanted to yell, "So much plastic, ladies! So much waste! The Gulf of Mexico is filling up with this detritus. Is it really necessary for you to give us these?"

But then she remembered: she'd wanted to carry along her own metal water bottle, but Monica had shaken her head. Said it was pointless.

"You can't take water through the security checks any more," she'd said. "And it's awfully hard to find a fountain to fill an empty bottle after you get to the other side. There aren't many."

And who wanted to drink the water, she'd added with a sour laugh, in airport bathrooms?

Rhodo was thirsty now, after the long wait. The air in the cabin had become devoid of moisture, her throat felt like it was being sandpapered. With reluctance, she accepted a bottle when the flight attendant arrived at her row. The woman was young and blonde, with too much make-up and a red patterned scarf tied crookedly around her neck. She looked tired. She said, "Sorry for the delay. We're leaving momentarily."

Rhodo opened the bottle, took a sip, peered out again. They'd departed from the de-icing crane, were inching slowly forward, but it took another tedious half an hour to reach the runway. She'd drunk the entire bottle by the time the plane pirouetted into position. The engines roared into action under her feet. The cabin shook. And off they went, roaring hell-for-leather down the long, white line in the middle of the tarmac. A couple of bins popped open as the aircraft went faster and faster and a bag fell out into the aisle. Whomp. No one made a move to pick it up. Rhodo felt relieved it wasn't her bag with the fish in it. Someone cheered again. She pushed against her seat back, let her water bottle slide on to the floor, clasped the armrests tight, braced for lift-off.

Then it happened — the feeling, always slightly magical, even though she'd experienced it many times, of becoming airborne.

For a few minutes, she forgot about pollution, about her book deadline, about the awful state of the world, about spring

bulbs that she wouldn't see, about Azalea being on her own —
Monica was dropping by and dispensing Whiskas every day—
and the salt cod stashed in the bin above her head.

It was if a veil had been lifted from her face as the plane
ascended up, up, up through the gloom hugging the city, into
pale blue light as clear as water, with a ribbon of puffy white
cirrus clouds strung out far away on the limitless horizon. So
this is why we do it, she thought, looking out. This is why we
sit cooped up like farm animals in pens shaped like long cigar
tubes, waiting for hours, unable to move, not even allowed to
get up and go to the bathroom and relieve ourselves. It isn't
good for the environment, the planet is suffering as a result,
the future looks grim. Yet what a relief it is to get away, to
swap the life we are living for something else that might just
be an improvement — if only for a week or two.

She felt glad now, about this trip. Settled back into her
seat. Relaxed at last. But then she thought of the time. Holy
moly, the time. She wriggled around, alarmed, trying to find
her cellphone in a pocket of her jeans and eventually realised
that she was sitting on it. Somehow, she managed to extricate
the little device without getting up. Anxiously examined the
little illuminated screen. Such a long delay… nearly three
hours added to the trip… would she make the connecting flight
to Guadalajara from Mexico City?

The prospect was so alarming, she told herself not to even
contemplate it. She put the cellphone away and fell into a doze.

Chapter 8
Ajijic, Mexico, 17th April, 2017

ABBY

Abby needed to stock up. The only things in her fridge were a carton of milk past its sell-by date, a plastic container of Mexican coffee, and the bag of almonds Eve wanted for her Italian cake. Conchita at the health food store had recommended storing the nuts in the fridge. But the kitchen store cupboard was even emptier: nothing but the cinnamon, a half-eaten bag of tostadas and the Oaxacan chocolate, sitting forlornly side-by-side on a long shelf. So with the first of the Sisters, Rhodo, due to arrive in a few hours, she had loads of stuff to buy.

She headed off to the Tianguis, the outdoor market still known by its Aztec name, held once a week in Ajijic.

The shopping list tucked into the pocket of her cream cotton pants was precise. Tensie (who would arrive tomorrow) wanted three pounds of chicken thighs, onions, potatoes and garlic and sour cream to make her Ajiaco. Also, her guest from Colombia was particular about the potatoes.

"They should be *papas criollas*, a small round kind sold frozen in bags at every supermarket in Bogotá," she stipulated in an email. "But you may not be able to find them in Mexico."

A tall order. Rhodo had also requested potatoes and

onions, Hannah needed fresh salad greens, avocados, garlic, 'a good oil, preferably olive', and wine vinegar. Then for Eve, some eggs.

Finally, Abby had her own must-haves: some of Herminio's *bolillos*, plus raisins, *piloncillo*, and a chunk of mild cheese to grate into the Capitorada.

The market was crowded, the stalls jampacked with the usual hodge podge of fresh produce and dry goods offered for sale in markets throughout Mexico. Stems of green bananas rubbed shoulders with racks of red thong panties, jeans, polyester shirts and cheap plastic shoes. Bins crammed with watermelons and mangoes in every stage of ripeness squeezed in beside the ubiquitous Frida Kahlo knock-offs, painted in even more lurid colours than the artist herself used. And the market was crowded. Buyers speaking both Spanish and English thronged the one narrow aisle that ran the length of the market, calling out "*¡Paco! ¿Que hubo?*" and "*Hola*, Dave and Mary! Long-time no see!" bringing commerce to a halt while they stopped to chat at the Oaxaca cheese stall or the table where a cheery woman wearing a green bandanna sold the custardy Mexican dessert known as flan, in individual decorated pottery bowls that buyers got to keep. Yet in spite of the inevitable bottlenecks, no one was in a rush. The Tianguis, like so much of daily life in Mexico, was relaxed and unhurried. Shoppers treated it as more of a social occasion than a time to replenish the larder. In fact, Abby sometimes succumbed to twinges of loneliness at this market, because she didn't yet have a circle of acquaintances with whom she could share greetings and a hug while doing her shopping.

Still, she experienced no such pangs today, with the imminent arrival of the Sisters.

She found the chicken thighs — they had alarming bright yellow skin, but smelled fresh — plus all the produce, except *papas criollas*. After checking with every eager vendor and getting nothing but, "*Lo siento. I am sorry, señora. I don't have*," in return, she concluded that Tensie would have to make do with regular-sized spuds, and cut them into small pieces.

On impulse, at a stall presided over by a smiling, old man with pale pink gums and no teeth, she also picked up a *Jicama*, a brown, rough-skinned vegetable rather like a big round potato. Peeled, cut in slices, sprinkled with chili powder and dipped in lime juice, *Jicama* would make a novelty starter to the lunch, she decided, with a jug of margaritas.

The remaining items, minus the *papas criollas*, she tracked down at two different supermarkets on the Carretera. Satisfied, she started for home. But the overhead sun was hot. Her sandaled feet ached from contact with the bumpy cobblestones. Hauling two big, cloth shopping bags filled to the brim was proving heavy going. She felt as droopy as a pot of parched petunias. Before undertaking the trek up the mountainside to Emiliano Zapata — and the task of manoeuvring her purchases over Campeon's prone bulk in order to get into her house — she wanted a pick me up.

Ixchel, a coffee shop she liked on the Carretera, beckoned. She crossed the street and went inside.

***

"Well, hullo there. Mind if I join you?"

No sooner had Abby sunk down on a seat with her *café cortado* than someone bounced up to her table.

"No, go ahead," Abby said, keeping her eyes firmly fixed

on her mug, not acknowledging the newcomer, because truthfully, she was eager to enjoy a few minutes on her own, in order to get her breath back. She felt too exhausted, not in the mood to make small talk with anyone.

"Ta, love."

She looked up, recognising the voice instantly. And yes, it was Gillian, the wacky Brit she met yesterday. This time the girl was weighted down with two heavy backpacks that pulled her off balance, making the mug of coffee in her left hand almost spill into Abby's lap. But with a nonchalant, "Whoops, sorry, love," she chuckled, straightened herself up and sat.

"Well, *mucho gusto*. Fancy seeing you again," Gillian said grinning broadly. "It's Abby, isn't it?"

"Yes, hi. Good to see you," says Abby, smiling.

Then what struck her immediately was how different Gillian appeared to be from most of the foreigners patronising the coffee shop. For a start, there were her clothes: the same grubby, grass-stained jeans torn at the knees as yesterday, plus a man's outsize, red check shirt, the sleeves rolled up, revealing muscular forearms. Her dusty boots — Doc Martens, by the look of them — had mismatched laces, one brown, one pink. And that tattered straw sombrero, the kind *campesinos* wore toiling in the fields, was much too big for her, falling lopsidedly over her face. As well, Abby detected the same youthful, mischievous manner that she noted at Aguacate, as if life was a wild ride for Gillian and she was determinedly making the most of it. To top it off, besides the backpacks, she was hauling a brand-new garden fork, a price tag still hanging from the handle.

Gillian peeled off the backpacks and let them fall beside the table, thud, thud, making Ixchel's wooden floor vibrate.

She dropped the garden fork too, with an even louder thud. Two Mexican women uniformed in frilly white blouses and aprons looked up and frowned from behind the counter, where they were serving a line of customers. She shot them a 'So what?' glare, took her hat off, placed it on the table and leaned back on her chair with the air of a corporate executive about to hold court with his underlings. And now that Abby could examine her face closely, minus the huge head covering, she realised that she'd been right in her assessment.

For Gillian was young. Not exactly in the bloom of youth, but less than thirty-five, she estimated with an inquiring, freckled face, alert eyes, chubby cheeks, hair the colour of carrots and not a scrap of make-up. Flakes of skin were peeling off her sunburnt nose. And while she couldn't be called pretty in the conventional sense, she was a perfect example, Abby thought, of what Mexicans like to call a '*muchacha muy viva*' — a girl full of life and sex, a description she'd read in a book somewhere — who was probably immensely attractive to a certain kind of man.

True or not, Gillian was an anomaly in Ajijic. Almost all the other foreigners going about their lives in the town were twice her age. They didn't haul heavy backpacks around and they mostly adopted an unofficial kind of uniform. For the men it was knee-length shorts with lots of pockets, loose shirts, sandals and baseball caps, the latter often to conceal balding scalps. Many sported goatee beards, too, an attempt at roguishness, perhaps — either that or they're simply tired of shaving — yet the sparse white and grey hairs clinging to their chins like shreds of coconut matting tended to make most of them look older than they probably were. The women wore similar shorts and shirts, but if they'd gained a few pounds, they favoured loose flowing cottons — what Abby was wearing today herself — to hide the inevitable lumps and bumps of advancing age. And their hair was often long and frizzled-looking, dried out by the tropical sun and pinned back behind their ears with barrettes. Yet whatever the wardrobe of expats, she never saw any of them wandering around in soiled work clothes and boots like Gillian's. Only Mexican labourers wore those.

They both looked down at their coffees, lapsing into the awkward silence that descends over people who've only just become acquainted and wonder whether they want to go further. Then, after a few moments, Gillian lifted her freckled face, stared hard at Abby and asked, in a teasing tone,

"So what's your story, Miss Abigail?"

Abby felt mildly taken aback by the abruptness. She briefly explained that her name was Abelia, not Abby, and how that came about. Then she hesitated.

"I don't know what you mean by my story," she said, with a puzzled look.

Gillian grinned again.

"I mean your background, your history. The reason why you came here. What are you running away from?"

"Excuse me?"

"Oh come on, love," Gillian's voice took on an impatient edge. "Every foreigner you meet in Mexico is running away from something. Didn't you know that? And we get all kinds showing up in Ajijic, you know. Believe me, there's a real mish-mash of dubious characters around here."

She shook her head.

"You're kidding me. Like who?"

"Oh, runaway wives and husbands, gamblers who can't

pay their bills, escaped criminals, druggies, and worse. Did you know..." she paused for effect, widening her eyes and dropping her tone to a conspiratorial whisper, "...we even get murderers in our midst."

"Murderers?"

Abby's mouth dropped open in disbelief. Ajijic's expats had struck her as a uniformly quiet, peaceful crowd, who retired early and kept their noses clean, probably because they were all past the age of wanting to kick up their heels. And contrary to what the MacDonalds told her, she hadn't found the town particularly noisy. In fact, she often observed wryly, it was quieter than summertime back home in Darien. With all her neighbours hauling out their gas-powered lawnmowers and weed-whackers — or hiring landscape companies to do the cutting and trimming for them — there always seemed to be a cacophony coming from somewhere, making it impossible to enjoy her backyard in peace. Then when fall came, the disruption got even worse, thanks to their detestable leaf blowers.

But in Ajijic, mercifully few residents had a lawn to cut behind their high walls. And although the town's plentiful trees did regularly shower the streets with leaves, these were quietly cleaned up with rakes and straw brooms wielded by a squad of men and women in the early mornings. As for radios and people partying, while she occasionally did hear loud pop music wafting over her own walls, the only really intrusive sound came from a propane gas truck which rattled around the neighbourhood almost daily, its driver playing a monotonous tape which repeated the word "GAAAAS... GAAAS... GAAAS" over and over again, like a muezzin issuing a call to prayer at a mosque. In fact, most nights, the town was as calm as a graveyard, the restaurants closed, streets empty, all the local residents — Mexican or expat — seemingly tucked up in bed by 10 p.m. So what on earth was Gillian referring to? She couldn't picture any of the people she saw running around town with murder on their minds.

"I presume you mean the drug cartels?" she concluded, looking quizzically at Gillian.

"No, the narcos are mostly in the north, up near the US border. They haven't reached here, thank heavens. Not yet at least."

Gillian frowned, drew a breath, then twisted her mouth into an odd kind of smile.

"I'm talking about rogues like Pete Gomez," she said. "You must know about him?"

Abby looked blank.

"No. Who's he?"

"Ah, Petey boy. He was the talk of the town. But perhaps it was before you got here." Gillian shook her head reflectively, grinning now, as if at some private joke. "Such a charmer. He was from somewhere in the States, I forget where. But his dad was Mexican, the reason why he wound up coming down here. Weird thing is though, he hardly spoke a word of Spanish. Couldn't seem to pick it up. His mother was a Yank and just didn't want to know about Mexicans. Bad marriage, I presume. Anyhow, he quickly talked the knickers off an American woman down here, a widow, quite wealthy. Then he opened up a café, using money this woman gave him, and it became a popular hang-out with expats. But then he pissed her off, screwing around with other ladies. And…"

She paused, took a long draw on her *café macchiato*.

"…she blew the whistle on him. Turns out he nearly

strangled her after an argument in her house one night. She wound up in hospital. Also, that he'd had a wife back in the US who he bludgeoned to death. Then he'd hid her body in the basement. I forget exactly where they lived, I think maybe New York."

She sighed.

"Nice bloke, eh? So they extradited him, and he's in jail now. New Jersey, I think, awaiting trial."

Gillian paused to stare, frowning, at a wall of the coffee shop, which bore a poster of a smiling boy on a donkey, hauling sacks of coffee beans.

"But it was a shame, really," she resumed, turning back to Abby, with another odd smile. "You'd never know it to look at him. So good-looking. Dressed cool, you know? Suave, sophisticated. A real gentleman, everyone thought. And..." she took another sip, clearly relishing the drama and Abby's surprise "...we were all sorry to see him go because he made the best coffee in Ajijic."

She wrinkled the sunburnt nose, picked up her mug again, and drank, wiping froth off her lower lip.

"He liked experimenting with different kinds of coffee you know? He got us all to try it the traditional Mexican way, with cinnamon, brown sugar and a bit of cocoa. And whatever he did, it tasted so much better than the swill they serve here."

She pulled a face again at the women behind the counter.

The remembrance concluded, her eyes became bright with curiosity again.

"But what about you, love? I saw you the other day when they were doing that bread pudding thingummy down by the *Malecón* and I thought you looked sort of lonely. So I'm just wondering what brought you here, that's all. Do you, um..." a throaty chuckle, "…have a dodgy past like our Petey Gomez?"

Huh? Abby felt discomforted, unsure what to say. This outspoken Brit, who peppered her conversation with bewildering British slang, was amusing for sure, but getting kind of nosy. She picked up her own mug. Looked pointedly away, out of the open café doors, to a *Tabebuia*, the tree of spring in Mexico. Its blossoms overhung the Carretera in a picture postcard cascade of golden yellow against the azure sky. She couldn't wait to show off this gorgeous tropical specimen, commonly called the primavera, to the Sisters. She knew they'd ooh and aah over it.

Oblivious to Abby's hint, Gillian barreled on.

"With me, see, it was my old man," she said. "Lazy sod. Always with his mates down at the pub. So one day, I said 'Bollocks to all that. I'm going to pay you back'."

She looked up at the ceiling, letting out the cackle of laughter that was becoming familiar. An elderly couple bent silently over coffees at a nearby table turned, frost on their faces.

Gillian ignored them.

"Went online, I did, bought a ticket to Mexico and debited our savings account," she continued gleefully. "Then I went down to our bank and cleaned the whole lot right out. We were supposed to be saving to visit his Aussie cousin in Perth, but they didn't need his signature for me to withdraw the funds, they said. So I said 'Give it all to me, then. In cash. I need it now.' And they did, which was a bit of a surprise. So then I went to a lav in Starbucks near the bank and stuffed the wads of notes in my boots."

She paused, swung her legs out from under the table and wiggled the Doc Martens, like a child showing off new shoes, as if the memory of her escapade still thrilled her to the tips of her toes.

"Then at the airport, see," she took a breath, "I just converted the whole lot into pesos and flew away. Free as…"

She nodded at two mourning doves cooing at one another on a branch of the *Tabebuia*.

"…those two little love birdies up there."

Abby did smile then. Still at a loss for words, hearing such blunt talk from someone she'd barely met, she nonetheless found Gillian's candour refreshing. Besides, she was learning things about Ajijic that she didn't know. The truth was, she hadn't had an encounter like this since arriving. A couple in their sixties from California who attended Spanish lessons with her proved pleasant enough, they'd had lunch together after class, yet they kept resisting her overtures to become better acquainted. And she'd made no other friends. Ajijic is as clique-ish as any small town, she'd concluded a while ago. You have to find the crowd where you fit in and do your socialising there. Thus far, she'd discovered an artsy crowd, a sporty crowd, a gourmet crowd that ate out together once a week in the town's restaurants, and a crowd of fiercely patriotic fellow citizens, who celebrated every US holiday with a fervour she'd never witnessed at home. But Abby wasn't sure she wanted to do any of those things. And though she hated to admit it, Gillian's observation struck an uncomfortable note. She probably did come across as lonely, walking around town, always unaccompanied. The realisation of how she might appear to others was unsettling.

"Well, since you ask," she said, more formally than she would like, but thinking that she may as well open up a little about her own past, "I lived in Connecticut for about thirty years with my husband, but we are now separated and getting a divorce."

"Aha, I knew it!" crowed Gillian, slamming a hand down on the table, as if she'd hit the jackpot playing poker. "I could tell. So many women like you here, fed up with their husbands."

She reflected for a moment, impatiently pushing a tuft of red frizz away from her eyes. A flake of sunburnt skin drifted off the back of her wrist and floated in the air, before coming to rest on the wooden floor.

"But there's plenty of blokes too, going solo after being married for years, you know," she continued, "except they always do it differently."

A cynical chuckle.

"How do you mean?"

"Well, the blokes ditch the trouble and strife back home, and within a few weeks of getting here, they've shacked up with some cute, little *camacha* in tight pants. They don't like being on their own, I guess. No one to do the laundry and cook."

Another chuckle, followed by a snort.

"Lazy buggers. Most of the women stay single, though. They don't want to get hitched again. But they still like their bit of you-know-what. Oh boy, do they ever. You should see them…" Gillian raised her eyebrows "…all tarted up, hitting on the Mexican men at *La Campamocha* every night. Doesn't matter how old they are."

"Oh," said Abby, with a chuckle herself, surprised. "Well, good for them. Is that a bar?"

"Yeah, a couple of blocks down that way…" she inclined her head "…on the Carretera. Spanish for praying mantis. Very appropriate. You should check it out."

Abby wasn't sure that she wanted to get 'all tarted up' as Gillian put it, and go out looking for a man — Mexican or otherwise. Yet solitude's not so welcome sister, loneliness, sometimes made her presence felt at night, after long evenings with only a bag of tostadas and the big, black, flat screen in the living room for company. She'd watched so many unmemorable movies and TV shows on Netflix, her eyes sometimes burned by the time she went to bed. And a trip to this bar, on the Carretera— it was unmistakeable, thanks to a huge, lurid-green praying mantis made of fibreglass on its flat roof — might be an entertaining thing to do with the Sisters during their Titan Reunion.

"I have three girlfriends — well, four now — coming on a visit," she said, checking her watch. "One of them is arriving in a few hours from Toronto. Perhaps I'll take them out for a drink at this place one night."

"Yeah, they might find it cool," Gillian said. "Be sure to try their margaritas, even if you don't like the male talent. They're the best, made with fresh lime juice."

She yawned. Got up. Stretched her arms high above her head as if trying to reach the ceiling fan that went, tock-tock, tock-tock, like a metronome, stirring up the burnt coffee bean air of the café. Then the sombrero went back at an angle on her head, partly obscuring her face.

"Well, I gotta run," she said. "My boyfriend, Egg is picking me up at the bus station and we're heading home in our truck. We live north of Joco, out in the sticks, see. Love it out there. Couldn't stand being in town, with all the oldies."

She pulled a face in mock horror. Then remembering who she was talking to, she clamped her hand over her mouth and looked sheepish.

"Whoops, sorry, didn't mean you, Abby," she said. "Really I didn't. You're younger than most of 'em."

Abby smiled tolerantly.

Gillian leaned over again and picked up the garden fork.

"I just came into town today to get this," she said, waving it in the air. "Broke mine the other day, hitting a rock. Gawd, the soil is so stony out in Joco. I have two hectares, all bad. But I love my crummy, little house, just right for me and Egg. I bought it after my ex and I sold our place back home. It was advertised on Craigslist, believe it or not. Cheap too. The owner, a sad, old gringo had cancer. He just wanted to get rid of the place and go home to die. He even left his motorbike behind. I take it out sometimes, although it's got no springs left and gawd, the seat kills me arse."

Another cackle of laughter. Then, hoisting one backpack on each shoulder, Gillian explained that she raised herbs, heirloom tomatoes and cut flowers to sell at Ajijic's organic market on Wednesdays. She also supplied two health food stores, one of which was Aguacate.

"Yes, I was just there again a few minutes ago," said Abby, "buying chocolate."

"Yeah, great place. Conchita's a love, isn't she?"

She checked her watch again.

"I better go. Egg will be waiting," she said, but continued to hover. "He teaches Spanish, see. Intensive three-month courses at the *Centro Cultural*. You should check them out, Abby. Lots of expats sign up, because he's good."

She raised her eyebrows expectantly.

"Thanks for the tip," Abby said, smiling, "but I'm already signed on with Mike…"

"Yeah, I know, the American bloke," Gillian turned her mouth down in displeasure. "Nice guy, but Egg's Mexican and he'll get you speaking Spanish right away, instead of learning from books. You'll learn Mexican slang, too, instead of tourist Spanish. Like *chela*."

"What?"

"It's the word Mexicans use for beer. When you're in the mood for a cold beer, you say '*Tengo ganas de un chela*'. I'll bet you didn't know that, didjer?" Another snorting laugh. "You probably always ask for a '*cerveza*' right? Like all the gringos do."

"Well, um, yes, I guess I probably would. But as I'm not really a beer drinker, I haven't…"

"Anyhow," Gillian interrupted, "taking Egg's course really worked wonders for me. I met him at the *Centro Cultural,* see. Two years ago. Acquired me own personal coach in the art of talking like a Mexican. Taught me a lot of naughty expressions, he did. Ha ha," she chuckled mischievously. "But I'd better not get into those, being as I'm here with a lady like you."

She groaned and sighed. "Egg makes all the dosh. I don't. Farming in Jalisco is tough. People keep telling me I'm a nutter."

"Why do you call him Egg?" Abby asked. "Do you keep chickens?"

"Oh no. I mean, we do have our own chickens, but they have nothing to do with his name. You think your name is weird, Abby? Well, get this," she rolled her eyes. "His is Egidio. It's pronounced Ay-hee-dee-oh in Spanish. No hard g. Name of a famous saint, I hear. Quite a mouthful. But I just call him Egg. So do all the other expats. And he's a good egg.

Does his share. Not like Brian, my bloody ex."

A grimace, then another chuckle.

"Toodle-oo, then. Must go." Gillian got set to leave at last, straightening the backpacks into a comfortable position on her shoulders. "Bring your friends to see me at the organic market."

"Yes, I will."

At that moment, three American women walked in, blocking the entrance to the coffee shop. Arms linked together, they looked to be in high spirits, gossiping and joking like old friends who had just reconnected after a long time apart. Abby thought again of the Sisters. Soon they'd be sharing that kind of togetherness. Yes, she had been lonely. She couldn't wait for their arrival.

Gillian stood aside to let the women pass.

"Watch out for that Petey Gomez, won't you, if you go to *Campamocha*?" she called out in a voice that could be heard all around the cafe. The old couple looked up again disapprovingly. She pulled a face at them.

"He used to hang out there and he's bad news, but women can't seem to resist him. And I heard a rumour the other day, you know…" that grin again, "…that he's done a plea bargain or something, got himself a new name and is on his way back to Ajijic."

"Be warned, love." She winked at Abby. "He loves older women like you."

Then Gillian was gone, hoisting the garden spade on to her shoulder like a rifle. She marched out of Ixchel's open doors as if on parade duty, her boots going clomp-clomp-clomp all the way down the Carretera.

--

Abby looked at her watch again. With a start, realised that she'd better get moving herself. The perishables she bought needed to go in the fridge. Then she'd call the accommodating Juan, find some less sweaty clothes and head out to Guadalajara to meet Rhodo.

She pondered Gillian's revelations as she plodded back up the mountainside carrying her bags.

What a whirlwind the girl was, with her non-stop chatter. But was any of it true? The bit about murderers sounded kind of farfetched.

Even so, Abby observed her fellow expats with new eyes heading home. None of them appeared to be anything but decent, ordinary folks who'd had the smarts to retire somewhere warm and sunny, where a comfortable life wouldn't cost them an arm and a leg. Yet at that moment, as if to contradict the image of normalcy that had become lodged in her mind, a middle-aged, white man with a greasy, pockmarked face and a belly like a soccer ball came into view as she crossed the street by Herminio's store. And he did kind of fit Gillian's description. No, she was being too generous. This guy was definitely on the seedy side. He had the furtive, hunched-over air of someone who might be hiding something and he avoided meeting her gaze, stepping off the sidewalk on to the cobblestones as they passed each other. There was a pronounced smell of booze on his breath. She noticed food stains on his shirt, purple bags under his eyes. And he looked as if he hadn't slept for days. Could she attribute his beat-up appearance to wild sex every night with some pretty Mexican *muchacha* wearing a frilly nightie or those red thong panties she saw at the market? Or worse, was he concealing a past life? Did he kill his wife back in the US then run away to Ajijic to escape justice?

"I've been naïve," she concluded as the man disappeared around a corner. "I've been living in a bubble of fantasy about what goes on in Ajijic. This town clearly has clearly a dark side."

"I just haven't encountered it. Yet."

Chapter 9
Mexico City Airport, 18th April, 2017

TENSIE

Tensie noticed him at once, walking across the departure lounge. He had the kind of looks that all women notice. Thick, glossy black hair. Skin like toasted almonds. Laughing eyes. A full, sensuous mouth. A confident, easy way of moving his muscular, well-oiled body as if he was aware of his magnetic appeal to both sexes — and revelled in the power that it gave him.

He was a good height, too. Tall, but not overly so. Clearly Latin. Probably Mexican. Tensie was not enamoured of the American ideal of masculinity, the men like awkward giants, towering over her on their beanpole legs. And they wore their suit pants too short. The socks always showed — and why did they insist on picking such silly, childish colours and patterns? American businessmen were always coming into the Embassy dressed like that. She found them very unattractive. But this man was stylish, sexy, gliding across the lounge in a pale-green, linen suit with pants that fitted smoothly over his thighs and extended long enough to just cover the tops of his polished, nut-brown lace-ups. She liked to see that kind of look on men. Lamented that she rarely did any more, unless they were gay. Straight males who took trouble with their appearance when they travelled were a vanishing species. Nowadays, they all dressed — and behaved — like overgrown babies escaped from the nursery, running around airports in baggy shirts and falling-down jeans that revealed the cleft between their buttocks.

Once, in an airport in France, she'd watched a bored toddler go up and poke a finger down that cleft. The person whose cleft it was, a young American with a shaved head and tattoos down his arms, was squatting in the departure lounge repacking his luggage. He'd turned around immediately when he felt something touch his backside. But he wasn't mad. He'd simply laughed and said, "Hey kid. Don't do that, will ya? It tickles." The toddler ran off, back to its parents, who were sitting a few yards away. They laughed too. But then the man made no attempt to pull his pants up and cover his nakedness. He just stayed there, bent over, fiddling with his luggage, showing off his hairy cleft for everyone in the airport to see. So uncouth and lacking in manners, Tensie thought at the time. She'd been mildly shocked.

A dark, blubbery youth with an angry face blocked her view of the handsome man for a few moments. The kid was so fat, he waddled like a duck past where she was sitting, waiting for her connecting flight to Guadalajara. In his mouth he had a lollipop, which he sucked noisily. On the front of his enormous red sweatshirt, in white capitals, were the words: STOOPID WEIRDO. Tensie shook her head, wondering if he was Mexican or American. Why, she thought, smoothing her grey pencil skirt, shifting in her seat, inspecting her fingernails — in preparation for this trip, she'd had them manicured and painted oyster pink at a beauty salon in Bogotá — why would anyone choose to advertise themselves to the world this way?

Why was this young guy so proud of being an idiot?

Then she spotted the handsome man again. A better view, showing part of his face. Her heart lurched because he reminded her so much of Juan Diego when he was in his mid-forties. He had the same build, the same self-assured way of walking. Yet, if she was honest about it, this hunk of a man was even better looking than Juan Diego. He had a nicer nose, a not-so-fat neck, bigger, gentler eyes. They weren't hard and sharp like her estranged husband's.

His eyes also made her think of someone else she and Juan Diego had both known when they were very young. She remembered how that boy would look right into her with eyes like that, making her blush and squirm and go all hot inside. She felt a pang for him, had never forgotten how he charmed her into doing that terrible thing, the secret she's had to keep to herself all her life. She wondered, for the first time in years, what happened to dear sweet Paquito. Remembered how she'd once ached to find him, to run to his arms, crying, seeking consolation in the aftermath of what they did. But not any more. Wherever he was, she simply hoped his life had turned out happier than hers.

The man went up to the AeroMexico desk and asked the girl behind it a question. She was clearly beguiled by his good looks too, because she turned all fluttery and giggly. She blushed, looked down, then up into his eyes again, batting her eyelashes. He flirted with her in the practised manner of a man who is used to getting what he wants, leaning in over the counter, pouring on the charm. It seemed that he didn't have a ticket for the flight to Guadalajara and there wasn't one seat left. Yet the girl looked down again, checked the manifest behind the counter, frowned, did something on her computer terminal, smiled again and within a minute, she was printing out a boarding pass for him and handing it over. His thank-you sounded smooth and mechanical as she ran his credit card through the machine. Watching, Tensie thought that the girl wouldn't have done the same thing for her. No way. She'd have been told: Sorry, *señora*, we're full. You'll have to wait for another flight.

Yet the man surprised her. She overheard part of their conversation and his Spanish sounded jerky and hesitant. It clearly wasn't his native tongue. In fact, the girl switched over to English to accommodate him. So he wasn't what she thought. He might be American after all. Or another nationality even. Something of a mystery, in fact. Perhaps that aura of the unknown was what made him so intriguing. He carried with him a hint of danger which was hard to put a finger on. Yet if she were still as young as that airline clerk, she'd probably ignore the warning signals, bend to his wishes, do what he wanted, because she couldn't resist him.

Then she lost him again. After tucking the boarding pass into his breast pocket, he went off to sit in an area of the departure lounge where she could no longer see him.

When the flight was called, he got ahead of her in the line-up. She hoped that the seat the girl gave him was close to hers. Even though, at sixty-one, she was beyond the age of having anyone flirt with her the way he did with that ticket clerk and she presumed that she would never again feel her insides tingle at the closeness of a male body — a reality which saddened her deeply — she still liked being around attractive men. The sexual energy they gave off made her feel young again, as though she was still in the game. She could kid herself for a few moments. Luis did that for her, back at the farm. Such a handsome young man, earthy, confident, with his firm thighs and tight little backside. She suspected he was a good lover to his pretty girlfriend, Michaela, who worked in one of the greenhouses disbudding carnations, but hoped they wouldn't produce a baby too soon. Tensie needed him at her side too, unfettered by the demands of domesticity. She wondered if Luis was taking care of everything during her absence, felt reassured that he must have been, because he was so responsible, and wanted the farm to be a success as much as she did. She looked for her seat, located it on the aisle, at the rear of the plane — and sat down.

The man went somewhere else. She forgot about him. She settled in, did up her seatbelt, started thinking about Abby and the Sisters and their lunch party. She'd sent Abby a shopping list by email. She still felt awfully nervous about being in Mexico, couldn't shake the feeling that something unexpected was going to happen to her there. But fear didn't overwhelm her, the way it had when she received the invitation. Perhaps whatever happened would turn out to be pleasurable, not upsetting.

For thus far, everything had gone smoothly. Her direct flight from Bogotá was uneventful. Alejandro had driven her to the airport, hugged her, kissed both cheeks and told her to go and have a good time with her gardening friends, to forget about the farm for once. It would do her a power of good.

Then her arrival in Mexico City airport went without a hitch. She'd debated about bringing the *guascas*, wondered if she should, in case it was mistaken for marijuana by the customs people. But *guascas* is an essential ingredient in *Ajiaco,* she couldn't make the dish without it, so she simply neglected to mention the little bag of the dried herb tucked into her carry-on bag. And the officious little man in army fatigues, cocky as a rooster, standing behind the immigration desk, gun swaying in the holster on his hip, didn't ask if she was carrying any food or agricultural products. He just told her to go over and press a button on a post. When it turned green, she was waved through. No one the other side asked to look in her luggage.

After the flight reached Guadalajara, she saw him again. He was ahead of her, heading out of the big, plate glass doors of the terminal building. She craned her neck to watch. A glamorous tanned woman with big sunglasses, dressed in a silky, turquoise shirt, rushed up to him outside on the white hot, glaring pavement. She looked American, this woman, and seemed older than he was, had perfectly straight, greyish-blonde hair framing her face in a silver helmet. In spite of the glasses, Tensie thought she could detect the joy of a lover on the woman's face when she flung out her arms to him. He pulled her close. They hugged and disappeared behind the line-up of taxis waiting at the sidewalk.

She wondered briefly where they were going. But then Abby was there in front of her, hands on hips, a broad grin on her face. Dear Abby. She looked happier than when they'd last met in New York. Healthier. She'd lost weight. Adopted a shorter haircut that was flattering. The new glasses suited her too. Less bookish. There was a glow about her friend now. Moving to Mexico definitely seemed to have been a good idea although she couldn't help wondering why. She'd liked Larry, had no idea they were so unhappy together.

Behind her stood Rhodo, already arrived from Toronto. Still in her jeans shirt as always, no make-up, looking a bit tense as she often did. Yet such a good person to spend time with, because she was so knowledgeable about plants, particularly shrubs. And she had so many good ideas. They'd become accustomed to exchanging emails — useful emails, not just idle chatter — whenever *Flores Rojas Hernandez* was planning to introduce a new cultivar to the North American market. This Sister from Canada was a whiz at dreaming up names that would fire the imagination of American and Canadian consumers. Tensie thought of the mini-hydrangea with creamy-white flowers which Alejandro had just hybridised at the farm. So exciting. She couldn't wait to tell Rhodo. She'd know exactly what to call it.

She kissed both Abby and Rhodo on both cheeks and the three Sisters piled into Juan's taxi. Then off they went, thankful to get out of dusty, overwhelming Guadalajara and on to the highway.

Ahead lay the blue-green serenity of Lake Chapala, full of promise under the tropical sun.

The Party

"If you are a disciple of one of those calorie counters who turns the joys of eating into a form of punishment, then close this book at once. It is too lively and aggressive for you."
— Salvador Dali
In "*Les diners de Gala*"

Chapter 10
Ajijic, Mexico, 19th April, 2017

Myra MacDonald would be so happy to see this, Abby thought. Her state-of-the-art kitchen, with its professional appliances, cooking pots and capacious chopping board was finally back in action, getting the work-out Myra had designed it for. She could almost hear the fridge, gas stove, food processor and shiny saucepans whispering in a chorus: 'Thank you, ma'am. We were feeling kind of redundant, you know. It's good to be needed again'.

For with the safe arrival of all the Sisters — the accommodating Juan had driven her to Guadalajara last night to meet Hannah and Eve after their long journey from Heathrow — they'd settled on tomorrow for their Titan Reunion lunch. Now it was early afternoon, the sun high above the *boveda* roof, but the air felt agreeably cool indoors, and the kitchen was buzzing like a hive of worker bees. Crucial ingredients were getting peeled, chopped, sauteed, simmered, boiled, whisked, whirled in a blender and baked in the oven in preparation for the feast.

Abby sat on a stool at the centre island, relaxing, sipping wine, not doing much herself today. She'd baked the *Capitorada* yesterday before going to the airport and done last-minute shopping on the Carretera this morning for a few other ingredients — like fresh corn on the cob that Tensie wanted for her *Ajiaco*. Now, she felt as happy as a clam, watching the others at work. It had always been fun, meeting up with the Sisters, but this idea of preparing a whole, spectacular meal together was proving to be even more of a blast. She wondered why she had worried that it wouldn't be a success. Such affinity, such affection, such a sense of solidarity had developed within the group now. Having a passion for plants in common had meant, right from the beginning, that they'd never run out of things to talk about. But in the course of cooking together as well, they were becoming even closer, more like true sisters.

And how they all loved the rule they'd informally developed for their reunions: women only, absolutely none of the male species invited. Today they recalled — as they usually did — the men they met at the Titan Arum flowering in the Brooklyn Botanical Garden.

"Remember that awful Dutch botanist Jost, who came with Mieke, the one with bad breath who made vulgar jokes when the stalk on the Titan Arum kept getting bigger?" asked Abby, pulling a face and chuckling as she took a sip of wine.

"Yes, who could forget him? He tried to grope me, you know, then I discovered that he was doing it to every woman there," Hannah said indignantly.

"What a creep," said Rhodo with a shudder. "I told him to fuck off. Poor Mieke, being stuck with him."

"Yes, she couldn't offload him because the Dutch bulb information centre paid for them both to go to New York," said Abby.

"I don't remember him at all," said Tensie. "But some of the other guys were nice. I had a good conversation with a man from a botanical garden in Florida who was trying to get kids interested in plants. He hoped that getting a Titan Arum there might help, because it was so freaky-looking. And..." she smiled "...I recall being quite taken with a handsome, young man called Michael who had a TV show in California."

"I remember him too. The cute gay guy with the yellow suit and purple bow tie," chipped in Abby.

"Oh, was he gay?" said Tensie, laughing. "I guess I just like well-dressed men."

**

On the reminiscing went. And while their lunch tomorrow might prove worthy of a five-star restaurant, it equally well might not. Yet whatever the outcome, no one was going to care. The joy was in the doing. Just as Shakespeare said. Looking around the kitchen, Abby felt grateful that three of the Sisters had taken the trouble to come and see what her new life was like in Mexico.A chef's outsize, white apron (unearthed by Abby from a hall cupboard) wound around her waist, Rhodo stood bent over the gas stove, peering into a pan of simmering salt cod. Yesterday she soaked the fish three times, as Matilde instructed — outside in the courtyard, where she could pour the discarded water down an open drain — vastly easier than manoeuvring wobbling bowls of stinky liquid around her cramped Toronto kitchen. She didn't spill a drop. Next, she was making mashed potatoes. But she kept shooting awed glances at the big earthenware olla containing Tensie's contribution to the meal — the *Ajiaco*. It was cooling on the counter beside the stove, a wisp of steam rising from its rich, creamy interior. And it had a tantalising smell of chicken, garlic, butter and something herby that Rhodo didn't recognise. Tensie cooked the dish this morning, while the others loafed over a long, lazy breakfast in the courtyard, because she'd wanted to have the kitchen to herself. She'd spent an inordinate amount of time cutting into bite-sized pieces the potatoes that Abby had bought for her. Then she'd disappeared for a nap in one of the spare bedrooms. Rhodo and Hannah were sharing the other one. And in spite of a glass of wine at her elbow, which she hadn't touched yet, Rhodo felt a familar a wave of anxiety engulfing her. The *Ajiaco* was intimidating. So were the obvious cooking skills of the other Sisters. Would Tensie's dish outshine her humble cod cakes, which they'd agreed to start the meal with? Would everyone rave about Hannah's salad? Were they secretly going to dismiss the comfort food of her Canadian childhood as bland and boring, compared with this exotic Latin American stew that none of them had tasted before? Cooking meals with other people, she concluded worriedly, her brow wrinkled, was rife with unspoken rivalries.

Hannah, meanwhile, long, grey hair pulled back into an untidy bun, jaw set in a determined way, stood over the chopping board. With a sharp knife, she was cutting, into a neat pile, the celery-like green leaves she'd sneaked into Mexico from her garden. None of the Sisters had tasted lovage before, she'd been pleased to discover. So with a grin, she'd refused to hand out samples in advance "…because I want you all to be surprised by how good lovage tastes in this salad dressing."

Eve stood shoeless at another counter in a black halter top, the seam of her skimpy, white shorts pulled tight between her buttocks. Abby stared, remembering how she once had a firm, shapely backside and legs like Eve's. Now her thighs were dimpled with cellulite and her entire lower anatomy bulged in all the wrong places. Not that anyone ever got to see either anymore. Some brave retired women walked around Ajijic in shorts, baring raddled legs crisscrossed with varicose veins, but she didn't intend to follow suit. The ankle-length white pants which came with her from New York or a long, loose concealing cotton skirt acquired in Ajijic right after her arrival constituted her habitual wardrobe now.

Eve was trying to grate by hand a slab of hard, dark chocolate. But after two full glasses of wine to Abby's one, her coordination had gone off kilter. She suddenly screamed, "Ouch!" making the others turn around in surprise. Then she let rip a string of curses worthy of potty-mouthed British celebrity chef Gordon Ramsay.

"Shit… fuck… *porca misera. CAVALO!* Why didn't you use the bloody food processor, you fucking idiot." she wailed, leaping back from the grater as if scalded. For Eve's right index finger had been caught — and gashed — on the grater's metal teeth.

She hopped around, sucking on the wounded finger, swearing like a stevedore in English and Italian.

Abby slid off her stool, hurried to the bathroom, was relieved to find a first aid kit. "Thank you, Myra and Bruce," she murmured. Yet Eve's wound wasn't serious. An impressive amount of blood, but after the digit in question had been rinsed at the sink, dried on a piece of gauze, smeared with salve and bound in a white bandage, Eve pronounced that she felt fine. Fueled by another glass of wine, she resumed grating.

"I trust you folks won't mind if you find a part of me in your slice of cake. But if you do…" she declared, turning her head back from the counter and flashing a wicked look "..I've

143

been told in Italy that I'm a *piatto gustoso*, a tasty dish."

Abby laughed. Loudly, throwing her head back. Kind of inebriated herself by now, she was enjoying Eve. While Hannah's sister certainly was too free with foul language, too fond of making the rest of them feel old with her not-so-subtle references to her prowess with the male sex, her exuberance was infectious. People like Eve are an asset at a party, she concluded. Having this extra guest descend unexpectedly on them was not proving to be the unwelcome intrusion she'd anticipated.

"Okay, Eve," she joked, waving her glass in the air and taking another large gulp, "I'll let you know if those guys were lying."

"Yeah, you do that." More laughter.

Rhodo and Hannah didn't join in the banter. Brow furrowed, Rhodo was wondering how many potatoes to peel. Six? Ten? Even more? She remembered doing half a dozen when she'd made the cod cakes for Monica, but five of them tomorrow — not two — would make a big difference. She wished she'd checked Gramma Mercer's instructions more thoroughly. Worried that her dish would be a disaster, with not enough mashed potato to mix with the cod. Yet she didn't want to look foolish by asking any of the others for advice. They were all so accomplished in the kitchen.

Hannah, whirling oil, vinegar, Worcester sauce and dry mustard in the blender, had one ear cocked to Eve's histrionics about the bleeding finger and held her tongue. What a relief, she thought, it wasn't serious. Also, that Eve was making a good impression so far. Indeed, Abby seemed to be quite taken with her.

Yet Hannah remained as wary as a cat sensing the

nearness of something threatening, like a dog off its leash. Past experience had taught her to be.

Taking her first cautious sip of wine, she prayed that this good-natured acceptance of her self-centred sister would last — and not cause her grief later on.

***

At dusk, most of the prep work for tomorrow's lunch complete, three of the Sisters and Eve retired to the courtyard to relax. Abby lit candles, whipped up a jug of margaritas, brought out snacks, laid glasses and plates on the table, told everyone to help themselves.

Tasting the Mexican cocktail for the first time, Hannah took a sip and said thoughtfully, "I like it."

She swallowed slowly, twisting the glass in her hand, examining the pale green liquid, nodding with pleasure. "I always like anything made with limes."

"Yes, but be careful not to gulp it down too quickly," warned Abby. "Margaritas can fool you. They don't taste strong, but the tequila can knock you out. It's not like drinking lemonade. And if you use a cheap brand of tequila — they often do in bars here — just one cocktail can give you a terrible headache."

She took a sip from her own glass and nodded.

"Mmm. Not bad. Could do with a bit more lime, I think. But don't worry about getting a headache," she added, noticing Rhodo's look of concern. "I used a good brand in these. Tequila is relatively cheap in Ajijic because Jalisco — that's the state we're in — is where most of it comes from. "

"How do they make tequila?" Rhodo asked.

"With a plant called Agave, a succulent. They use the crown — they call it the *piña*. It's a huge, kind of roundish ball that develops at the base of the plant."

Pleased that Rhodo asked the question, because she was personally fascinated by the whole process of making tequila, Abby settled down in her chair to explain.

"If we go to Puerto Vallarta to visit the botanical gardens, the bus will go through the agave fields on the way down to the coast," she said. "And they look amazing — thousands of these huge, spiky blue-green plants planted in wavy rows, often on dry, barren mountainsides that are quite steep. But agave doesn't mind that because it's like all succulents, as you know."

Rhodo, nodded knowledgeably. So did Hannah.

"It grows anywhere that's sunny and hot. But the incredible thing is, it takes about seven years for each plant to get big enough to be turned into tequila — and the distilling process is unbelievably complicated. I took a tour to a farm after I arrived here, and I was bowled over by the amount of work involved."

"I'd like to see how they do it too," Rhodo replied. "But as we're not here for long..." she smiled persuasively "...what I'd prefer is to visit the... um... the botanical gardens in Puerto Vallarta."

She put down her glass and raised her eyebrows with a tentative look at Abby.

"A friend in Toronto told me about the Vireya rhododendrons they have, and I'd love to see them," Rhodo added. "Do you think we'll have time to go?"

"Yes, I think so," Abby assured her. "I've checked into it and we'll need to stay overnight down there, after a three-hour

146

bus ride down to the coast. But that's not a problem nowadays. Mexican buses are real luxurious. I was quite surprised when I went to the botanical gardens with a tour. No chickens on the roof any more. And the drivers are great. Very careful and courteous. Trust me," she laughed, noting Rhodo's familiar wrinkled brow, "you won't wind up at the bottom of some ravine."

"Well, that's good to know," said Rhodo, chuckling.

Abby described the Vallarta Botanical Garden in rapturous terms — how it was started by an American who bought thirty hectares of rainforest along the Sierra Madre, south of Puerto Vallarta, and how, in only a few years, aided by private donations and a squad of dedicated volunteers, he'd managed to transform the area into a paradise of tropical plants. But probably the most impressive aspect was the orchids.

"They've amassed an amazing collection, because they got in touch with botanical gardens and plant organisations not just in Mexico but all over the world," Abby went on. "The US sent them plants. So did Brazil and China. They now have over forty-five different species, and literally hundreds of hybrids, and they're propagating some of the ones that are endangered in Mexico."

"Like what?" asked Rhodo.

"Oh, one called *Mormodes*. And an *Oncidium* called Sotoanum which is indigenous to Central America," said Abby. "A very pretty pink."

"I think I know the *Mormodes*. They're the ones whose petals have a strange shape. Like a lip," said Hannah.

"Right. But there's a lot more to see than orchids," Abby said. "They have your beloved Vireya rhododendrons,

147

Rhodo…and the biggest collection of magnolias ever… and a vanilla plantation…and cycads…and giant tree ferns. Oh, I could go on and on. But you know…" she paused to take another sip of her margarita, "…the discouraging part for them is that they get no help at all from the government."

"Why? How come?" asked Hannah, surprised. "I imagine that a place like that would be a big tourist attraction."

"Who knows? The Mexican government seems to be stuck with the mindset that people just come here for sun, sea and sand," Abby said, shaking her head. She laughed. "But at our ages, let's face it. Who wants to lie around a pool all day, showing off our sagging boobs and bellies?"

More laughter around the table.

"Don't know about you," she grinned, "but I'd much rather stay covered up and go look at gorgeous plants. And there must be many tourists who think the same way as us."

Rhodo and Hannah nodded in agreement.

Eve said nothing. She'd become uncharacteristically quiet and sulky. The word 'succulent' somehow made her think of oral sex and she missed Fabio. Added to that, she had no idea what a cycad was, she found the endless talk about plants tedious, and — contrary to what Abby contended — she'd have loved to be loafing on some Mexican beach at that moment in a skimpy bikini. But she stayed silent. Nearing the end of her second margarita, she sat curled up in her chair deciding — not for the first time — that gardeners had to be the biggest bores in the world, always tossing around weird Latin names and terms like hybrid and species even though no one else had a clue what they were talking about. When Hannah used to call her in Rome and start going on about the plants in her garden, Eve remembered, she would quickly cut her off, saying, 'Sorry. Have to go. Something's burning in the oven'. But here, there was no escape. With a whole bunch of bloody gardeners around her, yapping non-stop, what on earth could she do? Just get drunk?

Yes. Eve leaned across the table for the jug of margaritas, poured herself a third cocktail, grabbed a handful of tortilla chips from a big, ceramic bowl, shoved them in her mouth, then leant back again, sighing. After a few more minutes of talk about plants - Tensie told Rhodo about the new mini-hydrangea Alejandro had successfully hybridised — mischief entered Eve's mind. She decided it was time to spice the party up.

"So c'mon tell us the truth, Abby," she butted in, with a provocative smile. "Did you leave your husband for some hot new Romeo?"

Abby was in the middle of raving to Hannah about an extraordinary vine from India called *Thunbergia mysorensis*, which festooned the Vallarta Botanical Garden's main building with cascades of reddish brown and yellow flowers shaped like dolls' slippers. She stopped in mid-flow, momentarily tongue-tied. Stared at Eve with an uncomprehending look. Then she exploded with laughter.

"A Romeo? What, at my age?" she asked "I wish. You get to sixty, Eve, and you're invisible. The pickings are small. Just remember that. But to answer your question…"

She turned pensive for a moment.

"…no, there's no one else. For me or him. The honest truth is that, when I think about it, we just got bored with each other."

It was the first time Larry had been in her thoughts for ages. She felt vaguely surprised that she didn't miss him and wondered if she should. While their ordinary day-to-day routines of cohabitation were hard to break — they had become as deeply ingrained as fissures in the trunk of the hated black walnut — she'd gritted her teeth and told herself to smarten up. She wasn't too old to change her habits. Lots of people became single after living with someone else for years. And now, she reflected, my new life is so different, everything here in Mexico is so different from what I once had, that already it's becoming hard to remember how things were with him.

"Yes, husbands can get awfully boring, can't they?" quipped Hannah, so relieved to be away from Charles and his iPad— and also feeling the effect of tequila for the first time — that she made this observation loudly, with a surprising bark of laughter.

Yet mild-mannered to the core, Hannah felt instant remorse. Never before in her life had she criticised Charles behind his back to other people. It seemed so disloyal, something she'd resolved never to do when they got married. She was shocked at herself, wanting to bite the words back.

"But of course it's entirely natural that boredom enters into a marriage after..." she added hastily, floundering, trying to put things right.

Yet Eve couldn't have cared less about Hannah's remorse or her attempts at corrective measures. Oblivious, not listening, she charged on with her inquisition, going around the table.

"Okay, but what about you Rhodo?" Eve demanded. "Are you married? Is there a man around?"

"Nope," said Rhodo crisply.

"Lovers?"

"Nope."

"Never?"

"Well...um... there were a couple..." Rhodo blushed and looked away. Then she scowled, wishing Eve would stop this interrogation. She didn't like the way people discussed sex so casually nowadays — as if it was as routine and uncomplicated as brushing teeth.

"Women, maybe?" Eve asked with a sly grin.

"No, not at all. They were both men," she replied indignantly. "But it was a long time ago."

She realised that she hadn't been on a date for nearly thirty years. Briefly recalled the clumsy fumbling with a fellow student at university whose name she could barely remember, but then, with such painful sharpness — still like a knife in her guts — the rejection by Russell, the only man she'd ever loved. Russell had a red beard and chest hair that she liked to stroke during their brief unsatisfactory encounters in suburban motel rooms, and their affair, conducted in secret because he was married, went on for two long years. It all came to nothing in the end but the effect was long-lasting. His decision to stay with his wife — and the way he broke the news, callously, a couple of days before the bleakest Christmas in her life — made Rhodo resolve to stay away from romantic entanglements forever.

And she had.

"So what do you do for sex?" Eve persisted, raising her eyebrows suggestively, enjoying herself, unwilling to let the matter drop.

"Sex? What's that?" Hannah butted in, attempting a joke now, seeking to divert Eve's attention from Rhodo, who, she noticed, was practically squirming with embarrassment.

Hannah also realised that until this exchange, she'd known nothing about Rhodo's personal life. The subject had simply never come up during their previous plant-focussed reunions.

Abby broke in too, seeking a similar diversion, realising much the same thing as Hannah.

"When you've been married forever, you do start to wonder if it ever really happened," she said, shaking her head with a wry laugh.

Indeed, she couldn't remember when she and Larry stopped being intimate. Concluded that it was probably during a World Series years ago. They'd shared a cosy dinner with a bottle of wine (Hollis was doing a sleepover at a friend's house) and she'd felt amorous afterwards, but he'd brushed off her overtures to go to bed, because he wanted to watch the Mets. How agilely her spouse had leapt up from the dining table and rushed off to his study to turn on the TV. She had never forgotten that. The insensitivity hurt, and perhaps as a consequence — or perhaps, she reasoned, simply because they'd been together for nearly twenty years by then and desire had died a natural death — she'd lost interest herself. She took to regarding sex as a not-very-urgent chore, on a par with cleaning the hard water residue off the tiles in the bathroom shower stall. Both probably needed attending to, she'd probably feel better afterwards if she did, but it really wouldn't matter if she didn't, would it? So why bother? And she knew that Larry felt the same way about the sex (he never cleaned the bathroom) because he took to staying up late to watch TV, clearly hoping she'd be asleep when he came to bed.

Hannah's and Abby's attempts at diversion had no effect on Rhodo. She didn't laugh. Lips clamped in a thin line, she sat staring straight ahead, outwardly calm but inwardly furious, her cheeks going hot. She wondered if Eve was going to ask if she had a dildo next and what the damn woman was doing at their reunion in the first place. She pointedly got up from the table, headed for a corner of the courtyard to examine the potted *Datura* in an effort to put some physical distance between herself and Eve. With darkness tumbling over the town at surprising speed after the sun went down — the usual course of events in the tropics — the plant's white bell-shaped blooms had taken on a spooky quality, like fake ghosts suspended from trees on her street in Toronto every Hallowe'en. She squatted down, turned up a bloom to her face, breathed in deeply, savouring the hypnotic scent. Combined with the margarita, it made her slightly dizzy.

An awkward silence followed. No one spoke up except Eve.

"Oh dear, ladies, I suppose you won't want to hear about my love life, then?" she said at length, smiling coyly, having written Rhodo off as a dried-up old maid and eager to turn the subject back to what she liked talking about the most: herself.

"You're right," muttered Rhodo out of earshot, keeping her back turned towards the table.

"No, wait a minute. Maybe we do want to hear," piped up Abby, abruptly coming to life and gripped by a what-the-hell mood, induced by drinking most of the afternoon without eating anything. "Go on. Do tell us, Eve. Brighten our boring old lives with some salacious details."

"I'm embarrassed," said Eve, putting on a demure look, tucking her bare, tanned legs underneath her with feline grace.

"What you?" Hannah murmured, rolling her eyes. "Impossible."

Peacemaker Hannah sensed that the conversation was

starting to take a dangerous turn. Yet unaccustomed to alcohol — and under the influence of two margaritas by now — she wasn't sure how to move it back into safer territory.

"So how many men have you slept with, then? A dozen? Two dozen? More?" Abby egged Eve on with undisguised delight.

"Oh, lots more." A giggle. "But I've no idea, really."

"Wow. Any of them stand out?"

"Not particularly. Let's see…in the past couple of years, there were Francesco and Alvaro and Tonio and the last one, Fab…" She counted off her conquests one by one on her fingers, then her voice wavered. Hannah looked at Eve's face, but didn't expect a flood of tears this time at the mention of Fabio. Eve's last *inamorata* was toast. She knew that already. On the flight from Mexico City to Guadalajara, her sister didn't stop ogling a handsome Mexican sitting across from her on the aisle and deliberately let her handbag slide off her lap on to the floor of the aircraft cabin, so he could bend forward and pick it up for her. And the man had obliged, with a flirtatious smile.

"I truly have never kept count of how many men I've been with. But I confess that I do… I do love to fuck," said Eve, flashing a cheeky grin, then looking away abruptly, out into the courtyard.

She blushed, bit her lip, wondering if she'd gone too far, making such a candid admission to a bunch of women older than she was, whom she hardly knew. And she had. When she shot a nervous glance across the table at her sister, Hannah's face was contorted with rage and she was mouthing the words, "Stop this."

Unusually for Eve, she obeyed. Another awkward silence

descended over the table, as the women continued to sip their margaritas and look at each other with bemused expressions, wondering how to proceed.

Once again, Eve broke the silence.

"But what about you, Abby?" Eve finally asked, in a light tone, recognising a need to change course. "Have you met any attractive men here yet?"

"Ha. Not much chance of that." Abby shook her head. "All the single guys I'm likely to meet in this town have either run away from their wives back home or..." she paused and grinned... "they've murdered them."

"What?" Hannah and Eve expressed shock in unison. Rhodo even turned around from the *Datura*, surprised by the revelation too.

"Well, not quite," Abby corrected, chuckling. "But I've learned some interesting gossip about Ajijic from a British girl I've met. Oh boy, I had no idea."

She shook her head again, told them about her coffee with Gillian at Ixchel, about the colourful stories she related, and about the brutal wife-killer Pete Gomez.

"It was like being hit by a whirlwind, the things she said," she continued. "And according to Gillian, this Pete Gomez is on his way back here, seeking another older woman to bilk out of her life savings. But she's a colourful character and a lot of what she said sounded kind of exaggerated. So..." she brought her glass to her lips, smiling, "...I don't know whether to believe her or not."

Abby swallowed the last of the margarita and cleared her throat.

"But to answer your question Eve," she said, "the last thing I want in my life now is a man. Truly. I'm so happy to be on my own, doing what I please, not having to fit in with somebody else."

"Me too," muttered Rhodo from her corner of the courtyard.

"Well, count me out on that," said Eve, draining her own glass, unfolding her legs and stretching them out in front of her. "I would miss the...er..." She stopped. "But what time is it? I think I'd better be getting back to Tosca's don't you?"

She rose from her chair unsteadily.

Rhodo said, "Thank God," under her breath, straightening up. She returned to the table and sat down again.

At that moment, Tensie suddenly appeared in the courtyard doorway, looking rumpled and sleepy, a tuft of hair sticking up from the back of her head. She held her palms out to the group in an apologetic gesture.

"I'm so sorry everyone. Rude of me, I do apologise to you all," she said. "I don't know what happened. I went off for a nap, lay down on the bed and didn't wake up all afternoon."

"No problem. It's good that you had a long sleep. You're probably tired and needed to rest," Abby said.

Tensie nodded and took a chair.

Abby asked if she wanted a drink or anything to eat. She shook her head.

"Well, the rest of us have drunk far too much for sure and I, for one, am ready for bed," she said, getting up, eager to conclude the evening's festivities. "Hangover central here tomorrow morning, probably."

Everyone laughed in the tired manner of party-goers who realise the time has come to fold up their tents and head home to sleep.

"But stay up as long as you like, Tensie," she added. "Help

156

yourself to anything you want in the fridge."

"Yes, I will, thank you."

After the others had said goodbye to Eve at the front door and headed off to bed, Tensie went into the kitchen. She poured herself a glass of white wine, tasted the *Ajiaco*, added a bit of salt, tasted again and decided: *si, suntuoso.* Sumptuous. The best *Ajiaco* she'd ever made. The Sisters were bound to like it. She returned to the courtyard, sat for a long time sipping the wine and watching the thin sliver of a new moon mount slowly over the hulking shapes of mountains to the west of Ajijic. The mini-moon ascended into a sky of black velvet, stippled all over with pinpricks of stars. She thought of Juan Diego in New York, how he used to love the way she made *Ajiaco.* Pictured him sitting across from her at a table in their Upper East Side apartment, dipping his spoon in, then looking up at her with a warm smile and saying, "*Gracias, mi amor. Buen provecho.*"

She felt sad, desolate, that she'd never hear him say those words any more. Wondered if Cecilia cooked *Ajiaco* for him. Thought about their boy Javier, the son she was never able to give Juan Diego herself, realising with a start that the child was coming up soon for his fifth birthday. She wished the knowledge didn't hurt so much.

For some unaccountable reason, the handsome man she noticed in the departure lounge at Guadalajara also came to mind. She saw his face with vivid clarity. He'd looked so much like Juan Diego., perhaps that was why. He even had the same kind of swaggering walk. An instinct hit her that — somewhere, somehow — she was going to see that man again. And soon.

Then she spotted a shooting star. It flashed through the heavens and was gone, in barely a second. She recalled stars over the Savannah doing that in her childhood, how they'd fascinated her and what her grandpapa had always said.

"A shooting star means change is coming to your life, *niñita*, especially if you see it at a new moon."

Change. What kind of change? She shook her head, dismissed the thought and went to bed.

Chapter 11

Ajijic, Mexico, 5 am, 20th April, 2017

The neighbours' rooster woke Abby before the sun came up. His usual habit. Pale green dawn was barely colouring the sky above the mountains east of town when he started crowing. *Cocka rocka doo E... Cock rocka doo EEE.* As insistent as a cellphone tune. "Get up all you slothful folks," he seemed to be saying. "Get out of your beds and face the day. Right NOW."

Vato (what Carlos and Santiago called the bird. She thought it meant 'dude') didn't bother Abby. She'd concluded long ago that if she wanted to live in a small Mexican town, roosters would be part of the package. In fact, she rather liked her natural alarm clock. Most mornings she rolled over and dozed for another hour, until the first fingers of light started seeping into the courtyard. Yet today, in spite of too much to drink yesterday, she felt wide awake the moment he started up — the consequence, she knew, of being the host and of the need to be considerate to her guests. She wondered if Vato had disturbed the Sisters too.

Apparently not. She got up, crept into the kitchen in her bathrobe, made a pot of coffee. Felt only a mild headache from mixing wine with too many margaritas. Good. A relief. With no sign of anyone stirring from the other rooms, she poured herself a mug — black, no sugar, definitely no cream this morning. Returned to her own bedroom. Checked her laptop for emails.

Five messages. Four were from the other Sisters — Lola, Mieke, Nathalie and Jing-Jing. They all said how sorry they were not to be in Mexico and sent best wishes for the reunion.

"One day, you will all come to visit me in Guangzhou," wrote Jing-Jing, and Abby could almost hear her high, chirrupy voice, carefully enunciating the words. Dear Jing-Jing. So warm, so friendly, and quite famous in China, with her own TV gardening show. She spoke excellent English, acquired at school. Abby wished she'd been able to learn Chinese. Thought what fun it would be to all meet up where Jing-Jing lived.

The fifth message was from Hollis. And very brief.

'A model friend of Jaz called Clare, is going to be in Ajijic. Quite a coincidence. So I said to drop by your party. I just provided your street address. Have fun. H.'

A surprise, this. The strain between Abby and Hollis had grown more pronounced since she arrived in Mexico. Tired of a constant stream of text messages from her daughter about drug gangs, cilantro fields infected with E-coli and other negative aspects of the country she had chosen to live in, she'd wanted to scale back the contact for a while. And the best way, she concluded, was to pretend that she'd gotten rid of her cellphone, due to hassles with the service provider in Ajijic — which was partly true anyway.

"From now on..." she'd texted back to Hollis over a month ago, "...you can't text me. Call the landline at the house. It's included in my rent. Or you can email." But Hollis didn't call. Or email. Nor did she react to an excited email

Abby sent herself, saying three of the Sisters — from Canada, the UK and Colombia — were coming to a reunion she'd organised. Yet Abby wasn't concerned. She'd wondered if she was a bad mother because she felt only immense relief at Hollis's silence. She just didn't want to be bombarded with that kind of negativity any more.

What she felt now was irritation. No, outright annoyance. Who was this Clare? Some friend of Hollis and Jaz? She'd never heard either of them mention her. Didn't the girls realise that her little reunion was private, for close friends only? It wasn't a casual get together, open to anyone who felt like dropping by.

A strange girl joining the lunch, far younger than the rest of them, would spoil everything. Conversation was bound to be strained. What would the Sisters talk to her about? Certainly not plants and gardening. The eyes of her daughter's generation glazed over the moment the words were mentioned. Yoga then? Mindfulness? Drumming? Smoothies? Hollis and Jaz had become preachy bores about all four. And the girl was a model, so probably the only thing she'll be interested in was fashion, which bored all the Sisters, except Tensie, rigid. The black coffee turned sour in Abby's stomach as she contemplated this new development. Yet perhaps, she told herself hopefully, it won't happen. Perhaps, by some quirk of fate, this unwelcome guest wouldn't manage to find her little house, tucked away behind the high, yellow wall on Emiliano Zapata. Yes, there was certainly a glimmer of possibility of that, as she lived in Mexico. Although her black front door was certainly inscribed, at the top, with some barely visible tiny white numerals, the whole matter of numbering streets in her new home tended to be as haphazard as the observance of time.

She'd found that out a few weeks ago, while pacing up and down, looking fruitlessly for a store that did computer repairs on the Carretera. A Mexican youth eventually stopped and offered to help, saying politely, "I will walk you there, *señora*." Then he'd led her to a store front marked 3245, which proved to be mystifyingly sandwiched between numbers 3238 and 3239. When she'd commented on the mix-up, he'd shrugged, smiled and walked away. Perhaps Hollis's friend would have a similar experience. Flummoxed by the illogical sequencing of numbers, she'd give up.

Deep down, though, Abby knew that wouldn't happen. This Clare WOULD come. With a sinking feeling, she realised it was predestined, somehow. The girl would be young and beautiful and very thin. She'd make the Sisters feel fat and old and out of it. And her eagerly-awaited Titan Reunion would be a disaster.

Over at the *abarrotes*, picking up a paper sack of warm *bolillos* for the Sisters' breakfast, Herminio cheered her up.

"Another person coming to your party? Why is that a problem, *Señora* Abbee?" he asked, puzzled by her frown. "You Americans are so funny, worrying about such things. When Mexicans throw a party, we don't care how many people come. Everyone is welcome, no?"

Indeed, a couple of weeks ago, Herminio invited her to a huge silver wedding celebration for a grey-haired couple in his family. She wasn't sure who the celebrants were. He seemed to have dozens of cousins — and they were always dropping by the store. The anniversary partygoers gathered beneath two big, green tarpaulins erected on a soccer field near the lake. Steaks and chicken sizzled on barbecues, booze flowed, the live band was deafening. Herminio made an effort to include Abby (she suspected that he felt sorry for her, a woman on her own in a country where family is everything) and introduced her to his rotund wife, Eufemia and their two grown up sons, both of whom wanted to move to the States. They sat together on a low wall which ran alongside the field, while she attempted to answer their questions in a hesitant mix of English and Spanish. Yet after the boys went off to find their girlfriends, she'd felt out of place, not knowing a soul, wandering around solo amid discarded beer bottles and paper plates smeared with tomato sauce and chicken bones. A drunk sprawled on the grass had leered at her. She left.

The Sisters were sipping coffee in the courtyard when she returned to the house, stepping over Campeon, who lay sunning himself in his usual spot outside the door. She put the *bolillos* on the table, brought out butter, the pineapple jam she bought at Aguacate and slices of watermelon. Made more coffee. They'd agreed to eat a light breakfast in view of the upcoming feast that day. She told them about Hollis's email — and Clare.

"Well, I wouldn't worry about it," Hannah said shrugging. "She'll hardly be a monster with two heads, will she?"

Hannah, like Herminio, wondered why Abby was upset. Uninvited young guests were nothing new at the Dorset farmhouse. Friends of her own daughter, Alice, who still lived periodically at home, were always showing up, intent on scrounging a free meal. Only a week before she'd left for Mexico, a climate change activist with three rings in his nose interrupted their Sunday lunch of roast chicken. He'd promptly announced that he was vegetarian, lectured them about factory farming and gobbled all the brussel sprouts.

But the young always condescend to the old, she thought, recalling the encounter with amusement. It's a natural state of affairs. In our youth, we were undoubtedly insufferable know-it-alls too.

The prospect of an extra guest didn't concern Tensie either.

"I like having young people around," she declared, thinking of Luis, wondering how he was getting on at the farm without her, because an important shipment of *Alstroemerias* had to be dispatched to a wholesaler in Chicago that day. "I like their energy."

"Well, I guess I don't mind either. But I just hope she doesn't talk about sex all the time, like your sister, Hannah," grumped Rhodo, still sore about the way had Eve pestered her with personal questions the previous night.

"Which reminds me," said Abby, looking at her watch. "Where is Eve? Wasn't she supposed to join us for breakfast?"

Hannah sighed. "Oh, knowing Eve, she's probably slept in. She drank an awful lot yesterday, you know. More than the rest of us. We probably won't see her 'til lunch time."

She buttered a *bolillo* and dipped her knife into the pineapple jam. Spread it on liberally.

"No problem, but I think I'll get the *jicama* ready now. It's kind of a messy job," Abby said, getting up from the table. "Then I'll go and change."

"Yes, let's all wear something nice," decreed Tensie, looking around, cradling her coffee mug in her hand, smiling beatifically at each Sister in turn. "It is a special occasion, is it not, our meeting up and cooking together like this? So, *queridas*, we should celebrate it by wearing something special."

"But I don't have anything special," objected Rhodo, with a tense look.

"You didn't bring a dress with you?"

"Nope. I don't do dresses. Haven't worn them in years."

"Well, what about a pretty shirt and necklace?"

"Sorry. I never wear jewellery. Rings get in the way when I'm planting stuff. And I hate jangly things hanging around my neck. They're a nuisance too. But if you insist, Tensie…" Rhodo drained her coffee and rose from the table, anxious to be agreeable and aware that the others probably were thinking she overreacted to Eve's probing last night "…I'll go look in my bag for a nice, clean T-shirt."

Tensie smiled again. "*Bueno.* I will go and get myself ready too."

She disappeared into her bedroom. Hannah and Rhodo did the same. In the kitchen, Abby pulled out a vegetable peeler and pared the rough skin off the big brown *Jicama* she had bought at the market. It was a tedious task. Reminded her of peeling butternut squash in fall back at home, to make a soup that Larry had always liked. Yet she had already become a fan of this Mexican tuber as a snack with a cocktail, particularly a margarita. *Jicama* had the crunchy texture of a radish, but was sweeter, almost like an apple. And it had few calories. She cut the pulpy, white flesh into slices, put them in a bowl of cold water. Right before the meal, all she needed to do was drain off the water, arrange the slices on a platter, then douse them with lime juice and mild chili powder.

She eyed Eve's chocolate cake. It sat on the counter, resplendent on one of Myra MacDonald's lacy doilies which Abby had found in a drawer. Topped with sieved icing sugar, the finished product looked quite modest in size. Served in small portions at the same time as her *Capitorada*, it would probably be delicious — very nutty, with all those ground almonds, but not too filling.

Rhodo's annoyance notwithstanding, she felt glad Eve had come. She'd be fun at the lunch.

***

The Sisters gathered again in the courtyard just after noon. Hannah had changed into white cotton pants and a short navy jacket, with a pale blue top underneath. Abby got out the embroidered *huipil* that she'd bought on impulse at a market in nearby Chapala, right after arriving, but then put it away, because she decided, after a long hard examination of herself in the mirror, that folkloric costumes only looked good on Mexicans. But nothing else was clean in her closet, she hadn't got around to doing a load of laundry before the Sisters' arrival, so the *huipil* plus slightly grubby white pants would have to do. Rhodo wore her usual jeans, topped by an outsize green T shirt, with the words 'Rhodos Rock' in Day Glo pink across her chest.

"Sorry. It's kind of garish, I know, but it was a door prize at a symposium of the Rhododendron Society," she said. "I don't have anything else."

Abby and Hannah laughed and exchanged glances.

"You're fine. Your usual self," said Abby.

"I think you all look very nice," pronounced Tensie. She glided into the courtyard later than the others in a knee-length dress of violet silk, shiny purple pumps with kitten heels and pearl stud earrings. She'd put on pantyhose and piled her hair up in a chignon. Applied more make-up than usual. Smelled of something flowery, like gardenias. And around her neck was a glittering, gold necklace with a centrepiece of a huge emerald.

"Oh my god, Tensie, you look gorgeous!" Abby said, with a twinge of envy.

For even at sixty-one, how, elegant, how feminine, how like a career diplomat's wife Tensie still looked. Her heart-shaped face, over which she'd smoothed a layer of foundation, showed few wrinkles, her lips were full and voluptuous, not thinning and turning down at the corners, and her widely-spaced, brown eyes stood out, perfectly enhanced with mascara and violet shadow. The way Tensie had transformed herself triggered a memory for Abby of a similar dress and necklace Tensie wore once at a Colombian embassy cocktail party (she and Larry were there, although she couldn't remember why) and back then, she recalled, her friend had swanned around playing the perfect hostess, clearly enjoying her role. Abby felt guilty now, belatedly realising that Tensie, with her new life at the farm, probably didn't get much of an opportunity to dress up any more. So to humour her, she should have made more of an effort. Done what was asked. Worn something 'nice'. So should Rhodo and Hannah. Yet the fact was, her enthusiasm for beautifying herself had kind of withered away over the years — the only beauty that commanded her attention now, was the kind found in gardens — and she suspected that the other two Sisters felt the same way. And it was surely too late for any of them to go and put on a dress now.

Abby poured margaritas and brought out the platter of *jicama*. Everyone gave the novelty hors d'oeuvres a thumbs up.

"I like it," pronounced Hannah, crunching the crispy flesh

between her teeth and feeling chili burn her tongue. "It's sweet, but then you get the fire. An interesting combination."

Rhodo agreed, thinking it was the first Mexican food she'd truly liked.

"In Colombia, we have a similar vegetable but we call it *yacon*," Tensie said. "We shred it and make a salad, with lime juice and onion. But I usually order it in a restaurant, because the tubers are difficult to peel."

"Aren't they just?" said Abby pulling a face. Her fingers ached from peeling. "Enjoy *jicama* while you can, Sisters!"

The platter got emptied quickly. More margaritas were poured as the conversation drifted comfortably down memory lane once more. With raucous laughter, the Sisters recalled how, at Lola Honeybone's in Texas, they'd all got so involved in examining Lola's prize-winning collection of cacti — she kept them in a special greenhouse at one end of her long, ranch-style bungalow — that the steaks grilling on the barbecue at the other end of the garden caught fire and the neighbours called the fire brigade. Then there was the scary moment at Nathalie's outside Paris when Hannah nearly drowned in the river Seine. It was springtime, the river a raging torrent after the winter. Hannah stepped backwards to get a proper look at a soaring *Liriodendron* in the garden, intending to take a photograph, and almost lost her footing on the muddy bank. Rhodo, standing close by, prevented a disaster by grabbing the hood of Hannah's duffel coat.

Reflecting that she had never told Charles about the incident, Hannah observed with a chuckle, "It's dangerous to love plants as much as we do. Gets us into all kinds of trouble, doesn't it?"

"Yes, but we can't help it. We're addicts," said Abby, her

heart overflowing with happiness to be sitting here, sharing such memories with the Sisters. She reflected that the best times of her life had been spent in the company of women.

***

There was still no sign of Eve. Abby looked at her watch. She and Hannah agreed that she'd better call Casa Tosca. Abby went to the cupboard in the hallway, felt glad she'd made a note of the number when she made Eve's reservation, picked up the phone.

No one answered. After a dozen rings, the voice of the imperious girl came on. "Casa Tosca is closed during the day. Please call back later, after four p.m. This telephone does not record messages."

"Oh boy. Helpful lady, huh? Where can Eve have gone?" Abby asked, rejoining the others in the courtyard.

"She's probably still in bed," Hannah sighed. "I'm sorry, Abby. I'm so sorry, all of you. My sister is so... so..." She stopped, embarrassed.

Abby shook her head and thought for a moment.

"It's not your fault, Hannah, but I guess we'd better go on without her," she said. "What do you think, Rhodo? Want to serve the cod cakes now?"

"Sure," replied Rhodo, getting up. "It'll only take me a few minutes to get them ready."

Rhodo went to the fridge, removed her container of cod patties, took a frying pan off a long, wrought-iron hook hanging from the ceiling. She'd shaped the patties with her hands yesterday and partially cooked them. All that was left to do was refry the little discs for a minute or so in hot oil, then drain them on paper towels, so they'd taste crisp, not soggy, when brought to the table. She poured vegetable oil into the pan and lit the gas stove.

The frying pan went on the heat just as there was a violent hammering on the front door.

Bam, bam. Bam, bam. Whoever waited out there clearly wanted someone inside to pay attention.

Hannah groaned, smiled apologetically, put down her margarita glass, made a move to get up.

"That'll be Eve now," she said. "I'll go let her in."

"No, don't worry. You stay here. I'll go," said Abby.

It was indeed Eve. She stood on the doorstep yawning, tangled, black tresses flopping over her face, a white crumpled bed sheet wrapped around her torso. Underneath the sheet, she appeared to be naked, Abby noticed. She had no shoes on either. Her bare feet were coated in fine, grey dust.

"Oh hello," said Eve wearily. "That bloody dog…" She gestured crossly at Campeon who had sloped off with a villainous look to the sidewalk across the street. "He's a nuisance. And he stinks. You should tell the neighbours to stop letting him lie here."

Abby shrugged. "I guess. But he was here before me. So were they."

Eve snorted and, with delicate steps, entered the house.

"I'm not too late, am I?" she said, bunching the sheet up under her armpits, pulling it tight over her breasts. On her way through the hall, a leg caught in a hanging length of the fabric, and she tripped, just missing falling flat on her face.

"I've had the most awful time," she wailed, grabbing at the wall to steady herself. "I overslept and missed breakfast. So I took a sheet off the bed and went over to the dining room to see if I could at least get a cup of coffee."

She collapsed into an armchair.

"But there was no one around. Not in the dining room or even the kitchen. Can you believe it? Just opera music playing. What a place. Then I found I'd locked myself out of my room. You have to open the door with one of those card things you stick in the lock. I'd left mine in my bag in the room. So all I could do was walk over here."

She leaned over the table, exhausted from the ordeal of walking barefoot for a couple of blocks and smiled feebly at Abby.

"I got some funny looks on your street, let me tell you. There were two young guys sitting in a mini-van and they called out something obscene, I think. Then they roared with laughter and one made a rude sign with a finger at me. But I couldn't understand what they were saying. And *Dio mio*, those cobblestones were as hot as hell…"

She checked the undersides of her feet, which did indeed look red and sore.

"See? I hope you have some ointment," she said, showing them off to everyone in turn. "But can I have a cup of coffee first Abby? Please, please…" her tone turned plaintive. "I have the most terrible headache. Must be all that wine yesterday. What were we drinking? Some ghastly Mexican plonk?"

Abby made an exasperated noise in her throat, explained that it was chardonnay from California, and added, with barely concealed impatience, that there was no such thing as Mexican plonk, because hardly any wine grapes are grown in Mexico and wine is not a popular drink.

"It must have been the tequila. It's strong stuff," she concluded tartly. "You probably aren't used to it, Eve. But I'll go make you some coffee."

Hannah followed Abby into the kitchen, fluttering around like an anxious bird and whispering apologies.

"Sorry, sorry. I shouldn't have brought her. I knew something like this would happen. She's much younger than Ada and me and…"

"No, no, it's not your fault, Hannah," Abby interrupted, waving a hand to shut Hannah up. "But I'll admit that this IS annoying. I've so looked forward to our little lunch and now it seems that everything is getting screwed up."

She gave Hannah a long, reassuring hug, telling herself to stop making such a big deal out of Eve's behaviour. It would only spoil everything and put a dampener on the whole lunch. Rhodo stood awkwardly beside them both while this was going on, glancing anxiously at the stove, wondering what to do about the cod cakes.

"The frying pan is starting to smoke," she interrupted at length.

"Omigod. No! NO!"

Abby's reaction was swift — and tinged with hysteria.

"Turn the damn gas off," she screamed, abruptly releasing her hold on Hannah, spinning around to look at the smoking pan, visions of Bruce and Myra MacDonald's cosy Mexican hideaway going up in flames right before her eyes. Once Rhodo extinguished the gas, she calmed down and apologised for getting into a flap.

"Sorry. But whew, that was close, wasn't it?" she said, her heart still racing. "Just imagine if…" Words failed her. "But thanks, Rhodo. Many thanks. Let's forget about the cod cakes for now, shall we?"

"Sure."

Smoke from the overheated fat still wafted around the kitchen. It made Rhodo cough. Abby and Hannah waved their hands around in an attempt to clear the air. Then grabbing an insulated kitchen mitt, Abby lifted the white-hot frying pan off the burner, and carried it out carefully out to the courtyard, still sizzling and spewing smoke. She put it on the tiled floor. The cod cakes were returned to a shelf in the fridge and Rhodo retreated outside, her lips clamped in a straight line again as she silently cursed Eve.

Abby took a deep breath, told herself to smarten up and said out loud, "Right. Coffee." She went over to the sink with the kettle.

There was suddenly another knock at the front door. Softer, more polite-sounding, than when Eve had barged in.

Hand on the faucet, she stopped. Thought, 'Who the hell is that?' Remembered. Oh no. NO! Not now, on top of everything else. Not that fucking girlfriend of Hollis. She'd completely forgotten about her. She rolled her eyes, suppressed another urge to scream, shook her head, went out into the hall.

She approached the door unwillingly. Pulled it open, fighting the urge to slam it shut again.

Her jaw dropped open.

A man — an astonishingly handsome man — stood on the doorstep. Mexican by the look of him. About mid-forties, and very smartly dressed. Close-fitting designer jeans in pale blue, leather sandals and a bleached white Yucatan *guayabera*, left open halfway down his chest, clearly with the intention of showing off the rippling muscles beneath. He had dark, curly hair, which shone in the sun. Bright, alert eyes. And as he regarded her, she detected a hint of insolence in the

173

intoxicating smile, as if he knew already what kind of effect he was having, because it happened with every woman he met. In his left hand, he carried a bottle of something in a decorative gold bag.

"Well, hello, you must be Abby," he said in flawless, unaccented English, his voice smooth, deep and self-assured. He held out the bag bowing his head slightly, as a courtier might, delivering a gift to a queen.

"Hollis told me to drop by," he announced to her shocked face. "I am Clare."

Chapter 12

Ajijic, Mexico, 19th April, 2017
1.10 p.m.

Clare? CLARE? How could this Greek god of guy have a girly name like Clare?

Abby was struck dumb, one hand on the door, only half-open. For a few paralysing moments, she couldn't think of a single thing to say. The man out there had so completely taken her breath away. He made her think of a suntanned statue of Zeus — with clothes on. Or maybe Michelangelo's David, so overwhelmingly male and in your face, but with shorter, better-proportioned arms. And such a total shock, when she'd been expecting some skinny model in black.

"Oh... er... hi..." she stammered, staring at the bag but not putting out her hand to accept it.

She looked up again, into his eyes, then lowered her own eyes again. Decided to concentrate on his white teeth, framed by the dusky skin, to avoid the penetrating gaze. To her dismay, she felt a flush spreading upwards from her neck, turning her face pink. God, how utterly ridiculous this is, she thought. So annoying and embarrassing. I am over sixty, for heaven's sake! But this man is so... so unbelievably handsome.

For a brief, panicky moment, she wished the floor would open and swallow her up.

"Yes... um... thank you..." she mumbled eventually, recovering her composure. "I'm sorry, but I... um... I didn't know. Hollis didn't make it clear... You see I kind of presumed that..."

She drew a deep breath. The man continued to hover on the stoop.

"To be honest," she concluded with an apologetic grin, opening the door wider, "I thought you were going to be a gir..."

"I know. It's all right," he broke in, his voice commanding like a military man's, as if he'd heard people say the same thing a hundred times before.

"You can blame my mother." The seductive smile dissipated. He looked rueful. "She had a penchant for unusual names."

The gold, foil bag, tied with glittery cord, hung awkwardly from his hand and glinted in the sunlight as he waited to be invited in. Campeon, having hoisted himself up on wobbly legs, stood stolidly beside the man, a ribbon of dribble suspended from his open jaws. The old dog clearly wanted this unwelcome intrusion to disappear inside the house pronto, so he could reclaim his snoozing spot.

"I'll tell you about it sometime, if you want," Clare said in a resigned way. "Hollis should have explained. But for better or worse, my name IS Clare."

He tipped his head slightly to one side, as if willing her to believe him.

"Yes, I see. Well, um, please come in," Abby said at last.

They shook hands. She shut the door. Took the bottle bag. He explained that it was an Italian Pinot Grigio, bought yesterday at a store on the Carretera and he couldn't be sure how good it would taste, coming all the way to Mexico from Europe. But it was at least, chilled. She murmured thank you, very nice, it will be lovely, I'm sure, the words coming out in a rush. She worried that she wasn't being very gracious but couldn't stop feeling flustered.

She dropped the bag on a narrow table in the hall and motioned for him to follow her, through the house, out into the courtyard.

"Sisters," she announced, raising her eyebrows in a 'just look what showed up at my front door' kind of expression, pleased that he couldn't see her face. "This is... um... Clare. He's the friend of my daughter, Hollis, that I told you about."

She was tempted to add, 'Believe it or not' but stopped herself in time.

"Oh," Hannah and Rhodo said in unison, looking up at Clare goggle-eyed, surprised by his incredibly good looks too. Hannah was immediately seized by a mad urge to laugh because she was feeling the effect of the margaritas. Rhodo, less inebriated than Hannah, frowned and looked puzzled. After all the talk earlier about the possibility of a girl — a model — dropping by, what was going on? They both said, "Hi."

Tensie wasn't merely surprised. She let out an audible gasp. With lightning speed, she put down her glass on the table, patted her hair, smoothed out the lap of the elegant violet dress. Then she worried that her lipstick might have worn off. She recalled what was on her mind last night, when she'd sat alone in the courtyard looking at the new moon and the shooting star. Thought she must be developing psychic powers.

For this amazing apparition that stood before her was the

man she'd found so fascinating in the departure lounge at Mexico City airport.

Clare had a magical effect on Eve too. Yet her most immediate response was lust. Delicious, unmitigated lust. Her face went crimson, she felt a fluttering in her stomach, then between her legs. It had been a while since she'd encountered such a powerfully attractive man. And oh boy, this one oozed sex appeal like honey being poured from a jar. Forget Francesco and Alvaro and Tonio and Fabio and all the rest of them. Why did Italian men persist in thinking they were the cats' whiskers in the Latin lover department? Mexican men beat them hands down. She briefly recalled the man who sat across the aisle from her and Hannah when they flew to Guadalajara. He looked good enough to eat too. But this Clare, this specimen of *meraviglioso* masculinity... he was even better. How she wanted to melt into his arms, to do anything he wanted. She felt suddenly weak with desire.

Eager to be the first to experience his warm, inviting skin next to her own, she scrambled out of her chair. But in her haste, she forgot the sheet that had been clasped to her bosom ever since coming over to Abby's. A corner of cloth got snagged on the chair's wooden frame as she moved.

The sheet pulled taut. It ripped. The noise sounded awfully loud in the silent courtyard. Then Casa Tosca's high end, 480-thread count white linen bed covering fell in a heap around her feet.

Eve had — as Abby had surmised — nothing on underneath. Not a stitch. Everyone stared, open-mouthed. She said, "Whoops" and smiled coquettishly, bending down calmly to retrieve the sheet, swivelling her torso in Clare's direction, so that he was treated to a glimpse of her perky little breasts and shapely backside. Then, clutching the heap of crumpled cloth around her, she stepped forward boldly and thrust her right hand out at him.

"Hullo there," she said huskily, affecting a Mae West imitation. "I am Eve."

"So I see," he quipped, colouring slightly.

He shook Eve's hand and looked around at the Sisters, baffled.

"Well, pleased to meet you…er…ladies." he said raising his eyebrows. "Seems like I've stumbled on quite a party. Is it okay if I sit down?"

"Cod cakes… cod cakes… go make the damn cod cakes," muttered Rhodo, retreating into the kitchen, infuriated by Eve's theatrical showing-off. She concluded that Hannah's sister must be a nymphomaniac to be so obsessed with men. For it was surely obvious to him — and everyone else — that she dropped the sheet deliberately in order to show off her curves.

What a brazen bitch. Why on earth did Hannah bring her to Mexico?

Yet Rhodo wasn't exactly delighted either by the reaction of both Hannah and Abby to this man with the odd name of Clare. They seemed to be going gaga over him too — simply because he was admittedly handsome, in an old-fashioned, matinee idol kind of way. He reminded her of George Clooney.

But why did grown women always undergo an abrupt personality change and act like silly, little girls whenever good-looking men showed up? she asked herself, exasperated. She'd seen it happen so often. And this kind of development inevitably injected an entirely different atmosphere into a get-together that was meant to be exclusively female. It always ruined the whole thing.

Rhodo removed the container of cod cakes from the fridge once more. Lit the gas, feeling disappointed and short-changed. This Titan Reunion in Mexico, like the previous three, was supposed to be for the Sisters only, an opportunity for everyone to reconnect, reminisce and talk about their passion for plants and gardening. She'd been looking forward to telling them about her childhood connection to cod — and a certain herb — in Newfoundland. Also, about her new book, *Native Rhododendrons of North America*, which was due to be published next spring. But now she didn't want to even want to serve the cod cakes. She wished she hadn't come.

Why didn't she stay home with Azalea, working on the book in her comfortable little office? Then she could have gone downstairs periodically to take a break and witness her dainty little *Tête à Tête* daffodils coming into bloom. It would have been a much better bet.

In the courtyard, meanwhile, after introductions were made and Abby gave a cursory explanation as to why the women called each other Sisters, Clare headed immediately to Tensie's side of the table and took the chair that Rhodo had vacated. Her heart went pitter-pat as he leaned in close to admire her necklace. When she revealed that the huge gemstone at the centre of the necklace was a family treasure, an emerald mined years ago in Colombia, he murmured, "Beautiful. Must be worth a fortune," and reached out to touch it.

Abby disappeared into her bedroom, came back with a bathrobe and flip flops, and handed them over to Eve. She told her tartly, through pursed lips, that it would be a good idea if she returned to Tosca's and put on some proper clothes — and that she could surely find someone with access to her room if she looked hard enough.

"Try going through the kitchen," she said. "There must be a maid around somewhere."

With surprising meekness, Eve acquiesced, impelled by a grim glance from Hannah, who continued sipping her drink, saying nothing.

A tense bubble of apprehensive silence descended over the courtyard after the front door shut behind Eve. The kind where you could hear a pin drop. At length it was broken when Abby asked Clare if he'd like a margarita.

His face relaxed into a smile tempered with relief.

"For sure, I'd love one, thanks," he said, settling more comfortably into his *equipal*, "and don't worry about getting ice for me. I prefer them straight up."

"Okay. Coming up."

Abby drew another martini glass from a cupboard in the living room and filled it with the last of the contents of the jug on the table, thinking she'd better go into the kitchen and whip up some more margaritas. She handed the glass to Clare. Then she sat down again, desperate to get some kind of conversation going.

Hannah, sensing her discomfort and trying to help, gestured at a nondescript brown bird that was perched on a branch of the mango tree, chirping noisily.

"Does anyone know the name of that bird?" she asked brightly. "I've kept hearing it since we arrived and it has such a weird, raspy kind of song. It makes me think of scissors being opened and shut, over and over again."

Hannah and Eve looked blankly up at the bird, but Abby,

after a quick glance, chuckled. "I know what you mean. There's a pair of them. They're always here, every morning when I get up. I think they have a nest in the tree. Don't know about the scissors though. To me it sounds like they're saying 'Kick your rear! Kick your rear!'"

"Kick your rear. I love it," said Clare, shaking his head, chuckling too. "That's a good description. I'm pretty sure they are Mexican chickadees."

"Oh," said Abby. Then not wanting the conversation to dry up again, she turned to Clare and asked quickly, in a tone as chirrupy as the bird's, "So what brings you to Ajijic, Clare?"

"Oh, this and that," he said, leaning back, taking a sip of his margarita and looking up at the sky in a move that struck her as dismissive — and calculated to evade her question. "Like everyone, I wanted to get away, back to the sun. It's still pretty cold in New York, you know."

"Yes. I remember. So you've been here before?"

"Oh sure, I know Ajijic well."

"And you're American? I… um…" she hesitated, "I thought you might be Mexican."

"Well, yes, here's the thing… I might be Mexican or I might not," he said, his face now taking on an odd blankness, like a mask. "But…" he paused, clearly debating the virtue of what to say next, "…that's a complicated question to answer. And I think it's best if we leave that for some other time."

He abruptly switched on the seductive smile once more, which he directed mostly at Tensie.

"Okay," Abby said uncertainly, taken aback, as the others simply look confused. "Where are you staying?"

"I have a friend who owns a house in *Rancho del Oro*."

Hmm, she thought. Girlfriend? Tensie thought the same,

remembering the woman with hair like a silver helmet who had met him at the airport.

"*Rancho del Oro*. What a lovely name. What does it mean?" chimed in Hannah.

"The Golden Ranch," explained Clare. "There were gold mines there in the 1920s. And although the area has been turned into a *fraccionamento* — what a subdivision is called in Mexico — there are still street names like *Cajeon de la Mina*, which means Mine Alley and *Calle de los Mineros*, or Miners' Street. Some people even insist…" he took another sip, "…that you can still find flakes of gold if you go panning there."

"Really? What an interesting part of the world this is," said Hannah, with a wistful sigh. "I wish I had a house here too. I'd come for the whole winter and get away from the dreadful drizzle in Dorset. Do you think you'll buy a house here, Abby?"

Abby was thoughtful as she took another sip of her margarita.

"Perhaps, when my lease runs out. But I do worry that there are too many of us here already," she said. "I mean foreigners, the expat community, Americans and Canadians, and Brits like yourself, Hannah. I wonder if the Mexicans might wind up thinking we're the New Age Conquistadors."

"The Conquistadors?" piped up Tensie, with a curious smile. "I do not understand. What do you mean?"

"Well, they came to the New World and plundered it for gold, didn't they? And what we're doing is plundering Ajijic for the real estate. It's getting very expensive to buy a house here, you know."

Abby looked around the courtyard, at the high, whitewashed walls and the remarkable privacy they provided

— even though she was surrounded by neighbours, she felt barely aware of their presence — then at the collection of tropical plants the MacDonalds has amassed over the years. She was envious of them for owning this little piece of paradise.

"My landlord and his wife bought this house cheaply many years ago," she added. "But I'm not sure I could even afford something like it now. And that kind of situation is surely shutting out the locals, like my neighbour's kids, who will grow up and not be able to stay in the town where they were born."

She pictured Carlos and Santiago, such cute little boys, and so polite, playing hopscotch by the yellow wall after school and saying, "*Buenas tardes señora,*" every time she stepped out of the house. What would happen to them?

"But surely that's happening everywhere," objected Hannah. "Look at London. There's hardly an area of the city which hasn't been gentrified. Only the rich can afford to live there now. My son Edward can't. He has to live in the suburbs with his wife and two children and travel for hours to get to his job in the city."

"It's the same in Bogotá," agreed Tensie, nodding her head vigorously. "All the best parts of the city have become desirable and expensive. But as for your comment about the Conquistadors, Abby…" she narrowed her eyes and her voice rose, "…if you follow that kind of reasoning, none of us are entitled to live in the New World. Are we?

She looked hard at Abby, then brought a palm down gently on the table as if to emphasise her point.

"You know, of course," she added, her tone crisp and overlaid with anger, "…that I am probably directly descended from one of those awful Conquistadors who everyone despises for…"

"You are?" broke in Hannah, awed.

"Yes, my grandfather once traced our family back to a nobleman from Castile," said Tensie, pride displacing her displeasure at Abby's comment for a moment. "He received a land grant in return for military services to the Spanish crown — and we still own part of that land. It's in the valley outside Bogotá, where our farm is."

The look she directed next at Abby was defensive and accusing.

"Are you saying that we not entitled to own it, because indigenous tribes lived there before we did?"

"No, of course not, I'm sorry," Abby said, wishing that she had kept her mouth shut about the touchy issue of the Spanish explorers who rampaged through the New World.

"How fascinating that you can trace your ancestry that far back," Clare cut in. "I heard about you from Abby's daughter, and I want to learn more about Colombia. Could I take you out to lunch one day and pick your brains?"

He put down his glass and placed his palm over the top of Tensie's hand for a moment, smiling at her.

"*Claro que si.* Of course. I would be delighted," Tensie said, blushing, thrilled at the invitation and the intimacy implied by the gesture.

Abby smiled too, relieved that Clare came to her rescue and jumped into the conversation, to make up for her gaffe. Yet she felt uneasy, was starting to sense that he carried an aura about him that was distinctly odd. Why had he shown up like this at their lunch? Why was he so interested in Tensie? And why did he indicate such immediate admiration for her valuable necklace? She was undoubtedly still a lovely woman and looked beautiful in that silk dress, but that hand placed on hers seemed a bit too cosy for comfort, coming from someone Tensie — and the rest of them — had only just met. And why, in any case, would a guy his age seek out a gathering of women older than he is, then immediately turn on the charm to one of those women in particular — and in such an obvious way?

She suspected that this charmer who called himself Clare had an ulterior motive with Tensie. But what could it be?

A nerve in her neck started to throb.

***

Rhodo re-entered the courtyard bearing a tray. On it she'd placed six, small, decorated Mexican pottery plates, each containing a lettuce leaf, a small, round patty, and a quarter of lemon on the side.

"I hope you like them," she said, looking around anxiously at the group for approval, her brow creased in a familiar line. "They're my grandmother's recipe."

"I'm sure we will," said Abby, aware of the need to placate Rhodo, because Eve had annoyed her last night and today's shenanigans with the sheet had upset her even more. "They look delicious. I'll open Clare's white wine, shall I?"

Everyone agreed that would be a great idea. Wine poured, they settled down to savour the patties, along with a basket of quartered *bolillos* and butter, as Rhodo launched into a tale about her early life on the coast of Newfoundland.

"My grandfather was a fisherman. He and my gramma raised me after my parents split up and disappeared from my life. And they were poor and went through some very rough times. So she cooked an awful lot of cod because it was plentiful back then," she says. "But my brother and I hated having to eat fish all the time. The only thing we really liked was these patties, made with salted cod."

"Mmm, they are scrumptious," said Hannah, licking her lips. "What's that herb I can detect? It tastes sort of peppery."

"Yes, I was just coming to that."

Rhodo explained that it was summer savoury — and that Newfoundland was the only place in North America where people cooked regularly with this herb. A staple of gardens in summer, the fresh leaves were dried in the fall to use throughout the winter with poultry, pork, beef and fish.

"No Christmas turkey in Newfoundland would be complete without savoury stuffing. And some people even sprinkle it on baked potatoes," she added, her eyes twinkling at the memory of Gramma Mercer doing exactly that. "I thought that would interest you, as you're gardeners. I put two whole tablespoons of savoury into these cod cakes."

Hannah nodded with satisfaction, taking another mouthful, saying that she'd make a point of adding savoury to her herb garden in future. She also thought: great, another candidate for a *Dirty Fingernails* column.

"Yes, Newfoundland is fascinating. So wild, so few people, and they have unique traditions and expressions that you don't find anywhere else. I love it," said Clare unexpectedly, putting down his glass.

"You've been to Newfoundland?" Rhodo asked, astonished.

"When I was a kid. My mother used to rent a cottage for the summer on the Avalon Peninsula. We loved being on The Rock, although the first time we went, Mom was kind of put off because the owner of the cottage, who lived next door, kept going on about a 'bile-up' in the kitchen. She thought we were in for blocked drains, because the place was quite old." He laughed. "But the woman was in fact using an old Newfoundland term for a kettle. She'd equipped the cottage with a brand new one especially for us."

He took another sip from his glass.

"They have so many funny expressions like that. I loved being among Newfoundlanders. They're such down to earth, unpretentious people, and they'll talk your head off if you let them." He paused and laughed again. "I even got to kiss a cod."

"What?" asked Abby and Hannah simultaneously, make-believe horror on their faces.

"Oh, it's a silly ceremony someone dreamed up. If you kiss a cod, you become accepted as a real Newfoundlander," interjected Rhodo as Clare nodded in recognition. She shrugged dismissively. "But it's really just a gimmick to attract tourists. When I lived there as a kid, I never heard of any such thing."

Yet the fact that Clare was familiar with the ritual pleased her. She smiled at him for the first time, started clearing away the plates, feeling more relaxed. She rarely met anyone, even at home in Toronto, who knew anything about the rugged, rocky outpost where she was born.

Abby, meanwhile, was still feeling uneasy. She mentally scratched her head about the handsome newcomer. Travelling with his mother? Who was she? And to Newfoundland, of all places. It hardly sounded like the kind of regular holiday destination for a Mexican family. She only had a vague idea herself of where this part of Canada was. She pondered the possibility of posing more probing questions, but her musing got interrupted by a tap-tapping sound of someone approaching in the hallway.

It was Eve. Making a spectacular entry again. Having let herself quietly into the house with a key Abby gave her, she came into the courtyard throwing her arms wide, like a cabaret performer stepping on stage before an adoring audience.

"*Tra-la, tra-la,*" she sang, twirling around in a clumsy pirouette, bumping into Rhodo, almost knocking her and the tray of crockery flying into a tufa trough containing a huge *Mammilaria* cactus with wicked four-inch spines. "*La, la, la.* Here I am at last folks. How do I look?"

'Like a cheap little hooker,' Rhodo almost retorted out loud. 'Or a creepy female spider who lures males into having sex and then devours them.'

For Hannah's sister had squeezed herself into quite a get-up: skin-tight, silvery-black leggings topped by a low-cut, jewelled halter top that revealed a surprisingly large tattoo of a naked woman with pubic hair lolling over her right breast. On her head, turban fashion, she had a shimmering bandanna plus enormously long silver earrings that rattled like metal spoons being shaken in a box And her feet were encased in scarlet, ankle-strapped sandals with spike heels so high, they could have impaled the heads of ten traitors at the Tower of London, Rhodo thought sarcastically.

Everyone in the courtyard was taken aback again. They privately wondered how Eve could walk in such crippling footwear. And she couldn't. Not well, at least. Heading towards the table, breathless after her little performance, her rear end stuck out like a duck hobbling about on dry land, she stumbled and almost fell headfirst into Tensie's lap.

"Whoops. Sorry," she said, giggling. She flopped gracelessly into an *equipal* beside Abby.

Tensie swallowed hard, looked down, smoothed out a crease in the violet silk and stared resolutely into her wineglass, as if nothing had happened. Then she shot a furtive, disgusted glance at Eve's feet, remembering how Cecilia had staggered about in exactly the same kind of sandals — they were even glossy red too — at an embassy cocktail party. And how Juan Diego couldn't take his eyes off Cecilia all evening. He'd pursued the little *puta* around the room like a dog after a bitch in heat. Then they'd disappeared together after the party and started their affair that night.

Hannah squeezed the neck of her glass hard, wishing it was Eve's neck. Abby avoided looking at anyone, and suppressed a scream that was once more threatening to rise in her throat.

A pall descended over the courtyard again, as heavy and oppressive as a humid afternoon in Puerto Vallarta. No one could — once again — think of a single thing to talk about.

Except Eve, that is. Oblivious to the strained atmosphere, she was as chirpy as the Mexican chickadee, which still sat on a branch of the mango tree, chanting 'Kick-your-rear, kick-your-rear' at the group of people gathered uneasily below its perch. Eve demanded some wine. She batted her eyelashes shamelessly at Clare, who pretended not to notice. She fiddled with her bandaged finger, willing someone to pay attention and ask if it hurt. She whined twice that she was hungry and when was something going to be brought out to eat?

Ignoring her, Abby got up from the table and went into the kitchen for a bottle of wine. She found Rhodo hiding by the sink, scraping scraps of lettuce and squeezed lemon quarters off the pottery plates into a garbage bin, reluctant to return to the courtyard.

"My god," Rhodo whispered to Abby, rolling her eyes. "What's she going to do next? Jump into his lap? Can't you get rid of her?"

"I don't know how I can," said Abby despairingly. "She's Hannah's sister, after all, and I did say she could come."

Rhodo rinsed her hands off under the tap.

"Those ridiculous fuck-me sandals," she snorted, grabbing a tea towel. "I hope they're killing her feet."

***

With the appearance of another bottle of wine, the fourth Titan Reunion of the Sisters of the Soil staggered into life again, like a bird slowly regaining consciousness at the side of the road after being stunned by a passing car.

Abby filled glasses to the brim, desperate to rekindle a festive mood by any means, even if she had to resort to making her guests dead drunk. And the additional alcohol did have the desired effect. Tongues quickly got loosened again. Within a couple of minutes, Hannah and Rhodo were chatting companionably, comparing notes about their favourite herbs. Hannah loved basil, Rhodo opted for savoury, "...because of Gramma Mercer." Tensie told Clare about her farm in Colombia, the variety of flowers she grew there for export, her hopes for the future. He listened raptly, asking questions, his head turned at a sharp angle towards her, as if he was trying to shut out Eve, who sat opposite him. Peevish at the lack of attention, Eve gulped two glasses of wine in quick succession, belched into the glass, fiddled with her sandals (which were indeed pinching her toes) then her bandaged finger, and stared unhappily out at the courtyard.

"I want something to eat," she said in a little girl squeak, plaintive as a three-year-old now. "I'm starving. My stomach is gurgling. Can I please have a cracker to tide me over 'til you get around to serving some food?"

She put a hand to her forehead, making the earrings rattle.

"I feel faint. I think I'm going to pass out."

Go right ahead, Abby thought grimly, unmoved. Aware that the plea was probably genuine, because Eve had missed breakfast at both Tosca's and the house — as well as the hors d'oeuvres of jicama served with the margaritas — she didn't care if Hannah's sister collapsed in an alcoholic coma under the table. At least it would shut her up for a while. Why on earth did you imagine that Eve would be an asset to the party? she asked herself crossly. The damn woman is a walking, talking nightmare, the Guest from Hell everyone dreads showing up at an occasion like this.

Ignoring Eve's pleas, she bustled around like a server in a restaurant, laying out more plates, plus bowls, knives, forks and spoons and a soup ladle, in preparation for the next course.

Then, with a gaiety she didn't feel, she addressed Tensie:

"Ah-HEE-ah-co," she declared, pleased at her pronunciation of the word, rolling the syllables out like a pro, with hard aacch sound at the first and the third, as if she were clearing her throat. "Let's try your lovely *Ajiaco* now, shall we, Tensie?"

Tensie was more than happy to pick up the cue, having defused many tense situations at the dinner table during her years as the wife of a diplomat. In fact, she knew the formula off by heart: when things go wrong, act fast. Gloss over the behaviour of the difficult guest, bring something new to the table that everyone can focus on, keep the conversation going, avoid anything controversial. She stopped talking to Clare and headed immediately into the kitchen. The stew she made yesterday had been heating in the oven. Holding the huge heavy *olla* in front of her with kitchen gloves, she returned to the courtyard, triumph on her face, like a proud matriarch serving a festive dinner to her family. Clare located a decorative tile in the living room and put it on the table top, to protect the glass. She set the hot cauldron down. Lifted the lid proudly. A curl of steam arose from the rich, creamy-looking interior, which was flecked with green and ornamented by freshly-boiled cobs of corn. Everyone looked impressed, most of all, Tensie herself.

"*Bueno*. We are now going to eat a famous dish from my country," she announced grandly, as if addressing a banquet of business people at a Colombian Embassy dinner. "It is the pride of Bogotá and I'm very pleased to have the opportunity to introduce it to you here. Please smell it first."

Everyone did as ordered, like obedient kids, then made appreciative noises.

"But before we eat…" her tone turned mischievous "I want to hear you all say *Ajiaco* in Ajijic."

"Great idea, Tensie," said Abby, laughing, clapping her hands together. "Come on, everyone."

A master stroke, she thought, typical of a canny diplomat. For Tensie's request made the mood lighten magically — as one by one, the by now inebriated group struggled to wrap their tongues around the tricky, guttural Spanish combination of the two words. Eve, with her fluent Italian, fared the best, Clare the worst. The way he stumbled and comically mangled the pronunciation was a surprise to them all.

"Sorry, I speak hardly any Spanish," he admitted, to raucous laughter around the table.

"How come?" Abby asked, thinking aha, here's the chance she'd been waiting for, an opportunity to learn more about her mysterious guest. "You look so, well, Mexican."

"Yes, I know," he agreed, then stopped. The closed-off look flashed over his face for the second time since he arrived — quite briefly, making Abby wonder if this time she had imagined it. Even so, she picked up a distinct message that he was not willing to be subjected to any more probing into his background.

"Let's listen to Tensie now, shall we?" he said firmly, as the seductive smile got turned on again. "Isn't she a treat?"

His insistence disturbed Abby. It was a fleeting glimpse at a different side of him, but she left it at that, because Tensie stood expectantly at the head of the table, keen to launch into her culinary tale. In fact, she appeared as childishly eager as a ten-year-old showing off a school report with excellent grades. Clare watched, undisguised admiration on his face.

"There are many different recipes for *Ajiaco*," she explained, once she was sure she'd got everyone's attention. "But I like to make mine with garlic, chicken thighs, *papas criollas* — that's tiny potatoes — plus corn on the cob, and *arracacha* — what you call cassava. Oh, and sour cream."

She picked up a large ladle and thrust it into the *olla*, stirring gently.

"You can also add a garnish of capers, more sour cream, thinly sliced avocados and white rice. That's what they will often bring to the table in some restaurants back home. But I've skipped the garnish today, because we're having a lot to eat, and I thought it might be too filling. Also, it would mean too much advance shopping for Abby."

She exchanged a smile with her host.

"Thank you, Abby, for buying all the ingredients for me. I appreciate it."

"*No pasa nada*," said Abby, who'd recently discovered this expression and loved the opportunity to use it. She leaned towards Rhodo and Hannah and explained quickly that it meant 'No problem. No worries', and they'd hear it often in fatalistic Mexico.

Tensie resumed her little story.

"But although I skipped the garnish, Ajiaco contains one very important ingredient that I couldn't leave out. It is a herb called *guascas* which is unique to Colombia and not used in cooking anywhere else in the world."

"Really?" said Hannah, shaking her head. "That's a surprise. But I've certainly never heard of *guascas*."

"Nor have I," said Rhodo and Abby together.

"No one outside Colombia has. It is unknown. Yet here's the most interesting part," Tensie said. "When I was a volunteer at Brooklyn Botanical Garden, I discovered that *guascas* grows everywhere, not just in Colombia. But people treat it as a common weed. American farmers hate to find it in their fields and gardeners pull it out. I even discovered some growing wild in Central Park."

She paused.

"And in the US, its name isn't *guascas*. It's galinsoga."

Everyone except Eve shook their heads in wonderment.

She muttered, "So?" under her breath and continued to fidget. Bored by the botany lesson, frustrated by Clare's refusal to flirt with her, she felt ravenous enough to tear apart a whole chicken with her bare hands. Her stomach kept rumbling like a train going through the Alps. And she didn't like this friend of Abby's — so stuck up, so full of herself, rattling on about farmers and weeds and some park in New York City. Who the fuck cared? Hold the lecture, lady, she wanted to interrupt. Just get on with serving this bloody soup that you're so nuts about. *Dio mio*, what a fuss. I could whip up something just as good in less than an hour for Giuseppe back in Italy.

Yet Tensie was clearly in no mood to hurry. The unique nature of *guascas* was a subject dear to her heart.

"Galinsoga gets its name from an eighteenth century Spanish physician and botanist called Ignacio Mariano Martinez de Galinsoga," she explained. "He founded the *Real Academia Nacional de Medicina* and was a director of the botanic garden in Madrid. But over time, you English speakers..." she chuckled, "...got muddled up and started calling it 'gallant soldier.' And in Brooklyn..."

She paused again, wanting to spin the story out.

"...the kids in the children's garden where I volunteered have done something really funny with the name. They've garbled it even more. You won't believe what they call the herb now."

She looked around the table, smiling, enjoying the quizzical looks on her friends' faces.

"What?" said Hannah.

"Gallon of soda."

"You're kidding," said Abby, laughing.

"No, I'm not. Gallon of soda. That's the name given to this herb by the kids at Brooklyn Botanical Garden. We planted some galinsoga in the children's garden and we put a sign up about it. It was part of a project we introduced to celebrate herbs of the world."

More surprised murmurs from the gardeners ensued.

"That's a great story," said Hannah. "I'm going to write about *guascas* in my column."

"I have lots more historical background if you want it," Tensie told her happily.

"Ah, but what does it taste like?" asked Clare. Tensie thought for a moment, clasping her hands together, still standing in matriarchal fashion at the head of the table.

"Mmm... probably parsley is the nearest to it," she said. "But the flavour is hard to define. See what you think when you taste it yourselves. I brought a package of dried *guascas* with me, but we use it fresh in Colombia and it has more flavour then."

She picked up the ladle.

"*Buen provecho, todos*. Good appetite everyone. Who wants to try the first bowl?"

"ME!" shrieked Eve, her voice rising so loud, the chickadee in the mango tree took off in fright. It flew above the town's high walls in the direction of Lake Chapala and disappeared.

***

As anticipated, the *Ajiaco* did get rave reviews. Clare leaned close to Tensie again, said he had never tasted a chicken dish quite like it and that it was very clever of her to introduce it to them. She blushed. Hannah loved the unusual mix of flavours (privately thinking that Charles, a conservative eater, would hate the *guascas*). Rhodo agreed that it was very tasty then worried that her cod cakes weren't and that everyone preferred what Tensie made. Eve wolfed down her bowl like a starving Mexican mutt that's wandered in from the bush, then begged for a second helping and polished that off in a flash too.

And Abby dipped her own spoon in thinking, whew, at least that part had gone well.

Perhaps her lunch party was finding its proper rhythm at last.

Chapter 13
Ajijic, Mexico, 19th April, 2017
2.30 p.m.

They moved on to the salad course. But with the sun now shining directly into the courtyard, it was as if someone had thrown a thick, wool blanket over Abby's lunch party. Everything went suddenly quiet. The brilliant blue sky turned pale with heat, the air still. The chickadee didn't return. It had seemingly vanished. The mango tree drooped in a defeated way, while on the roof of the house next door, the laundered navy blue and white school uniforms of Carlos and Santiago went even limper on washing lines strung between crooked poles. Outside the high, yellow wall, Emiliano Zapata emptied of pedestrians. The drone of traffic on the Carretera became muted, with less drivers proceeding along it. Even Campeon retreated to a shady alley, three doors away.

Abby opened a red and white umbrella over the table to shield her guests from the glare and realised that her decision to throw a noon hour celebration in the tropics was the misguided notion of a transplanted northerner. For this was siesta time in Mexico. Everything slowed down then — and rightly so. Ajijic might not experience the suffocating humidity of the Pacific coast, yet it was still too enervating to eat a lot, to make intelligent conversation, to entertain ideas of doing anything but dozing off. Why didn't she schedule the feast over dinner, the proceedings starting at dusk, when the temperature had cooled off? With the courtyard lit up by candles placed among the plants, it would have looked beautiful — and been much more intimate and relaxing. She shot a worried glance around the table, trying to hide her dismay. All her guests appeared sleepy and satiated after Tensie's filling chicken dish. Any remaining conviviality was fizzling out of the courtyard like a slow leak from a balloon. On the foreheads of Clare, Tensie and Eve, beads of perspiration were forming and Hannah had just shrugged off her navy-blue jacket, thrown it over the back of her chair and, hand over mouth, was trying to stifle a yawn. Abby's own eyelids felt as heavy as pot lids. Retreating to her bedroom for a nap would have been wonderful. The others were clearly dying to do the same, she thought worriedly, but were too polite to propose the idea.

Yet, determined host that she was, anxious to keep her fantasy of an all-day reunion over delectable dishes and lots of wine going for a little longer, she announced with a forced air of jollity, "Well, folks, I think we're all getting full, so what do you say that we have a taste of Hannah's salad and hear her story? Then after that, I'll make some coffee and we can take a break, okay?"

Unanimous agreement followed around the table. So ever-amenable Hannah gamely went into the kitchen and came back carrying a big, multi-coloured ceramic bowl full of salad greens and cut-up avocado, plus the jar of dressing she made yesterday. She poured the dressing over the greens, tossed everything together with wooden serving spoons and doled out portions into bowls.

And Hannah was a confirmed promoter of lovage. She

had exhaustively researched the history of what she considered was an overlooked herb — and sung its praises several times in *Dirty Fingernails*. Yet she decided to keep her dissertation to a minimum, sensing — correctly — that no one wanted to sit through a story as detailed as Tensie's.

"There was once this crusty, old dowager called Lady Lilford," she began in a sing-song voice, mimicking a governess reading a nursery rhyme to children, "and she had a cook and maids. But she always insisted on mixing the salad dressing herself during her dinner parties, while her guests sat around the table watching in their fancy evening clothes. And this dressing — what I've put on the salad today — is her own invention. Its main ingredient is lovage."

Hannah stopped to draw a breath. "I found out about the dressing through a writer about gardening called Beverley Nichols. He liked the taste of lovage and wrote about this Lady Lilford in one of his books."

She smiled and stopped, looking around the table.

"That's it?" asked Abby.

"Yes. That's my story. Don't want to bore you with any more," she said cheerfully, wishing she could go on a bit longer, but restraining herself. "Beverley said lovage tasted like smoked celery. And it does, don't you think?"

Everyone picked up forks and poked tentatively into the salad.

Clare was the first to venture an opinion. He chewed, swallowed, thought for a moment and said, "Mmm, I don't know about smoked, but it sure does taste like celery."

Rhodo concurred. So did Hannah and Abby. Eve, still sulky and silent because the fuck-me sandals were indeed — as Rhodo hoped — killing her feet, interjected that she'd cooked with lovage in Italy.

"We call it *sedona di monte*, and put it in a vegetable pie. Also, soups," she said in an offhand way. "And it's okay, I suppose, although I think basil and oregano are better."

Mildly miffed by Eve's dismissal, yet pleased that her sister was at least familiar with a herb she'd grown to love, Hannah cleared away the plates and looked over at Abby.

Picking up the cue, Abby swung into action again.

"Coffee?" she asked, getting up from the table.

"Oo yes," shrieked Eve again, eager for a shot of caffeine to take her mind off the excruciating pain in her toes.

***

Clare knew his *robustas* and *arabicas*. That was obvious. For he promptly asked Abby what kind of coffee she intended to brew.

"Oh, Mexican," she said with nonchalance. "I like to buy local. So I get my coffee from a little guy who parks a white truck on the Carretera. He drives in from Vera Cruz and sells the beans, ready ground, from the back of the truck. "

She shrugged. "But I'm afraid I don't know what kind of coffee it is. *Arabica* or *robusta*, I'm no expert."

She laughed.

"Yes, I know the man. Nice of you to give him the business," Clare said. "But Mexican coffee tends to be quite mild, unless it comes from down south, in Chiapas. Someday, you should try something else — Ethiopian or Colombian, perhaps. Both are grown at a higher altitude than in Mexico, and the flavour is stronger. More robust."

Tensie's eyes lit up.

"*Si, si*," she agreed, leaning forward, ecstatic about Clare's endorsement. "Our coffee is the best in the world. Some day you must all come to my country and I will make it for you."

"We'd love that," said Rhodo, "and I want to see your flower farm."

"So do I," said Clare, winking at Tensie.

"We will arrange it — and that's a promise," she said, blushing and looking down at her lap.

"Well, since you have Mexican coffee on hand today," Clare went on, addressing everyone around the table, "why don't we make it the traditional Mexican way?"

"Sure, if you like," said Abby, trying to sound enthusiastic, but feeling as wrung out as an old dishrag. She glanced up at the colour-drained sky. Noted that her armpits felt sticky. Suddenly felt drained, wishing fervently that Clare hadn't initiated this discussion about coffee.

"But I've no idea how to do it and I think we're all kind of tired and..." she said.

"Oh, it's real easy," he broke in smoothly. "I can prepare it for you, if you'll let me. Do you have a heavy-bottomed saucepan?

The seductive smile appeared again.

"Um, yes, probably," Abby said, thinking what a too-obvious charmer Clare was, and that he was used to getting his way with women.

She personally ached for a cup of regular filtered coffee, but she led him into the kitchen, where he asked for cocoa and cinnamon sticks.

"And you don't happen to have some *piloncillo* on hand, do you?" he said, moving towards a store cupboard with the air of a chef taking charge. He looked back at her inquiringly. "It's raw sugar that comes in a block and…"

"You don't have to explain," she interrupted sharply, detecting condescension in his tone. "I do know what *piloncillo* is, you know. And it so happens that I bought all three things the other day. We needed them…" she forced a smile, "…for the desserts we're supposed to be having later on."

"Great," said Clare, touching her forearm lightly as if he sensed her displeasure. "And thank you, Abby. Thank you. Let's do it then."

The saucepan and other utensils located, she told him to help himself and left. Yet Clare was just too smooth, too sure of himself. Her unease about him kept on growing. And his offer struck her as kind of bizarre, because never before in her life had any man — let alone a virtual stranger — done this, insisted on making the coffee himself, after a gathering in her home. She and Larry hadn't entertained often — he was always too busy at the bank — but on the rare occasions that they had hosted a lunch or dinner, usually for relatives, he'd always left the post-prandial coffee-making to her, taking for granted that he didn't have to get involved, because he'd prepared the cocktails and served the wine with the meal.

So what was with this Clare? An awful suspicion about his true identity had started to form in Abby's mind. She recalled her conversation with Gillian. Could the guy perhaps be…? But no, that was impossible. Out of the question. Don't even go there, she told herself sternly, because how on earth would he have got to know Hollis and Jaz? You're being melodramatic. Stop getting carried away. You've had too much wine. Clare is undoubtedly simply one of those java fanatics who like showing off their knowledge about coffee to other people.

She re-joined the others in the courtyard, feeling woozy and a bit unsteady on her feet. She hoped her anxiety wasn't obvious. Indeed, it didn't seem to be, for Tensie simply looked up at her and asked excitedly, "So we're having traditional Mexican coffee are we?"

"Yup," said Abby, grateful to sink onto an enveloping *equipal* again.

"How nice. And how lovely to have a man doing the honours for a change," said Hannah, reflecting that Charles never offered to make coffee for her.

***

After what seemed like an eternity, when they were all stifling yawns, Clare came out of the kitchen carrying a tray of pottery mugs. To a decidedly mixed reception. Abby spoke first — and was in favour. She'd tried Mexican-style coffee before— at Ixchel on the Carretera. But this time the way he'd prepared it — heating the grated *piloncillo* with water and a cinnamon stick, then adding ground coffee plus a teaspoon of unsweetened cocoa, tasted better than the café's version.

"It's richer, not as sickly sweet. I like the addition of cocoa," she told him. He nodded, seemed gratified and looked inquiringly around the table.

Rhodo and Hannah liked the flavour too (although Hannah privately thought it wouldn't please conservative Charles). Tensie nodded assent. Yet Eve was horrified. She took one sip, put her mug down, announced that she only drank Italian espresso, strong and black, no sugar, and declined to taste another drop.

"Sorry, but this isn't coffee," she said. "It's... it's... I don't know what it is." She shot a seductive smile at Clare. "But I'm sure you know how to please a girl with some REAL coffee, don't you, Clare?"

She raised her eyebrows provocatively, in her umpteenth attempt to gain his attention.

But his gaze was cool as he shot back, "Sure, Eve. And I do realise that Mexican coffee is an acquired taste."

Then he quickly turned to the others one by one, saying: "Interesting to get your reactions, ladies. I've made this kind of coffee so many times — for so many people. And some become fans. Others think it's a travesty, a waste of real coffee."

"How come you've made so much coffee?" Abby asked.

"Oh, I've worked in a coffee shop..." he said vaguely, staring out into the courtyard, smiling to himself, letting his eyes linger on the trunk of the mango tree, as if struck by a memory of something pleasant.

Watching him, Abby had a flash of recognition. Coffee shop? Coffee shop? Didn't Gillian say that the guy who murdered his wife ran a coffee shop? Her suspicions — and worries — about Clare refused to go away.

"You know, I've grown to like Mexican-style coffee myself," he said at length, turning back at the women with a contented smile. "I'm a confirmed espresso drinker too, like Eve," he nodded briefly in her direction, "but I do like to have this as a change from the real thing."

He picked up his own mug and drained it.

"Sharing some with you today has brought back some happy memories."

"Well, I'm glad," said Abby, smiling, but wanting to ask: what memories?

Then, to everyone's surprise, her unexpected and baffling male guest did something that startled all of them. He propelled the Titan Reunion to an abrupt, and rather unsatisfactory, ending.

After putting down his mug and wiping his lips with a napkin, Clare pulled a cellphone out of his jeans pocket. He checked it, frowned and announced rudely, "Sorry, but I have to go. I'm summoned."

He pushed back from the table, rose to his feet and — with what struck Abby as indecent haste — put his hand out to shake hers, saying "Thank you for allowing me to spend time with you and your lovely lady friends."

Then, quick as lightning he was off, practically sprinting down the hallway, shiny leather sandals gliding noiselessly over the tiled floor.

The Sisters got up too, planning to say goodbye and shake his hand, but Clare had already vanished. Abby started after him, intent on opening the front door, but she was stopped by Tensie. Leaping into the fray, she said, "No, no. You stay here. I'll go."

The other women stood around the table, looking at each other perplexed, uncertain how to react as they listened to their Colombian Sister having a whispered, barely discernible conversation with Clare on the doorstep. Then the door shut and she came back into the courtyard, her face glowing.

"He's going to call about taking me out to lunch," she said happily.

"When?" Abby asked.

"Um, I'm not sure."

"Does he realise that you're only here for a few more days?"

"Oh yes," Tensie said. "And now, if you don't mind, I'm going off for a nap."

She bounced off to her bedroom, cheeks pink, feet light as a feather in the purple kitten heels, humming a tune as she went. Rhodo followed a few minutes later, looking puzzled. Hannah stayed in the courtyard, hovering beside Abby. Both women were in a kind of stupor from too much wine and food and the tension engendered by Clare's presence — along with his hasty departure. Besides, they were now wondering what to do about Eve.

For Hannah's sister hadn't moved. She was slumped forward in her chair, torso bent over the table, arms cradling her head. The bandanna had slipped off and fallen on the floor and the halter top had taken a ride skywards into her armpits, revealing another tattoo — of a naked man with an erection this time — in the small of her back. And she was sobbing her heart out.

"He didn't like me, did he?" she mumbled into the table, saliva smearing the glass top. "He didn't like me. He liked HER, your Spanish friend."

She lifted her head and directed an accusing expression at Abby, her nose running, mascara once again streaking down her cheeks.

"And she must be twenty years older than him. Why?" Her voice rose to a fever pitch. "Why? I don't get it. Men never brush me off like he did. What's wrong with me?"

The blubbering resumed as she flopped forward again.

Hannah sighed, went around to the other side of the table, put a protective arm over Eve's shoulder and made the comforting noises she'd been accustomed to summoning up in situations like this for years. Abby sighed too, but impatiently, wanting to murder Eve. She went to the phone in the hall and called the accommodating Juan. She dug out another cloth bag from a cupboard, then picked up the fuck-me sandals, which had joined the bandanna under the table. Providing support on each side, the two Sisters helped Eve to hobble — shoeless and whimpering that her feet hurt — to the front door. Abby noticed blood on the tiles, figuring that the cut finger she bandaged up yesterday had started bleeding again. But as they moved along, she realised that the drips were coming from Eve's toes. She suspected that Hannah had noticed them too, but neither of them saw fit to mention it. Juan arrived, nodded gravely when asked to drive Eve straight to Casa Tosca, and helped her into the car.

"*Si, señora*," he said, with a knowing look at Abby. "*Subito*. We go *subito*. We go quickly."

Hannah hugged Abby after the black SUV disappeared down Emiliano Zapata. She apologised over and over again and, with a quick look at the piles of dirty dishes in the kitchen, asked, "Shall I start cleaning up?"

Abby shook her head.

"No, leave it for now. But tell me: why does your sister act this way?"

"Oh, it's because of the way she was raised," said Hannah, shrugging. "She's never really grown up. As you can see, she's much younger than Ada and me and our parents spoiled her and treated her like a little girl right into her twenties. So she still thinks the world revolves around her."

"Tough for you to cope with, I guess."

"Yes, but I don't spend much time with her, since she

moved to Italy." Hannah sighed again. "I'll be so glad when she's gone back to Rome."

Then Hannah, looking tired, went off to her bedroom to sleep things off too, after being assured by Abby that the dishes could wait.

Finally alone, Abby headed for her own room, determined not to succumb to the seduction of a siesta like the others. Not yet, at least. Her head may be throbbing, she felt ready to collapse, but there was something she simply had to do. And right away. Sitting on the side of her queen-sized bed, she reached for her laptop, opened it, clicked on Mail.

"Hollis, darling," she typed. *"Your friend Clare showed up at my lunch party today. Please tell me about him. Who is he? Is that really his name? Where did you meet him? He's very interested in my Colombian friend, Tensie, and I wonder why. He's kind of weird — is he really a model? I think he might have a devious motive. Hope to hear from you urgently. Love, your mom."*

But would Hollis reply urgently?

With a sinking heart, she thought not. Perhaps there wouldn't be an answer forthcoming at all, given how she hadn't been getting along with her only child. But it was worth a try. She pressed Send.

Abby kicked off her sandals, heaved aching legs up on to the bed, undid the top button of her white pants, breathed out thankfully and leaned back into a pile of soft pillows.

In less than a minute, she was asleep, resolving never to throw a lunch party again.

The Aftermath

Chapter 14
Ajijic, Mexico, 20th April, 2017

Next morning, Vato woke Abby earlier than usual. His *Cocka Rocka DOO EEE* burst into a bizarre dream she was having about a purple, leather armchair flying through the air and crashing into a bubbling cauldron of *Ajiaco*. She sat up with a start, listened to the rooster for a few moments, detected the first truck of the day rattling along the Carretera. Then she swung out of bed, grateful to the bird. It was still dark, yet her usual urge — to roll over and doze off again — didn't surface. In fact, this particular pre-dawn clarion call by the pet of Carlos and Santiago was well-timed. It meant she had an opportunity to spend some time alone, to unscramble her thoughts about the lunch yesterday, to recharge her batteries before her guests got up.

Stumbling around the dimly-lit kitchen without putting on her glasses, she made coffee. Then she sat on a stool, blinking in the half-light at the plants in the courtyard, formless and grey at this hour, reflecting that, after they'd all had naps, the rest of yesterday didn't turn out badly. With Eve and Clare gone, the synchronicity the Sisters established at their previous get-togethers came back naturally, without any prompting from her. A suggestion of a walk down to the Malecón was received with delight. Rhodo and Hannah chattered like excited monkeys about the natural wonders they encountered en route: bougainvillea cascading over walls; huge, golden cups of flowers on a *Copa de Oro* tree; hedges of scarlet *Ixora* and sky blue Plumbago near the lake; a fragrance emanating from the frangipani tree ornamenting the Plaza — all the same sights and scents that had enchanted Abby herself when she arrived in Ajijic three months ago.

"Holy moly, I've never seen so many lovely flowers," marvelled Rhodo, peering through cracks in fences, wooden doors and towering concrete walls. She kept holding up her cellphone to the cracks, trying to photograph what was hidden on the other side. "I thought you were exaggerating in your email. But it's true, Abby. It must be sheer heaven to have a garden here. And they're so private, aren't they, behind these walls?"

"Yes, aren't they?" Abby said happily. "Just like my courtyard."

Tensie had stayed behind at the house, declining to join them. She'd pleaded fatigue, but Abby surmised that her guest from Colombia intended to sit and daydream about the intimate lunch that Clare had promised. She'd been giddy as a teenager after saying goodbye to him at the front door. But would the slippery guy really call? Abby hoped not. Although she hadn't revealed her suspicions to the others, she'd become convinced that his name wasn't Clare, that he was a fraud, that he'd shown up at her lunch party as part of some kind of peculiar charade. In reality, this charmer had to be Pete Gomez, the wife-killer who'd owned the coffee shop in Ajijic. It all added up, somehow: he knew so much about coffee, seemed so familiar with the place, made strange, elusive answers to questions about where he'd come from. He must have got out of jail and returned to the town intent on finding himself another, well-heeled, lonely, older woman to take advantage of, just as Gillian had predicted. Obviously, sixty-one-year-old Tensie — still emotionally fragile, after being abandoned by her bastard of a husband late in life — had struck him as the perfect target.

But how on earth did Hollis know this master manipulator? And why did she tell him to come to the Sisters' lunch? There were so many pieces of the puzzle that didn't fit. Questions kept going round and round in her head. Perhaps a plausible explanation would come soon. Yet even if her daughter didn't deign to reply to the hurried email she'd dispatched — given the growing distance between them, that seemed likely — an enormous weight would fall from her shoulders if neither she nor Tensie ever heard from this 'Clare' again.

And when yesterday night came, his name hadn't come up. To her immense relief. Perhaps remembering the tight rope atmosphere created by his unexpected appearance at their reunion, all the Sisters, even Tensie, studiously avoided making any reference to their surprise male visitor. They'd simply relaxed together in the courtyard over coffee (the regular filtered kind this time), discussed going to Puerto Vallarta and enjoyed the desserts that no one had been in the mood to try after Clare's hasty departure.

Her cinnamon-scented Mexican bread pudding was declared delicious. But the real winner in the dessert department proved to be Eve's flourless chocolate and almond cake from Capri.

"Fabulous," agreed Rhodo and Abby.

"Yes, she's a very good cook. Works for a top caterer in Rome," said Hannah proudly.

"What a pity the poor girl isn't here to hear us say how much we all love it," mused Tensie.

Yet Abby didn't think it was a pity. On the contrary. Hannah's neurotic sibling hadn't returned after being bundled into the accommodating Juan's taxi and sent back to Tosca's clutching the bag containing her fuck-me sandals. If Eve was now languishing with bleeding toes in her bedroom there, sobbing her heart out, well, too bad. Being free of her — if only for a while — felt wonderful.

**

Abby dumped her empty mug in the sink. It wasn't even six a.m. Her guests hadn't moved in their respective rooms. Well, good. She would take a long, solo walk down to the *Malecón* to clear her head. She crept out of the house softly (fortunately there was no Campeon to step over; he tended to show up on the stoop after nine) and headed south at a steady clip. In the semi-darkness, a soft breeze was blowing off the lake. The air smelled clean and fresh. She'd always been a morning person, loved the promise of new beginnings that prevailed before the rest of the world came to life. During Connecticut's spotty summers, she'd regularly risen before Larry and gone out to putter solo in the garden. This time, after the stress of yesterday, she relished the surprising peace and quiet of pre-dawn in her little Mexican town. Few people seemed to be out yet. She encountered only two: a teenage girl in patterned leggings, heading along Emiliano Zapata clutching a sequined cellphone purse, who stepped off the sidewalk to let Abby pass, smiled sleepily and left a trail of cloying perfume in her wake; and, near the Carretera, a muscular youth, cleaning the windshield of an ancient, rust-red Volkswagen Beetle, who nodded and said, *"Buenos dias, señora,"* as she went by. She responded in kind, thinking how courteous Mexicans were to foreigners like her.

Lake Chapala was tranquil, the colour of ink, save for a few pelicans, white as ghosts, lurking in weeds at the edge. A lone fisherman sat on an upturned boat, patiently untangling a net. A few retirees were already out on the boardwalk, determinedly marching up and down in their big, boat-like running shoes. One, with woolly, white hair and legs like chopsticks, was sitting on the ground, doing vigorous sit-ups. Bony hands clasped behind his head, he gasped with every heave, his face the colour of fuchsias. She'd seen Fuschia Fred (her nickname for him) before, hoped for his sake that he didn't have a heart attack.

As dawn ascended rapidly above the mountains to the east, she went all the way to the end of the *Malecón* and back. Then, climbing circuitously through a maze of narrow sidestreets, she returned to the Carretera. Traffic had started to heat up. Restaurants and stores were opening, staff pushing up floor length shutters with a rattle, lining up colourful wares on the sidewalk. And she could smell coffee.

She went by Ixchel and was taken by surprise. Clare was there. At least, she thought so. He sat at a table near the entrance, where the morning sun had started to stream in, lighting up his glossy, black hair. A distinguished-looking Mexican in a grey business suit occupied a chair beside him. They had a sheaf of documents in front of them on the table, and from the grave looks on their faces, they were involved in a serious discussion about something. Abby reached the traffic light opposite the cafe, debated crossing the street to say 'Hi,' then stopped in her tracks. She didn't really want to know this guy any more, did she? So what was the point of going over and being friendly? A tank-like SUV arrived and parked in front of Ixchel, blocking her view of them. She resumed walking.

A couple of blocks further on, there was another surprise. Gillian. The battered sombrero still on her head, she was outside Aguacate, once again in her scruffy jeans and work boots, unloading milk crates from a black truck which had a decal depicting some kind of plant, in green and white, on the driver's door. She beamed as Abby approached.

"Well, hullo, love. It's Abby isn't it?" she said warmly. "What are you doing up so early?"

"Oh, I'm taking the air, getting my quota of exercise, trying to stop my aging body from seizing up," Abby said, smiling, feeling her knees burn after the climb to the centre of town.

"Good for you. Did your friends arrive?"

"Yes, we had a great day yesterday," said Abby, thinking with disappointment, no, not that great. Stressful. In fact, incredibly stressful.

Then a brilliant idea struck her. "Um… would you mind doing something for me?"

Gillian looked mildly put out. She dumped the milk crate on the sidewalk, straightened up, rubbed her back and grimaced.

"Well, okay. Sure, why not?" she said, glancing over at the health food store's window with a frown. She consulted her man-sized watch. "But it better be quick. It's organic market day today, you know. I have to get back. Egg's there, setting up our booth and I just came over to deliver some bunches of thyme to Conchita."

"This won't take more than a couple of minutes, I promise," Abby said. "Please, please…" She stared anxiously back in the direction she came from. "Can you come over to Ixchel and identify somebody for me? He's in there right now."

"What? You mean a man sitting at a table?"

"Yes."

"And you think I know him?"

"I know you do."

Gillian looked puzzled. Another frown.

"Well okay, I'll come." Her response was hesitant. "But this all sounds very James Bond-ish, love."

"I know, but it's nothing much. Truly. Just something I need to confirm. Please. I'll explain if you'll just walk over there with me."

"Hang on for a tick then."

Gillian picked up the milk crate again and went into Aguacate. She was inside the store for what seemed like an eternity while Abby paced up and down outside, whispering "Hurry up… hurry up." But in fact, after only a couple of minutes, the young Brit, sombrero flopped sideways, emerged again. She clomped over in her Doc Martens to rejoin Abby and the two women headed east on the Carretera towards the coffee shop. As they walked side by side, their pace slower than Abby would have liked, Gillian got an earful about the strangely unsettling man who showed up for lunch yesterday, and about Abby's suspicions that he might be Pete Gomez.

Gillian grunted, stopped on the sidewalk, and shook her head forcefully, making the sombrero wobble.

"No way."

Then she immediately reconsidered.

"Well, it could be, I suppose," she allowed with a dry laugh, as they resumed walking. "I wouldn't put it past him. There's no knowing with Petey baby. He uses all kinds of names. Gets up to all kinds of mischief. And…"

She paused and looked thoughtful.

"… I did hear a rumour that he was back in town."

"You did?"

"Yup, a friend of Egg's said he saw him in *Campamocha* the other night, chatting up a bunch of ladies sitting on the patio."

"Oh boy," said Abby. This was exactly what she wanted to hear. The prospect of Gillian confirming her hunch made her heart start thumping wildly. She couldn't wait to hurry back to the house and warn Tensie that the scheming con man had indeed come back to Ajijic — and she'd be well advised to steer clear of him.

They reached the traffic light opposite Ixchel. Abby endured more waiting for a crossing signal. Then, reaching the other side of the Carretera, they circled quickly around to the front of the parked SUV. Yet it was clearly not her lucky day. The male customers whom she'd spotted only eleven minutes ago, ensconced at a table out front, had vanished. In their place were two elderly American women with cloth sunhats tied under their chins, chatting in quiet tones over frothy cappucinos.

"*Ay, disculpe, señora*, those men just left," the frilly-uniformed barista informed Abby after she rushed up to the counter at the back of the cafe to check. And no, she didn't know who the men were.

"But the older man, he come in here a lot," she added, trying to be helpful. "I think he a lawyer."

A lawyer? Abby's imagination ran wild. Then for sure the man who called himself Clare WAS Pete Gomez. The other man had to be his legal representative, who was dealing with the Mexican immigration authorities on his behalf, cutting a deal so that Pete could stay in the town.

Yes, that was it. She just needed to confirm it! But how? Wanting to scream with frustration, she thanked the barista, rushed outside again, peered up and down the street, didn't see any sign of the pair. She turned to Gillian, who was waiting patiently on the cobblestones, chewing her lip and looking anxious to leave.

"Shit. This is so infuriating," Abby said. "They've gone."

"Oh, too bad," Gillian said.

"But thank you, anyway. Thank you very much for doing this."

"Sure, love. No prob," Gillian was sympathetic now, putting an arm over Abby's shoulder as they headed back to Aguacate. "Sorry you're disappointed. But you should bring your girlfriends over to the organic market today. It's just a short walk from your place. They'll enjoy it. And maybe..." she grinned and added "... Pete Gomez will show up to buy something. Then I can identify him for you."

"Sure, I'll bring them over, if there's time. We're thinking about a side trip to Puerto Vallarta, though."

"Ah, nice. I miss the sea. But you know..." Gillian added as they reached the pick-up and got ready to say goodbye, "...if you really want to find out if that man who came to lunch is Pete, I have a better idea."

A challenging grin with a hit of mischief spread under the hat — the kind of grin that was becoming familiar now.

"Take your friends out to *Campamocha* one night. If Petey

baby IS back in town, he'll be hanging out there for sure, looking for a new conquest."

***

It was a day of surprises. Later, one came for Hannah. After polishing off her second breakfast *bolillo* (she'd developed a fondness for Mexican pineapple jam) she pushed back from the courtyard table, blotted her lips with a napkin, and announced without enthusiasm that she'd better go check on Eve.

"Oh yes, I guess you should," agreed Abby, feeling guilty that she'd hardly thought about Eve since her departure yesterday. It had been such a relief to get rid of her. She started to clear the breakfast dishes away. "Um, I hope she's all right — and in a happier frame of mind this morning."

Hannah let out a little snort.

"Well, knowing Eve, she's bound to still be asleep, or lying around feeling sorry for herself," she said. "And I'll have to sit through another wail and whimper act. But I'm used to it."

She sighed, pushing her hair off her face.

"Poor you," said Rhodo, who'd been greedily sucking an Ataulfo mango like a dog with a bone. She put the stone down on her plate, licked her fingers, wiped the sticky juice off her chin and looked up at Hannah with concern.

"You have my sympathy, Hannah. I don't know how you put up with her."

"She's my sister," replied Hannah, a hint of defensiveness creeping in her voice. "I don't have much choice, do I? And I do love her in spite of everything. I also know that she's never

222

going to change."

Tensie, who'd been quietly sipping coffee, nodded supportively. "You are a kind woman, Hannah. Family is important."

Yet over at Tosca's something had certainly changed. The imperious girl in black leggings opened the front door. She led Hannah into the courtyard. When Hannah explained, with an apologetic smile, that she'd come to check on her sister who was 'probably still in bed', the girl shook her head and nodded in the direction of the dining room.

"Your sister is not sleeping, Mrs. Luxcombe. She's in there, having breakfast," she said, a superior smile escaping through her purple-painted lips. Then she disappeared through a wooden door in the courtyard wall.

To Hannah's astonishment, the girl was right. Eve sat at one of the tables with checked cloths, talking animatedly with two men. Yet she leaped up the moment Hannah entered the room and bounded over, looking wide awake, well-groomed and not at all tear-stained in a white, cotton mini dress and sandals — flat ones this time, Hannah was relieved to note.

"Oh, there you are," Eve said eagerly, grabbing her arm. "I thought you'd all forgotten me. Come and meet Sanjay and Guillermo."

Hannah was pulled over to the table. The men stood up as introductions were made. Sanjay was Indian and plump, with little, round glasses like Gandhi's, a long black beard and the fey disconnected air of someone who talks all the time about enlightenment. Instead of shaking Hannah's hand, he put his palms together, steepling his fingers and bowing like an impresario. "Namaste," he said, his voice high-pitched and girlish. "It is my supreme pleasure to meet Eve's beautiful sister."

The other man was Mexican, stocky and beefy, with a hard, chiselled face. His handshake was firm. Unlike Sanjay, who sported a saffron-coloured kurta, he had on an open-necked, check shirt and sports jacket. There was a briefcase open on the chair beside him. An odd couple, Hannah thought, wondering if they were lovers.

"Sanjay and Guillermo are from Mexico City and they're partners," Eve said adding, "business partners," with a glimmer of amusement as if she'd guessed Hannah's thoughts. "We met yesterday afternoon after Sanjay locked himself out of his room, just like I did."

She giggled. So did Sanjay.

"So he knocked on my door and I told him to try going through the kitchen. We both discovered an old man out there who sits in a shed all day, watching *telenovelas* on an old TV. I think he must be the gardener. He was very nice. Let us both into our rooms. But honestly, that girl…"

She rolled her eyes. So did Sanjay.

"Awful girl," he said, giggling again. "Very awful girl."

"But enough of her," Eve said dismissively, clearly dying to impart some news and to curtail Sanjay's uncontrollable giggles. "We all had dinner at a super Italian place down by the lake last night and Sanjay and Guillermo told me about an old resort with log cabins that they've just bought."

The men nodded in unison, Sanjay trying with difficulty to suppress another giggle.

"It's in a place called Mazamitla, up in the mountains, on the other side of the lake. And they're turning it into a yoga retreat. Sanjay will be in charge of the wellness programs." She shot an affectionate smile at him. "Guillermo will handle the business side and probably stay in Mexico City, but visit now and then." Another smile, this time at the Mexican. "And guess what, Hannah?" her voice rose with excitement. "They need a chef who can do vegetarian meals, especially vegan. And it looks like I'm it."

She chortled with excitement.

"Yes indeed, we are impressed by your sister's credentials," Guillermo said in English, turning to Hannah and carefully enunciating the word 'credentials' as if he'd used it many times before interviewing prospective employees and placed great emphasis on it. "I know Giuseppe di Vitale in Rome. Good man. Imaginative way with food. Eve, with her kind of training, is just what we are looking for."

Eve looked at Hannah, her eyes sparkling.

"Isn't that terrific?"

Hannah, momentarily speechless, wasn't sure what to say. This was all too sudden to take in. Her mind moved quickly, as it always did, considering the practicalities of such an undertaking. Surely Eve would need a permit to work in Mexico? Were they that easy to obtain? And what about her apartment in Rome, still leased as far as she knew? Yet she felt happy that her sibling's mercurial moods had swung over to the positive side of the pendulum. It was a welcome change. So she offered congratulations, but declined to join them for coffee.

"Thanks, but I have to get back. We're going to the market today. Abby is taking us to meet a woman who grows organic herbs."

"Did you say organic?" said Eve. "*Dio mio*, I want to come too. Tell me where it is and I'll be there."

At Tosca's entrance door, she hugged Hannah, then held

her by the shoulders with a beseeching expression on her face.

"Be glad for me, Han," she said. "Please be glad. I want to change my life and this is the opportunity I've been looking for. I'm sorry I've been such a trial to you and Ada. Really I am. And I've thought about it and decided…"

A wry chuckle.

"…I'm done with men."

Chapter 15

Gillian told a lie, Abby thought, inwardly cursing her new British friend. The walk to the organic market was certainly short, but it also turned out to be hot, dusty and unpleasant. From her house on Emiliano Zapata, the Sisters had to traverse a traffic-laden strip of the Carretera, on the outskirts of town. It wasn't easy going. As she, Rhodo and Hannah trudged in single file along patchy pavement punctured with cracks and holes (Tensie once again had declined to join them, hoping Clare would call) she wished they'd summoned the accommodating Juan and gone there in his nice, cool taxi. Nasty, stinging grit kept getting flung in their faces from passing trucks and buses. More dirt somehow managed to penetrate through their clamped shut lips. The taste was foul, kind of metallic, and the stink of diesel fumes suffocating. By the time the trio reached the brick-fronted community centre that housed the market, they were sweaty and tired, throats raw, and Rhodo had a coughing fit, like the one when the frying pan caught fire.

"Help. I cu... cu... cu... can't breathe," she gasped, collapsing on a bench inside the entrance.

She clutched at her throat, her face purple, squeaking out in a panic-stricken voice "I have asthma, you know."

A white woman with a kindly face and a big, cloth apron rushed over from a stall called The Lemonade Lady. She held out a Styrofoam cup. Rhodo grabbed it and downed the contents in a couple of gulps. To everyone's relief, her recovery was quick. After getting her breath back, Rhodo called the freshly squeezed drink 'nectar of the gods' and wanted more. Lots more. So Abby bought them all the giant size and they lingered on the bench, chatting with the Lemonade Lady.

"The dust is terrible at this time of year before the rainy season. Even worse than in Tucson, where I used to live," she lamented. "You're brave to walk along the Carretera. I wouldn't."

Abby said she wasn't aware of the dusty conditions, living in the centre of Ajijic, and apologised to Rhodo, mortified that she didn't know about the asthma either. They watched as more customers arrived, a steady stream through the wrought iron gates into the market, carrying cloth bags. Most were retired expats about the age of the Sisters, but some much older, with wobbly legs and walking sticks like Bruce and Myra MacDonald. From her vantage point on the bench, Abby could see their cars jamming the parking lot outside. She reflected how different this market was from the one where she regularly shopped.

At the traditional market, the Tianguis — held downtown on another day of the week — Mexicans operated virtually all the stalls. Their customers, who tended to arrive on foot, were mostly foreigners too, like at the organic market. Yet at the Tianguis, transactions often took a comic turn, with the Spanish-speaking vendors seeking to improve their English at the same time as the shoppers made strenuous efforts to improve their fledgling Spanish. The result was confusion, with everyone interrupting each other. Meanwhile, at the organic market (which had been started by an American retiree), the language of commerce was solidly — and to her mind, embarrassingly — gringo. The patrons rarely bothered to speak Spanish, even when they were buying from a Mexican — a contrast that made her cringe. She wondered what her plant-explorer dad would have thought. He'd travelled the globe, learning several languages, in the course of plant-collecting for Chicago Botanical Garden and he had drummed into his daughter at an early age that it is cultural arrogance, lacking in respect, not to at least try to learn the language of the country you are living in.

"Expecting everyone to speak in English to us is the reason why Americans are disliked abroad," he'd lamented with an exasperated sigh.

She never forgot that warning. Thus, right after arriving in Ajijic, she'd signed up for Spanish classes with Mike Kravinski, a bilingual American recommended by the MacDonalds. Her dad's admonition had also rung in her ears during her only previous visit to the organic market. She'd stayed away after that, reluctant to be considered just another clannish gringo, unwilling to learn about Mexican culture. Yet this time, she wondered if she'd perhaps been too harsh with her initial assessment. The place suddenly seemed bigger, less dominated by foreigners than before. She downed the last of her lemonade and turned to Rhodo and Hannah, eager to explore.

"Are you feeling okay now, Rhodo?' she asked.

Rhodo, colour back in her cheeks, insisted that she was fine.

"Okay good. Let's look around and go and find Gillian shall we?'

They all said goodbye to the Lemonade Lady, thanking her again. And as they ambled around the stalls in the aimless way of visitors to outdoor markets the world over, Abby noted with pleasure that the variety of wares was certainly broader and more reflective of Mexico than the last time she came. Amid the chicken pot pies, quiche, lasagna and pallid meat loaf slices with gravy aimed at homesick Americans and Canadians, she spotted, to her delight, roasted cacao seeds, granola sweetened with the raw cane sugar, *piloncillo*, *tomatillos* in green and purple to make *salsa verde*, local acacia honey and vegetarian *tamales*. She bought a bagful of tamales, thinking that little parcels wrapped in strips of banana leaf would be a novelty to Rhodo and Hannah who'd probably never tasted them before.

Gillian's stall stood at the far end, impossible to miss. It was decked out with a big banner reading 'Zinnia' in hand-painted, red letters, a name she had chosen — she told anyone who asked — because zinnias were native to Mexico and the word was conveniently the same in Spanish and English. Zinnias also happened to be her favourite flowers. She even liked the despised wild species of zinnia — called *mal de ojos*, evil eyes, by Mexicans, because they popped up everywhere and were difficult to get rid of.

"When locals tell me the *mal de ojos* are a curse, that they will take over and smother everything else on my land, I say '*No pasa nada*'. Who cares? I'll just pull them up if they get too overpowering," she was fond of saying, with a chuckle, to shoppers at her stall.

And while her primary focus was raising and selling herbs

— as seedlings or cut bunches to use in the kitchen — Gillian's passion for zinnias was obvious at the market that day. Bunches of the blooms, in scarlet, brilliant orange, yellow and two-tone shades surrounded the stall, kept fresh in buckets of water. They made her wares among the most colourful — and admired — in the building.

To the Sisters' surprise, Eve was already there. Earlier, saying goodbye to Hannah at Tosca's entrance, she'd sounded keen to see the market, yet Hannah hadn't taken her seriously. Her baby sister was clearly so caught up with her new friends, Sanjay and Guillermo, she'd be bound to forget. Being on time for appointments had never been Eve's strong point anyway. Yet there she was, examining a spindly potted plant with arrow-shaped leaves that a barrel-chested young Mexican with rimless glasses and a strong intelligent face had placed on the table between them. She still looked composed and lovely in the short, white dress and appeared to be listening attentively to what he was saying without attempting to flirt with him. Hannah was flabbergasted. Had Eve truly turned over a new leaf? It didn't seem possible. Time would tell, she thought soberly.

"Oh, hello everybody," Eve said, looking up as Abby, Rhodo and Hannah approached. "I'm hearing all about the marvels of *epazote*."

"The what?" said Hannah.

Abby and Rhodo looked puzzled too.

"Aha ha. Gotcha. Trumped all you gardeners for once, have I?" Eve chuckled. "You tell them, Egg."

The man she called Egg had a gentle smile, a ponytail and the patient, soft-spoken manner of a teacher who has explained a point many times over yet doesn't mind repeating it.

231

"This is a herb we cook with black beans," he explained in fluent English with only a hint of an accent. "A tradition in Oaxaca, where I come from. But hardly anyone outside Mexico has heard of it."

"I certainly haven't," said Hannah, shaking her head.

"And if anyone knows herbs, you do," said Abby loyally, squeezing Hannah's elbow. "All those books…"

Hannah looked embarrassed and blushed.

"But just wait 'til you smell the stuff," Eve said mischievously. "Go on, take a sniff, ladies."

Hannah dutifully bent over, held a leaf close to her nose and inhaled.

"Musty," she concluded, straightening up, looking at Eve then Egg. "Very musty."

Rhodo was less polite.

"Eeew," she said, wrinkling her nose and pretending to gag. "It smells disgusting. Like paint thinner."

"You're right. It does," Abby said, laughing, when her turn came.

"Yes, *epazote* has a strange smell. Very strong," Egg agreed, "but it gives a unique taste to black beans. Much better than cilantro, which you're all familiar with, I'm sure."

The Sisters nodded.

"My mother never prepares black beans without adding a few leaves of *epazote*. And if I eat these beans out somewhere, and they haven't been cooked with this herb, they don't taste right."

"Oh, I want to try this *epazote*," Eve said excitedly, clapping her hands together and bobbing up and down. "Absolutely, I do. Black beans with *epazote*. *Dio mio*, they sound so good together." She looked dreamy. "They'll be something different for me to put on the vegan menu at Mazamitla."

Hannah regarded her sister with disbelief. Was this really happening? Eve intended staying in Mexico, taking a job with this yoga outfit and not flying home to Heathrow with her? She felt piqued. The airline tickets she put on her own credit card cost a fortune. When she'd made the booking, Eve had looked so utterly wretched — and so desperate to get away — that she didn't bother to clarify who would be paying for what.

Would British Airways give her a refund? Probably not. So Eve was getting a bill before she left, Hannah decided.

***

Gillian was having a busy day. While the others got filled in on the peculiar allure of *epazote*, she stood negotiating a special price on an entire milk crate of fresh basil that an elegant, grey-haired American woman in a long, patterned skirt wanted to buy. A deal finally cut, the woman left, arms cradling two big, paper carrier bags containing bunches of the fresh leaves — which Gillian had carefully separated between sheets of newspaper so they didn't get crushed. The herb's unmistakeable fragrance wafted throughout the market as the woman walked, skirts swinging, clearly thrilled with her purchases from the delighted look on her face. Gillian, watching her go, felt thrilled too. She stuffed a wad of peso notes into the fanny pack around her waist and grunted, satisfied, then came over to the other end of the table to join the group.

"That was great. A big sale for once. She's making jars of pesto to give away to friends and wanted a discount, so I gave her a good one," she told them. "And I see that you've already met Egg." She flashed a warm smile at her boyfriend, linked a freckly arm through his, and regarded Abby's companions with curiosity.

"I'm Gillian, proprietor of this here establishment, ha ha," she said, chuckling, "and you are..."

Rhodo and Hannah introduced themselves. Egg watched as his garrulous girlfriend welcomed them to Ajijic. And he had such a look of love on his face, Abby experienced a flicker of envy. Oh, to still be as young as Gillian and have a man look at you like that. It was centuries since it had happened to her. Egg must be an unusual guy, she thought, for the object of his affection wasn't pretty and feminine in the usual sense. Gillian didn't put on pots of make-up or wiggle her ass provocatively in the tight, sexy clothes that Mexican girls habitually wore. Her forceful personality would undoubtedly also be considered a drawback by most men in this macho country. But Egg obviously adored Gillian. Abby felt glad for her, sad for herself. She'd never been considered pretty either, wore glasses from an early age due to an astigmatism in her right eye and could never adapt to contact lenses, yet she'd forged the same kind of magical connection with Larry when they were at university together in Chicago. Shockingly long ago now, she thought, appalled by the swift passage of time. But then they'd let the connection weaken and wither away, until there was nothing left to hold them together any more.

Gillian slipped her arm out of Egg's with a gentle motion and turned around to the back of the stall.

"*Hola, Roberto, ven aqui.* Come out for a moment," she called out.

Another dark-skinned man, younger than Egg, emerged

from behind a long, white sheet concealing a stack of milk crates full of more herbs. He was in the middle of eating something, dusted crumbs off his jeans, swallowed quickly, embarrassed. Then he stood rooted to the spot, as uncomfortable as an uninvited guest at a party, saying nothing, clearly reluctant to come closer.

The family resemblance between the two men was striking, Abby observed. Both had straight, silky, black hair, broad foreheads and alert dark eyes that indicated mestizo, or mixed ancestry. Yet Roberto's features were assembled into a more satisfactory whole than his cousin's and, in a contest over appearances, Roberto would be judged the better-looking of the two. Even so, he seemed as lacking in confidence as a wild animal forced out of his burrow to face the light. She immediately realised why. Unlike Egg, he didn't speak English.

"Everybody, this is Roberto, Egg's cousin," Gillian announced. "He sometimes helps us out at the market. He rides into town in the back of our truck and makes sure my lovely buckets of zinnias don't fall out and spill all over the Carretera. Right, love?"

She smiled in an encouraging way. Roberto smiled back but looked blank.

With unaccustomed boldness, Abby seized the moment.

"It is a pleasure to meet you, Roberto. I love my new home in Mexico," she told him in Spanish. And wow, how thrilling it was, uttering those complete sentences, one after the other. She'd done it at last. Spoken out loud in public, without hesitating, without obsessing about getting every syllable right before daring to open her mouth. The words came out effortlessly, smooth as silk. She felt so absurdly proud of this accomplishment, she wanted to cheer out loud.

But Roberto rewarded her apparent ease with his language by smiling broadly, then gabbling something unintelligible back in Spanish that made her as uncomfortable as he had been, after being summoned by Gillian in English. It was a relief when he disappeared behind the sheet again.

"Thanks for doing that," Gillian murmured in a low voice after he'd gone. "Roberto is a bit shy around people at the market. So few of them speak Spanish."

"Yes, I know. I've noticed," Abby said.

"But look at YOU, love," Gillian was effusive in her praise, throwing her hands wide. "Faultless pronunciation. You're certainly getting the hang of the old lingo, aren't you?"

"Am I?" Abby stammered, colouring. "I don't think so, but I do try. My dad taught me that it's important to try."

"He was right," said Gillian. "And you know, if you want to become properly fluent, Egg is starting another three-month course at the *Centro Cultural* next week."

She smiled hopefully at Abby, then at Egg.

"I think the course might be full already," he says. "But call the CC and ask, if you want to come. They can probably fit you in."

Abby said she would probably call. He pulled out a cellphone and glanced at it.

"And now I must go, *querida*," he said, kissing Gillian's forehead. "I'm meeting with some of the new students today and I didn't realise what the time was."

'Okay, no prob," said Gillian, hugging him. "Roberto and I can pack up the truck. You don't need to be here. We'll pick you up later. Who are the new lot this time? Anyone interesting?"

"Oh, the usual. Several American and Canadian couples, all retired, and a talkative widow who is from Ireland, I think."

"A nice group?"

"Sure, they're always nice — and very eager at the beginning. But then, half way through the course, the drop off starts. One by one, they stop coming…until at the end, I'm just left with two or three people who are truly keen to learn Spanish."

He smiled ruefully and shrugged.

"It always happens. But I'm not complaining. I still get paid, and I realise that it's difficult to learn a new language when you're older. But I do try to get them to overcome their shyness by emphasising conversation in classes. That's what's important, not learning grammar from books."

"He's a good teacher. Very patient even with dopes like me," Gillian told Abby laughing. "But I learned. I'm pretty fluent now, aren't I, love?"

He nodded.

"And you could be too Abby, at the end of the course. You should give Egg a try."

Abby said she would call the *Centro Cultural*, but after the Sisters had left. They were taking the bus to Puerto Vallarta tomorrow.

"Oh, lucky you," Gillian said. "Have a margarita by the sea for me."

Egg picked up a briefcase from behind the stall and got ready to leave — he would be walking over to the *Centro Cultural* — but then he stopped, remembering something.

"Now that I think about it," he said, "there's a single guy who signed up for the course and he's quite different from the retired couples. He's younger and seemed kind of odd to me."

"How come?" Gillian asked.

"Well, he looks Mexican — and does seem to be Mexican — but he's from New York, I think, and speaks virtually no Spanish. And he wouldn't tell me anything about his background. Yet he already knows his way around Ajijic. Has obviously been here often. I didn't have to explain a thing about the town to him."

"Oh," said Abby, and a little bell went ding-ding in her head. A possibility quickly occurred to her. Could this new recruit for Egg's Spanish course be Clare? He did mention something about wanting to take classes. And from Egg's description, it sounded awfully like the same guy.

The realisation made her feel foolish. Utterly foolish. If it was true, she'd been totally off base, indulging in some silly fantasy that Pete Gomez had been the guy who showed up at her lunch party. It clearly wasn't him. In spite of his wildly inappropriate name, Clare was real, likely just some oddball acquaintance of Hollis and Jaz. For unknown reasons, they'd told him to drop by. What a relief that she didn't tell the others about her suspicions. She'd have looked so stupid warning Tensie to run a mile from him, because he was a wife-killer, when in fact he was nothing of the kind.

"What's the name of this new recruit?" she asked.

Egg thought for a moment.

"Angel," he said. "Why? Do you know him?"

"No," said Abby, disappointed.

***

The Sisters loaded up at the organic market. They bought little greenish-yellow limes to make more margaritas, a papaya shaped like a bowling pin, bars of organic chocolate from Oaxaca for Hannah to take home to her grandchildren, an outsize watermelon, a bag of the Ataulfo mangoes Rhodo had fallen in love with, the container of *tamales*, plus bunches of zinnias, basil, cilantro and a packet of dried oregano from Gillian's stall. Abby was glad she brought two bags with her and felt in no mood to negotiate the dust on the Carretera. She asked Gillian if Pete Gomez had shown up at the market. When Gillian shook her head and said, "No, love. Sorry. I haven't seen him," Abby decided to call the accommodating Juan, so they could all ride home in comfort.

Eve opted to stay on at the market. She'd moved on from the *epazote* and was excitedly hearing about the tall plant called amaranth that Abby had seen Gillian take into Aguacate. Its tiny seeds were once considered a staple food by the Aztecs, Gillian was explaining, but they got banned by the Spanish invaders because the indigenous people used them in pagan rituals which involved human sacrifice. But now, thanks to the interest of organic farmers like her, the seeds — known as *huatli*, or the 'smallest giver of life' in the Nahuatl, or Aztec language — were being cultivated again. She had fledging plants for sale in her stall.

"You can make a candy known as *alegria* with the seeds. It's very nutritious and tastes good. Here," Gillian told Eve, holding out a thin bar, in which the cream-coloured specks had been solidified with honey.

"Yum," said Eve. "It looks sort of like quinoa — and it'll make a perfect vegan dessert."

She nodded with satisfaction after a quick nibble, carefully wrapped the rest of the bar in a tissue and put it into her shoulder bag. Then she announced to the Sisters that she intended meeting Sanjay and Guillermo at a restaurant near the *Malecón* later on and wouldn't need a ride.

"And tomorrow we're driving over to the other side of the lake and up to Mazamitla. They're going to show me the place they've bought. Isn't that great?" she added, her eyes shining.

Hannah felt her scepticism about this new development in her sister's life starting to fade, if not completely disappear. Eve seemed so happy for once. Perhaps the venture would work out, although she had her doubts about the one called Guillermo. He struck her as a wheeler-dealer, a tough nut who was adept at taking advantage of gullible innocents like his partner, that head-in-the-clouds Sanjay. Would Eve fall into the same trap? Then there was the matter of the apartment in Rome. Were she and Ada going to be stuck with handling Eve's undoubtedly irate landlord — and getting rid of her belongings there? For sure, she thought, annoyed. Eve wouldn't fly all the way back from Mexico just to take care of what she'd dismiss as 'a little detail' like that. She would leave it to Hannah simply because she knew that she could.

Still, going off to Italy could have a bright side, Hannah thought. It would provide the means for another little escape from Charles and his wretched iPad. The current break was proving such a tonic. She hadn't been force fed one item of depressing news since arriving in Mexico. Abby never shared what she read on her laptop, there didn't seem to be a radio in the house, and the big flat screen TV hadn't been switched on once during her entire visit. Good. Behaving like an ostrich in this Mexican town, turning her back on what was going on in the world, had made Hannah blissfully happy. And in clearing out Eve's apartment she could do the same — perhaps in the company of Ada next time.

After the Sisters disappeared in Juan's taxi, Eve, her face creased with worry, sidled up to Gillian and whispered in her ear that she'd like to get advice about something 'very personal and private'. Gillian's response was to raise her eyebrows with surprise. Then noting how tense Eve had suddenly become — twisting and re-twisting a Kleenex in her hands, clearly on the verge of tears — she called out in Spanish to Roberto to come to the front and take over manning the stall for a while. He appeared shyly from behind the white sheet. She led Eve over to a quiet bench at the back of the market, told her gently to sit, and sank down herself.

"Well, what is it, love? What's bothering you?" she asked in a kindly tone, putting an arm around Eve's shoulders.

Eve hesitated, fiddling with the tissue.

"This is very awkward," she said, looking down into her lap, not wanting to meet Gillian's gaze. "But I think I've caught something. I have — you know — a discharge." She hesitated again. "It's… um… green and smelly. And I'm having pain when I wee."

"Oh, too bad," says Gillian. "Where do you think you picked it up? Here in Mexico?"

"No!" said Eve vehemently. "I have admittedly slept with a lot of men…" she blushed, "…but I haven't been with anybody since splitting up with my boyfriend in Italy. My sister wouldn't believe me if I told her…" a dispirited sigh, "…but I honestly haven't. And I think Fabio must have given it to me."

"Who's he? Boyfriend?"

"Yes."

Eve wished a string of Italian curses on Fabio, presuming

Silvana had infected him, and then he'd passed it on. She hoped they were both suffering horribly as a consequence.

"Well, not to worry, love," said Gillian nonchalantly. "It's probably treatable and there are clinics here for that. I know of a place on the Carretera. I'll take you there tomorrow, if you like."

"Would you? Thank you so much." Eve's face brightened. "But you won't breathe a word of this to Hannah, will you? Please don't tell her or Abby or the others. Hannah will start lecturing me and…"

"Relax, love," Gillian butted in. "This is a secret between us. No one else needs to know. And by the way, I know what you're going through."

She flashed a cynical smile.

"My bloody ex back in Blighty," she snorted. "The fucker. He gave me the clap too. Twice."

***

Tensie was in an upbeat mood when the Sisters returned to Emiliano Zapata. She occupied an *equipal* at the table in the courtyard, where she was having a coffee and painting her nails with bright red varnish, clearly content. She greeted them with an expansive smile, said there was more fresh coffee in the kitchen, and quickly revealed the reason for her cheerful demeanour.

"Clare called while you were out," she said triumphantly, with an 'I told you so' glance in Abby's direction, as if wanting to convey the message that her host's scepticism about this new admirer of hers was way off base. "He is taking me out to lunch tomorrow."

"Oh, nice," Abby replied, deciding to stay neutral. "Where are you going?"

Tensie said she didn't know but it was a restaurant somewhere near the Carretera.

"Yes. There are lots of choices in this town. We're lucky."

Abby still felt unsettled about Clare, still thought he was playing some kind of strange game, still wondered if he might actually be Pete Gomez. But she'd resolved not to worry about Tensie any more. After all, her friend from Colombia wasn't a teenager but a mature adult who'd led a sophisticated life. She could very ably take care of herself. And perhaps they'd know more about who he was and what his intentions were when she got back from this lunch.

Yet those revelations would have to wait, she realised, because they were leaving early in the morning.

"You're aware, I guess, that we're all going off on the bus to Puerto Vallarta tomorrow?" she told Tensie. "So if you stay behind to meet Clare, you'll miss seeing those fabulous botanical gardens."

"*Si, Si*, I know, I'm sorry. But I'd prefer not to come. I hope it's not inconveniencing you too much. Um…" Tensie waved a manicured hand to dry in the air, looked distracted, then sheepishly around at all the Sisters. "But I…um, have been to a lot of gardens like that and I…"

"*No pasa nada*, Tensie. Not a problem," said Abby, cutting her off with a smile. "You don't have to make excuses. You go and have fun with Clare."

Tensie, relieved, bent over her nails again. Her face had turned as prettily pink, Abby noted, as a new flower that had just opened on a pincushion cactus in the courtyard. Oh my. It looked like her Colombian Sister was falling in love.

***

While the others napped during the afternoon, Abby took the opportunity to check her laptop. Four emails. Two were from other Sisters — Lola and Jing-Jing — asking how the Titan Reunion went. She wasn't sure how to respond, decided to reply later. The other messages were the usual junk. There was no word from Hollis. Disappointing. But she knew it was a long shot, given the current state of their relationship.

Hannah and Rhodo loved the *tamales*, as Abby hoped. She heated them up for supper in a steamer she found on the bottom shelf of Myra MacDonald's well equipped store cupboard. She suggested going for a drink at *La Campamocha* afterwards, thinking that Gillian had a good point. A visit to the bar might finally set her mind at rest about Clare. If he was in fact Pete Gomez, their server could probably identify him for her, because Pete hung out there. Yet there were yawns all round at the mention of *La Campamocha*. No one was interested in the margaritas made with fresh limes, recommended by Gillian. No one wanted to stay up late. No one was the slightest bit enthusiastic about going anywhere, in fact. Tensie shook her head emphatically. Both Hannah and Rhodo were even mildly shocked by the suggestion.

"You want to take us out to a BAR?" Hannah said, with a burst of laughter. "Oh my, Abby, I'm much too old for bars. Our son Toby dragged us out to some trendy place in London last year, to celebrate his birthday. The music was so loud, Charles stuffed Kleenex in his ears. We had a miserable time."

"Bars are full of leering jerks with wandering hands," said Rhodo, shuddering. "At least, that's been my experience.

Haven't been to a bar for years. And don't we have to get up early, to take the bus?"

"We do indeed," Abby said.

She dropped the idea of *La Campamocha*. Before they all headed off to bed, Tensie asked Abby if she could recommend a beauty parlour on the Carretera. She wanted to get her hair done in advance of meeting Clare tomorrow.

Abby feared for her friend. She was making such a big deal about this lunch. Would it live up to her expectations?

In her room, she debated emailing Hollis, asking again about Clare. Yet fatigue overwhelmed her.

She slipped under the coverlet, and drifted off, hoping she didn't dream about the damn guy.

Chapter 16
Boca de Tomatlán, Mexico, 21st April, 2017

Rhodo stood on a balcony overlooking the Pacific. She was biting into an Ataulfo mango shaped like a teardrop. The sweet juice kept dripping off her chin, in the manner of tears, making a mess of the Rhodos Rock T shirt she wore to bed last night. Yet Rhodo didn't care. She couldn't have been happier. This is pure heaven, she told herself. A mango should be always be eaten like this, out of doors, in the tropics, on a warm morning, with exotic flowers blooming, birds singing and the blue, bottomless ocean right there, in front of you.

"Never again will I buy a mango in a Canadian supermarket and eat it indoors wearing a wool sweater, with freezing rain falling outside my window," she declared out loud, sucking the last scrap of golden goodness from the stone, before turning back to the hotel room, to put on her swimsuit.

"What?" called out Hannah, from inside the room.

"Oh nothing," said Rhodo, laughing. "I'm just discovering how much I love Mexico."

She ripped off the sticky T shirt and dropped it on the tiled floor. "I'm going for a swim. You coming?"

Hannah, who was still in bed, declined, not being much of a swimmer. So Rhodo bounded down three flights of stairs and dived into the hotel pool. She'd in fact, preferred to have gone swimming in the ocean — she'd always loved the ocean since living in Newfoundland when there were only a few days in the year when the temperature rose high enough for her and Jeffy to splash about, shivering, at a pebbly beach near Gramma Mercer's house. But the rocks were sharp on this stretch of the Mexican coast. Perpetual worrier Rhodo was scared of gashing her toe. Or worse, encountering sharks. She found only one other person in the pool, a broad-shouldered man in a white bathing cap, doing laps. Too lazy to copy him, she rolled on her back and luxuriated in the lukewarm water, so different from the shock of the cold, grey Atlantic back in her childhood.

Rhodo, Hannah and Abby spent the night in this small hotel, a taxi ride from the hubbub of high-rises lining the beach in Puerto Vallarta proper. When they rode the *Primera Plus* bus down to the coast yesterday, Rhodo brought two Ataulfo mangoes from the organic market with her, stashed in her backpack. She wished she could take the rest back to Canada, because these mangoes tasted so much better than the ones she bought at home. Was it because they were riper? She wasn't sure, they looked identical in both countries, but perhaps the flavour was due to the location. For everything seemed to taste better in Mexico. Perhaps a warm climate brought out flavors of food in a way that northern countries couldn't. She recalled the night when she and Monica had shared cold pizza while the freezing rain kept going smack-smack-smack against her window. How terrible it had tasted. And how she'd pooh-poohed what her friend had said back then. Yet she was beginning to fall under the spell of Mexico herself now. So many aspects of the place she found captivating. The friendly people, the colours, the tropical vegetation, the warm, happy-go-lucky atmosphere, this glorious ocean. How Monica would laugh when she heard that. Rhodo thought of Azalea, had certainly missed her, but wished she didn't have to go back to Toronto the day after tomorrow.

In the room they were sharing, Hannah was thinking much the same thing. Propped up in bed, she had a view of the sea through the glass panel on the front of the balcony. And it looked so blue — unbelievably blue, dotted with whitecaps like the little frills on the uniforms of waitresses at her favourite teashop in Dorset. The English Channel was never that colour even on the best of days in summer, she thought. And the sky was always a grey monotone or overhung with scowling clouds because it never stopped raining. She pictured Charles hunched over his iPad, his face grim, digesting a daily diet of all the horrors happening around the world. She'd missed him, but not his constant companion. She wished she didn't have to go home the day after tomorrow either.

Getting dressed in the room adjoining theirs, Abby stared out at the ocean too, admiring the colour, the sky above and the great wide expanse of the Pacific, so different from being inland, surrounded by mountains. This side-trip was a great idea, she decided, a fitting end to the fourth Titan Reunion. Rhodo and Hannah had both got a kick out of riding in the swanky first-class, airconditioned bus with reclining seats. They'd peered out of the window at rolling agave and pineapple fields and trees heavy with mangoes and avocados, and at little fruit and vegetable stands set up by the side of the road under red, green and yellow tarpaulins. They'd kept wishing the driver would stop the bus. Then at the Botanical Gardens, a few miles away from the hotel, they'd loved everything. Rhodo went into raptures about the Vireyas, hauling a notebook out of her backpack and scribbling furiously. Hannah marvelled at the magnolias. They'd all chuckled when a young Mexican guide told them, tongue in cheek, about the 'gringo tree' *Busera simaruba*, so named because its trunk starts out green then turns as red as a sunburnt gringo. Then last night, they'd eaten at a simple café on a nearby beach, where a bare-chested server in long, electric blue shorts stomped gamely through ankle-deep, dry sand to show off the freshly-caught red snapper that the chef intended to barbecue for their supper. And they'd drunk lots of local beer, with Abby wishing she could order it the way Mexicans did — and getting frustrated because she couldn't remember the phrase Gillian had told her — then finally settling for the gringo word '*cerveza*'. They'd left the beach arm in arm, full of food and drink. So mellow and relaxed, she'd slept like a log. Yet Abby missed her little town on the edge of Lake Chapala. It was quieter, not as noisy and overcrowded as Puerto Vallarta. The weather didn't get as humid up there in the mountains either. Unlike her two guests, she was looking forward to taking the bus home that afternoon.

***

Clare knocked on the door of the house behind the yellow wall at precisely noon, three and half hours after the three Sisters had left for Guadalajara bus station in the accommodating Juan's taxi. Tensie opened it, hoping to appear casual and relaxed, but inside she felt so jittery with expectation, it showed — and he guessed her true feelings at once. The eagerness evident in her face worried him a little. He kissed her cheek in an affectionate way, and said that she looked just as beautiful as two days ago — she'd put on the violet dress again — making her blush with pride. How flattering he was, how charming, how attentive. She patted her newly-coiffed hair styled that morning at a salon on the Carretera, not quite believing her luck. For Clare made her feel young again and carefree, almost light-headed, still a candidate for the push and pull of love.

He took her arm, said smiling, "All right, shall we go?" and they headed on foot down Emiliano Zapata to Alex's Pasta Bar, a chic Italian place with minimalist black and white décor and doors opening on to a side street. After the server had shown them to a table at the front, Clare asked if she'd like wine. Or should we both have margaritas? he added, his eyes dancing and boring deeply into hers. She blushed and said, if it was all right with him, she'd prefer wine, because she'd drunk enough margaritas at Abby's in the past two days to last her a lifetime. He laughed at that, said, "Okay, wine it is." He ordered a bottle of Pinot Grigio. They sat in silence watching as the server went through the ritual of opening the bottle at the table and pouring an inch or so into Clare's glass.

Clare picked up the glass, took a sip, gave an affirmative nod to the young Mexican and said, "Mmm. Pretty good. Better than the bottle I brought to the party the other day."

"Oh, it wasn't that bad," Tensie said, with a girlish laugh.

The server smiled, poured them both wine, speculating on the status of this couple. Lovers? Mother and son? Just friends? They certainly weren't husband and wife.

Clare and Tensie clinked glasses, ordered food and chatted about Ajiic, then Abby's lunch party. She told him in detail about the extraordinary Titan Arum at Brooklyn Botanical Garden that had brought the Sisters together and how they now stayed in touch, discussing plants by email, then meeting up when they could.

He listened intently, head cocked on one side, and commented that it sounded like a great kind of friendship.

"How do you mean?"

"Close but not too close," he said. "As you only meet every three or four years, you aren't likely to get bored with each other."

"True," she said reflectively, pondering for a few moments his assessment of the bond the Sisters had acquired. "But you know, I don't think we would ever get bored. When you all love plants, there are always so many new exciting things to talk about."

When she'd finished, his expression abruptly changed. He became tense, his body taut as a kite string. He leaned forward on the table and regarded her uneasily, brow furrowed, as if he was gearing up to say something difficult and needed to have a glass of wine inside him — and to make conversation about ordinary matters for a few minutes — before he felt brave enough to go ahead.

"Listen, Tensie, he said slowly, clenching and unclenching his fingers underneath the table "you're a lovely woman. You truly are." He almost added 'even at your age' but decided that wouldn't be wise.

"Any man should be grateful to have you. You must have many admirers. But I hope I haven't given you the wrong idea. If I have, I apologise."

He sighed and stared out into the street.

"I've gone about this in the wrong way, I think. "He shook his head, annoyed with himself. "I'm such an idiot."

He turned back, brought out a hand from under the table and reached across the white tablecloth for hers.

Tensie was stunned. She blushed, lowered her eyes to the plate of pasta primavera that had just been placed in front of her. But her appetite has vanished. What was he saying? That he wasn't really attracted to her after all? A whole gamut of mixed emotions — hurt, confusion, bewilderment and acute embarrassment — flooded into her head all at once. She felt tears coming on, wondering what he was going to say next. She snatched her hand away.

He looked hurt, but carried on, leaving his own hand spread out, palm down, on the tablecloth.

"The fact is, though..." his expression turned almost pleading, like a puppy's, "...I'm not looking for romance... with you, with anyone. And I'm sorry about that. Truly sorry if I gave you the wrong impression."

He paused and took a sip of wine.

"But I would, if possible, like your help with something."

The dazzling smile that he'd used to such good effect at the lunch party appeared again. He raised his eyebrows, waiting for her to reply.

Tensie looked down, floundering, uncertain how to proceed. She picked up the fork beside her plate of pasta and turned it over, needing something to do with her hands. Her heart started beating wildly. She felt a rising sense of indignation and anger. How dare he do this? How dare this man, this charming seducer who was so evasive about revealing anything about himself, make such a monstrous fool of her? And why? Whatever for? What was his game? She almost picked up the fork and threw it at him.

"You want my help?" Her voice was icy as she placed the fork back on the table and straightened it so that it was precisely positioned beside her plate. She was still in no mood to eat.

"Yes, I do," he persisted. His smile looked nervous now. "Why?"

"Because you live in Colombia and because of... um... your family."

"My family? *No entiendo*. I don't understand."

"You will. But first, I need to tell you a story. If you'll indulge me, I'll do it right now. Here in this restaurant."

She looked out into the street. Two American women were walking by on the sidewalk right outside the restaurant, their conversation surprisingly audible.

"Doug has Alzheimers," she heard one say. The other one, shocked, said "Oh no, Carol, how awful," and put her arm over the first woman's shoulders.

Then the pair vanished, with grave faces, in the direction of the mountain. Tensie wanted to grab her purse, get up from the table and run after the women, across the Carretera, as fast as she could, all the way up to the black door in the yellow wall and slam it shut behind her. Anything to get away. But then she remembered. Abby and the others had gone off to Puerto Vallarta. How desolate and wretched she would feel, going back to that empty house, sitting in the courtyard alone, pondering, over and over again, why he had done this to her.

She regarded Clare coolly.

"Go ahead then," she said, shrugging, picking up her glass, even though she didn't want to eat or drink a thing. "I'm listening. I'm all ears."

So Clare did tell his story. And after he'd finished, Tensie did cry. Buckets.

***

Abby, Rhodo and Hannah returned late from Puerto Vallarta.

Their bus was delayed by a landslide outside Colima, they explained to Tensie, who'd already gone to bed when they arrived, exhausted, long after dark.

She got up in her nightdress to sit with them in the courtyard and hear about the trip. Yet as Hannah and Rhodo raved about the Vallarta Botanical Garden, saying that it was the best garden they'd ever visited and what a shame she'd missed it, Tensie was subdued, numb, barely listening to their tumble of words, her mind a million miles away.

Abby came out into the courtyard from the kitchen carrying a tray of mugs.

"I've made hot chocolate with Mexican cinnamon for us all," she said. "I figured we could use it after that long ride."

Hannah and Rhodo were enthusiastic, particularly Hannah.

"I love the way they use cinnamon here. I bought some at the market to put it in our cocoa at home, but Charles will probably pull a face. So I'll wind up keeping it for my daughter-in-law, along with the chocolate bars I got for the grandchildren," Hannah said with a smile, thinking that she was looking forward to seeing Edward's and Jackie's two boys.

Tensie perked up, deciding she wanted hot chocolate too. It would help her sleep, she thought. She hadn't yet. As she came close to the tray to pick up a mug, Abby was struck by how forlorn and careworn she looked, compared to yesterday morning. Her eyes were kind of red around the rims and slightly puffy as if she'd been crying earlier, but had made an effort to conceal the fact from the other Sisters by rubbing them hard with a washcloth. Hannah noticed Tensie's eyes too — she was familiar with that drained look on Eve, after her long sessions of sobbing — but thought it prudent to refrain from comment.

Yet Abby was curious. Someone, or something, had clearly upset Tensie.

"Well, how was your lunch with Clare?" she asked jauntily. "Did you have a good time? Where did you go?"

"Um, yes. He took me to an Italian place down towards the lake. It was good. I had the... um... the pasta primavera," said Tensie dully, although she couldn't remember eating even a mouthful of what was on her plate.

"I know the place," Abby says, nodding. "And?"

"And what?" Tensie looked irritated.

"I mean how was Clare? Are you seeing him again?"

Tensie cut her off coldly. "Yes of course I am going to see him. He's coming to Colombia. He ..."

She faltered, failed to finish the sentence. Her look at Abby was hard, almost a glare.

"Oh, I see," Abby said.

Yet she didn't see. Not at all. This hardly sounded like a budding romance. There was clearly something else going on. But she didn't want to think about Clare, or Tensie's troubled face, any more. It was all too weird. She dropped the subject and one by one the Sisters retired for the night. Abby was the last to go to her room, staying behind in the kitchen to wash the mugs.

After brushing her teeth, she checked her email. Surprise. There was a message from Hollis.

'Hi Mom, I'm in Paris with Jaz. She's here on business, checking out the collections. I'll be in touch when we get back. Don't worry about Clare. He's one of Jaz's regulars at Bloomie's fashion shows. I hardly know him, but I don't think he's dangerous. Hugs, H.'

Chapter 17
Ajijic, Mexico, 23ʳᵈ April, 2017

Leave-taking gets complicated when house guests are all departing on the same day, but at different times. Yet the accommodating Juan made sure that everything went off without a hitch when Abby bade farewell to her three Sisters of the Soil. Before Vato started crowing, before even a fingertip of orange sun rose over the mountains, Rhodo was the first of the trio whom he picked up for the ride out to Guadalajara airport. Her flight to Houston left at six a.m. From there she would fly on to Toronto.

At the front door, she hugged everyone in turn and told Abby that she wanted to come back. And soon.

"This trip has completely changed my mind about Mexico. I love it here," she said. "My dream is to retire in Ajijic like you, Abby."

She gave a mock shiver and laughed.

"And in the meantime, Sisters, wish me luck. I just checked my cellphone. It's zero degrees in Toronto. I'll probably run into freezing rain or snow when I get back. I just hope our plane can land."

"*¿Que?* You mean it's still snowing up there? But it's nearly May, Rhodo," said Tensie, aghast, feeling a shiver herself at the mention of snow, which she'd always hated while living in New York.

"Yup," Rhodo said, pulling a face. "But that's Canada for you. Our winters seem to go on forever now. They say it's due to global warming."

"Good luck then," Hannah said, thinking that going home to mild English drizzle didn't sound so bad. "And with your new book. Let me know when it's being published in the U.K. I'll plug it in my column."

"Ah yes, your new book on rhodos," said Abby, wishing she still had a gardening column, so she could give Rhodo a boost too. "I hope it's a huge success. And next, you must write a sequel, about the Vireyas."

"Yes, I've already thought about it and who knows? Maybe I can. I'll be in touch."

With a final grin, Rhodo hoisted her travel bag on to her back, straightened her ever-present jeans shirt, stepped considerately over Campeon (who this morning, for reasons unknown, had installed himself on the stoop far earlier than usual) and climbed into Juan's Toyota. The white SUV faded like a ghost into the pre-dawn darkness, with Rhodo ensconced in the front passenger seat beside Juan, waving an arm wildly out of the window.

A couple of hours later, after breakfast, with Juan barely back in Ajijic — and finding it difficult to secure a parking spot on Emiliano Zapata — it was Tensie's turn. Abbie had been glad to note that whatever upset Tensie yesterday, she seemed to have got over it. She was in a positive mood, although her bubbly air of excitement, as if she were walking on a cloud, had vanished like a wisp of wind off the lake. In the courtyard, the three remaining Sisters chatted companionably over their last fresh *bolillos* from Herminio's, Hannah spreading hers liberally once more with pineapple jam

— while Tensie said how proud she was to introduce them to *Ajiaco.*

"Our cuisine has many interesting dishes," she added. "And they are not well-known in the rest of the world. I think we should hold our next reunion in Colombia so I can introduce them to you. And I'd love to show you the farm. We grow so many beautiful flowers."

"Send us an invitation. We'll be there," said Hannah eagerly.

"You bet we will," said Abby.

"We will arrange it, then, *mis hermanas preciosas,* my precious sisters," said Tensie. "In three years' time."

She kissed them effusively, French-style, on both cheeks. Then Juan, waiting patiently on the sidewalk outside, booted Campeon out of the way, took her bag and bowing a little, escorted her to his automobile as if she were a celebrity and he her personal chauffeur. With a flourish, he opened the door to the back seat.

Tensie slid in decorously, keeping her slim legs together. She folded them under the same grey pencil skirt that she wore to travel to Mexico. He shut the door behind her. She looked back at the two women standing on the stoop with a cheerful wave, but Abby sensed that some sadness had taken up residence in Tensie now — and that it had nothing to do with being abandoned by Juan Diego. Wondering what the sadness was, she presumed her lunch with Clare didn't go as well as expected. Impulsively, she blew Tensie a kiss. Tensie blew one back. Then her Sister from Colombia was off with Juan to Guadalajara, bumping over the cobblestones, the sun high in the sky and beating down on the roof of the fortunately airconditioned Toyota.

After the car turned a corner and disappeared towards the Carretera, Abby realised that no one had mentioned Clare all morning. Hallelujah to that, she thought.

Tensie, sitting back in Juan's taxi, bowling along the dusty highway towards Guadalajara felt relieved too. Yet biting back tears, she couldn't stop agonising over what he told her yesterday.

***

Hannah's departure wasn't until late in the afternoon. She had a booking on a shuttle from Guadalajara to Mexico City. Then, squeezed into an economy-class seat, she'd face a long, tiring, overnight flight to Heathrow. Alone. Eve was adamant about staying on in Mexico, but had promised to drop by the house to say goodbye.

Abby and Hannah speculated about this development in Eve's life as they sat in the courtyard over farewell glasses of limeade.

"So she's serious, then," said Abby dubiously. "But what do you think, Hannah? Will it work out? Are those two guys who're starting up this yoga retreat on the level?"

Hannah shrugged.

"Who knows? Your guess is as good as mine. But Eve is very keen on the idea and does seem to be acting responsibly for a change. I'm amazed. She's paid you back, hasn't she, for that deposit you made for her at Tosca's? She checked out of her room this morning and settled up with them. When the girl asked for more to cover the loss of that torn sheet, she didn't quibble about it either. That surprised me."

"I was frankly surprised too, when she made an E-

Transfer to my bank yesterday. I got an email about it."

"And she's paid me back for her airfare. That's not like the Eve I know." Hannah gave a gentle snort at remembrance of things past and sipped her limeade. "Not at all. But she seems to be happy, doesn't she? So I'm willing to give her the benefit of the doubt about this... um... this wellness retreat, or whatever they're proposing to call it. For now, at least."

Hannah sighed and emptied her glass.

"It's her life after all. She's a big girl. I'll see how it goes and cross my fingers that she doesn't get into too much trouble. Or cause Ada and me a lot of grief, because you know..." she thought with a shudder, of the upcoming flight to London, how she'd be confined to her seat, dodgy knee getting stiff as a board from being forced to stay immobile for so many hours. "I'll be an awfully long way from Mexico. I can't come rushing back to pick up the pieces when everything falls apart."

"Yes, I know. But rest assured that I'm here, close by and more than willing to help if you need me to check up on her and..."

Their discourse was interrupted by a knock on the front door. Abby went to answer it. Eve, in her white, ass-defining shorts, stood on the stoop.

"*Hola*, Abby. Is Hannah still here? Can I come in for a minute?" she asked, looking agitatedly down through the hallway. "Something's happened and I'm in a bit of a hurry."

"Sure," said Abby, inwardly thinking, 'Oh no, not another drama'.

She consulted her watch as they headed out to the courtyard.

"But I hope you realise that Hannah is in a hurry too," she

260

said curtly, annoyed by Eve's tardiness. "She's leaving for the airport in um… precisely eight minutes."

"Yes, I know. I just came to say goodbye," Eve replied. "But I can't stay long because Roberto is waiting in the car."

"Who's Roberto?" asked Hannah, overhearing the name as they reached the courtyard.

"Roberto. You know, Egg's cousin. The shy one at the market." Eve chuckled. "He doesn't speak any English and I know about three words of Spanish, but we're managing to communicate somehow. And…"

She took a breath.

"…he's taken some time off from his job today to drive me up to Mazamitla to see the property again that Guillermo and Sanjay have bought. Guillermo says that I can live in one of the log cabins while they renovate the place, although they're quite primitive, and haven't been used for a couple of years. So we're going to check them out."

"And you're going up there with this Roberto?" Hannah said warily, a knowing look spreading across her face.

"Mmm, yes. He's a sweetheart. Very helpful. He has an old Volkswagen Beetle and it's fun riding around in it, although I'd forgotten how noisy the engine is. And those seats! *Dio mio…*"

Eve stopped, noticing Hannah's look.

"Ah, don't worry, big sister of mine," she said. "We're just friends. Your little sister is through with all that. Really I am."

Eve pictured the sober-faced, young doctor wearing a stethoscope and a white coat at the clinic she'd visited with Gillian. How he'd said her problem could be one of four things, but she should refrain from any kind of sexual activity until results of tests came back.

"And Roberto is only twenty-eight…" she added with a quick laugh, hoping her anxiety about the tests didn't show, realising that she wasn't the slightest bit interested in having sex with anyone. For a long time. "I'm much too old for him anyway."

"Good to hear that you think that," Hannah said disbelievingly.

Eve babbled on, explaining that, after going over to the other side of the lake, she and Roberto intended driving back this side to visit Gillian's farm, north of Jocotopec.

"I love Gillian. She's so friendly and funny," she said, feeling incredibly grateful to her fellow Englishwoman for this secret that they now shared. "Thank you for introducing me to her. She's going to supply my organic herbs once I get the kitchen started. She'll be a perfect contact. But the renovations won't be over for two or three months, so in the meantime…"

She paused and broke into a huge smile.

"…I badly want to learn Spanish and it shouldn't be difficult as I already speak Italian. So I've signed on for Egg's course at the *Centro Cultural*."

Oh my, Hannah thought, astonished. She seemed to have everything worked out. This was very good news. She couldn't wait to tell Ada, although Eve had behaved this way before. Then abruptly, all hell had broken loose. Time would tell. She wondered if Ada had got rid of the worm infestation in her sheep. Thought warmly of her twin, realising that she was looking forward to talking to her again. Although she'd only been away barely a week, it seemed like so much longer than that. Perhaps she'd even go up to Herefordshire after she got home.

Eve's chatter was interrupted by another knock at the

door. It was Juan, punctual as ever and ready to go, even though he would be embarking on his third drive of the day to Guadalajara and back.

With hugs and kisses, and promises to email, Hannah picked up her bag and left. Eve departed too, firm round buttocks bouncing like beach balls in the skimpy shorts as she headed down to the pensive-looking Roberto. He was waiting at the wheel of an ancient, rust-red Beetle with a dented hood, parked further down the street. Abby watched her go from the stoop, realising that she'd seen this car before on Emiliano Zapata and that Roberto must be a neighbour. In fact, he was the guy who had said, "*Buenos dias*," to her early one morning a few days ago.

Lingering as Hannah got into Juan's Toyota, something else hit her with an almost physical force. It was over. The fourth Titan Reunion. Oh boy. So eagerly awaited, so tense at times, so full of surprises. But done with now. Finished. *Terminado*. And all things considered, she'd call it a moderate success. Not perfect, by any means — Eve and Clare had certainly fouled things up — but okay. The Sisters — at least Rhodo and Hannah — saw a lot of plants, they all learned new things, they laughed a lot, they'd shared confidences and some very good food. The bond they'd established back in the Brooklyn Botanical Garden, watching the Titan Arum come into bloom, remained strong, in spite of a few bumps here and there. Strong enough for another reunion in Colombia, she thought with excitement, in 2020. She was sure up for it — and perhaps Lola, Mieke, Natalie and Jing-Jing could come to that one too.

Yet in the meantime her friends had all gone. The house was empty. Hushed. And the inevitable flip side of anticipation — a feeling of anticlimax — came over Abby. Sitting in the courtyard, finishing off the limeade, tidying up the empty glasses, reflecting on what she'd liked — and didn't like — about the past week, she was overcome by a fit of depression. And suddenly lonely.

Then she remembered. Egg. Yes, the Spanish course. Starting next week. Eve had reminded her. With the party over, she'd better hurry. Go put her name on the list at once. It would be another adventure, getting to know some new people and perhaps they'd be friendlier than the couple from California she'd met at Mike's. And from what she'd heard, Egg would help her get a better grasp of the language, so she could truly participate in the life of this vibrant, colourful country that she'd chosen to live in. *Peligro en demora.* There is danger in delay. So true. Now was the time to sign up.

She headed for the phone in the kitchen. Before she could pick it up, it started ringing.

***

The caller was Clare. He sounded edgy. No longer the suave, smooth-talking charmer who showed up at her lunch party, he spoke cautiously, as if expecting a hostile reception.

"Hello Abby. I hope you don't mind my calling like this," he said. "I wanted to know if Tensie got away safely."

"Well yes. I presume she did," she said stiffly, annoyed. With Tensie gone, she'd hoped to never see or hear from Clare again. The guy was too mysterious, too unsettling, too wrapped up in something she couldn't figure out. If Tensie intended seeing him, that was her business, but she wanted to close the door on him.

"But I didn't go to the airport to see her off, as my other guests were leaving today too as well. In fact, it's been a busy day all round and if you don't mind…"

"I understand, yes, I'm sorry to call you like this. Also very sorry that I gatecrashed your party. I know you weren't happy to have me there, but there was a reason why I came and I wonder…" his tone became more tentative and nervous, "…I wonder if I could meet up with you and explain?"

Abby thought for a few moments.

"When?" she asked abruptly.

"Soon. Could I take you out for a drink tonight?"

"No." Her voice was snappish. "I'm tired Clare. I'm going to bed early."

She felt a yawn coming on.

"Sorry, yes. I understand. Tomorrow then?"

"Okay, tomorrow," she agreed, more to get rid of him than anything else. "I could meet you at that coffee shop, Ixchel."

There was a pause at the other end of the line.

"Ixchel is kind of crowded and noisy," he said hesitantly. "I'd prefer somewhere more private, and quiet, if you don't mind. May I take you out to lunch?"

She thought again.

"All right, I guess so."

He named a restaurant on the Carretera that she'd never visited.

They settled on noon. Yet tossing and turning in bed that night, Abby wished she'd agreed to a drink after all. Unable to sleep, she kept wondering what he was going to tell her. And if they'd met at *La Campamocha*, she could have probably found out, once and for all, from somebody there, if Clare really was Pete Gomez.

Long before *Vato* crowed, she was wide awake, anticipating their lunch with a feeling of unease.

Chapter 18
Ajijic, Mexico, 24th April, 2017

Abby located Clare in a dimly lit restaurant, on a run-down section of the Carretera that she'd never bothered to explore. He was hidden behind an enormous potted ficus, grey with dust. The whole place had a forlorn air and was empty, apart from an old expat couple ensconced side by side in a corner, staring vacantly into space, not saying a word to each other. A half-empty bottle of white wine stood on the table in front of him and he already seemed mildly drunk when she arrived, although not in an offensive way. No server materialised out of the cavernous gloom to escort her over to the table, but he stood up courteously, pulled out a chair, and motioned for her to sit down.

"Thanks for coming," he said.

He took his seat again, poured her some wine, refilled his own glass and took a large gulp.

"This is going to be a long story," he warned, regarding her anxiously, his handsome features slightly reddened by the booze he'd consumed already. "So I hope you'll bear with me."

"Well, that's what I'm here for, Clare, aren't I? Go ahead. I won't interrupt." Abby's attempt at a joke sounded sharper than she intended, and she thought she probably came across as the prim, no-nonsense librarian she undoubtedly once was, peering short-sightedly at him through her glasses in the dark restaurant. But he was being obsequious. Irritating. It sounded so phony. At the same time, however she was intensely curious about what he had to say. She picked up her wine. Took a sip. A surprisingly good Sauvignon Blanc. Then she put the glass back on the table quickly. No way she was going to get drunk herself. Not in the company of this man she felt so uncertain about.

Sensing her resentment at being persuaded to meet him, he switched on the beguiling smile that he had used to such good effect at the Titan Reunion — and with the airline clerk at Mexico City Airport.

"First of all, Abby," he said smoothly, leaning towards her, across the table, his unsettling, brown eyes fixed solemnly on hers. "I do want to assure you that my name truly is Clare. I got the impression at your party that you didn't believe me, that you wondered how a man could have such a feminine name."

"True," she said briskly.

He sighed, swallowed more wine, the smile evaporating into a scowl.

"Well, believe me, I've hated being saddled with this damn name all my life. It's caused me all kinds of problems. But that's not the worst of it. There's more. I have two first names and Clare in fact comes second. The other one, believe it or not, is Angel."

He stopped, regarded her intently, waiting for this revelation to sink in, for Abby to put two and two together and be shocked, as he knew she would be. And it did happen, although it took a few seconds. She widened her eyes. Took a breath. Looked back at him with astonishment.

"Angel Clare," she said at length, slowly, incredulously, rolling the two names off her tongue. "You mean your name is Angel Clare? You've got to be kidding me. You were named after the hero in *Tess of the D'Urbervilles*? How weird that is, because I've actually just re-read the novel for the first time in years."

"Yes, the very same." He sounded weary. "I knew you'd get it. Most people don't, because hardly anyone reads the classics nowadays — or any other books, for that matter." A sigh. "But for better or for worse, Angel and Clare ARE my two first names. My surname is Lantzmann."

He emptied his glass, signalled to a server standing by the cash desk, absorbed in his cellphone, to bring another bottle.

"I know it sounds unbelievable, but my mother was an English literature professor at CCNY. She died when I was twenty. Her name was Ellen Lantzmann and she taught British classics, particularly Thomas Hardy. In fact, you could say she was totally obsessed with the guy. She made me read all his books when I was a kid — there are a lot of them…" he grimaced "…and she hauled me off to see his cottage in England three times. I had to sit in the garden while she gabbed for hours with a guide and went around making notes on every item of memorabilia about Hardy displayed inside the house. One time, I remember, it was raining, and I got soaked, sitting outside on one of those uncomfortable, wooden seats that they always seem to have in swanky English country estates, designed by some aristocrat with a funny name, Lootens, I think. I guess you would know who that is, wouldn't you, being a gardener?"

He raised his eyebrows speculatively. Abby smiled for the first time, his comment triggering a memory. She'd once badly wanted a Lutyens bench to put under the black walnut. But Larry had said, 'No.' He didn't like them. They were pretentious, too British. And too expensive.

"Yes," she said. "I do know Lutyens."

"Well, my mother didn't care about me sitting out there on that seat in the rain," Clare continued, his voice taking on a bitter edge, "and she couldn't understand why I hated Hardy. But I was a teenager, for God's sake! What American kid likes fusty old British novelists? She wasn't a good mother, when I look back, although she did try. Every summer, we would go off to a cottage she rented in Newfoundland, which I loved. I remember that as being the only happy part of my childhood. So I was interested to hear that your friend Rhodo comes from there."

He paused for another gulp.

"But I'm wandering off the point," he said, as the second bottle of wine arrived at the table. He shook his head. "Too much wine. Sorry, I'll move on…"

"No, no, wait a minute," said Abby. "I know I'm not supposed to interrupt, but even if your mother liked Hardy, why did she call you Angel Clare? Why the fascination with him? It seems like such a strange choice."

"To us, yes. But times have changed and *Tess of the D'Urbervilles* was her favourite of Hardy's books. She admired Angel Clare, said he was the most interesting of Hardy's characters, a social revolutionary, ahead of his time, rejecting the religious values of his father, bucking the British class system to become a farmer."

"Oh, come on, he was a self-righteous prick and brutal to Tess," snorted Abby. She vaguely remembered being disgusted by the novel back in high school. Bewildered too. Why on earth would Angel Clare abandon the woman he loved on the day they got married, simply because she'd had a previous relationship with another man? she'd asked her English teacher, confused. And the teacher, a lumpy woman with a severe hairstyle named Mrs Endicott, had said gravely: "Things were different for women then, Abby. Be thankful that they have changed."

Even so, re-reading the novel recently, sitting in the courtyard, it had still struck her how cruel and selfish Angel Clare's behaviour was.

Clare laughed.

"Mom acknowledged that he was a flawed hero. But she also said he was a man who stuck to his principles, with a strong sense of right and wrong. And she always liked people who bucked the Establishment, because she did that herself."

Abby shrugged and pulled a face. "Your mother was a very unusual woman. I'm not sure I agree with her. But anyway, carry on."

"She adopted me when she was forty-six. She'd never married and as far as I can tell, had difficult relationships with men, because she had rigid views about many things, not just Hardy. She was estranged from her parents, who were very traditional Jews, and didn't believe in women having careers. They disapproved when she went into teaching and did well at it. When she refused to quit and marry a man they chose, they cut her off.

"Then I guess she got lonely in middle-age, the way some single women do, and decided that what she wanted more than anything was a child. But at her age, and being single, it was hard to find one. I guess she wound up with me..." he laughed in a harsh way, "...because there was no one else available."

"She found me through an adoption agency run by Catholic nuns in Washington. They placed unwanted babies from Latin America with American families, and the nuns — and the agency — don't exist any more. Mom would never tell me which country I came from — I think perhaps she didn't know herself because the nuns kept that secret— and she always changed the subject when I asked her about it. But then just before she died, she did admit that she thought my father was either Mexican or Colombian and that my mother definitely came from an upper-class family in Colombia."

"That was why..." he stopped to pour himself another generous glass, "...I decided to drop by your party. I'm sorry I showed up uninvited but Jaz and Hollis had me over for dinner a few weeks ago and Hollis told me that you had a Colombian friend who would be visiting you. And that this woman could, amazingly, trace her family's origins back to the Spanish Conquest. So she sounded as though she belonged to the kind of society my mother referred to. And as I was coming to Ajijic myself, I wanted to meet her. I thought she might be able to help me find out who my mother was."

"Yes. You're talking about Tensie, of course," says Abby. "And you told her all this during your lunch together?"

"I did."

"And is she going to help you?"

Part of Abby hoped that Tensie had refused. That she told Clare to get lost. For during the reunion, he certainly gave no inkling of this, but implied instead that he had romantic intentions. All the Sisters — and Eve — had noticed how he played up to Tensie. Were she now in Tensie's shoes, she'd be feeling humiliated, not to mention embarrassed, to have discovered that her admirer simply wanted assistance with a

271

personal quest into his origins. But at least this confession had settled something in her own mind, she thought. She now realised why Tensie seemed so upset when they returned from Puerto Vallarta, why she'd been crying and was so subdued. She'd obviously felt disappointed and let down that her budding 'love affair' was nothing of the kind.

Indignant on her friend's behalf, Abby wondered if she wanted to hear the rest. Yet Clare seemed so wrapped up in telling his story, the words coming out in a mechanical way, as if he'd rehearsed them many times, that she stayed silent and let him carry on.

"Tensie has agreed to help, if she can. But Colombia is of course, a big country and I was born forty-five years ago," he said. "So it's probably a complete waste of time."

He took another gulp.

"Shall I go on?"

"Sure," Abby says.

"You seem to wonder why I know Ajijic well. I've spent a lot of time here because of a woman I consider my second mother. Her name is Maddy and she's retired now. She has a house in *Rancho del Oro*, the subdivision I told you about, that was once a gold mine. But she worked with Mom at City College for many years and she took me under her wing after Mom passed away."

"Mom had cancer and it was a slow, awful death. I kind of went off the rails after it was over. Dropped out of university, bummed around, got in with a bad crowd, did drugs. You know, the usual acting out stuff. But Maddy and her husband Burt — he died two years ago — straightened me out. I'm so grateful to them. And since then, I've had an up and down kind of life. I've worked at many different things, none of them very successfully, I'll admit. I tried to be a landscape painter for a while but didn't have the dedication to stick to it. I've done website design, run a summer theatre in upstate New York, taken jobs on cruise ships in winter, dancing with lonely, old widows. I was a barista in a trendy coffee shop in New York for a long time and truly enjoyed that job, making people different kinds of coffees and watching their reactions."

He raised his eyebrows. "I'm aware that my knowledge of coffee kind of annoyed you..."

He let his voice trail off as he sipped more wine. She said nothing.

"And recently," he went on, "...I've been working as a model."

The admission made him laugh, as if he was shocked at himself.

"That's how I know Jaz. I'm one of the cast she calls in for Bloomingdale's fashion shows — the hip, metrosexual swanning around in linen suits and pricey, brown lace-ups. That's me."

Another laugh.

"I even got to keep one of those suits. The manufacturer didn't want it back. And believe it or not..." the laugh subsided into a look of wonderment, "...Tensie saw me wearing that suit in Mexico City airport. We arrived on the same day, on the same flight to Guadalajara. But I didn't see her."

"Wow, quite a coincidence," Abby said. "She never told me. It must have been a surprise for her when you showed up at my house the next day."

"Yes. She couldn't believe it."

"I wonder why she never mentioned that to me," Abby

added, feeling mildly offended. "But... um... do you like being a model?"

He thought for a moment.

"Yes and no. The glamour business is bitchy, full of phonies, but I confess that I'm quite proud of my looks and how they open doors. Dating sites use me. I pose as the perfect suitor every woman is looking for." Another cynical laugh, then he frowned. "But I'm not gay, if that's what you're thinking. I tried it once, decided it wasn't for me. I like women. But I know I've hurt girlfriends in the past, because I've never been able to commit to anyone for long. I did marry briefly. My ex-wife knows Jaz. She's in fashion too, used to dress me and buy all my clothes. If I have a sense of style, it's because of her. We're still friends. But we split up a couple of years ago because she wanted to have a child and I didn't."

He took another large gulp of wine and stared moodily out of the restaurant entrance. The Carretera outside was blinding white under the noon day sun, the hoods of vehicles flashing by the open doorway like forks of lighting.

The brilliance made him blink. Yet he continued to stare, as if deep in thought. Abby almost wondered if he'd forgotten her. Then he abruptly turned back.

"Don't get me wrong. I may be vain, but I've nothing against kids. I'm just not ready for commitment and to be a father until I know who I am," he said, frowning again. "That's why I've come to stay in Ajijic for a while. Maddy has enlisted the help of her Mexican lawyer to see if we can find out whether my father was Mexican or not. It's become very important to me to know, although I know it's likely to be a lost cause, just as finding my birth mother will be. Yet Hector is determined. He's not going to give up, he says. And I'm sorry I had to rush off in the middle of your party, but he'd dropped by Maddy's place that afternoon — he lives in Guadalajara — and she'd wanted me to set up a meeting with him early the next morning as he was staying over in Ajijic to see some other clients."

'Ah, yes,' Abby thought, 'the distinguished-looking man sitting with Clare at Ixchel three days ago. He must be Hector.'

"And in the meantime, I've just signed on for a Spanish course at the *Centro Cultural*. I should have taken the step long ago, but I kept putting it off. I have a problem, I know, with motivating myself. I tend to take the easy way out and not bother."

He shook his head, clearly annoyed with himself for procrastinating.

"I feel so ridiculous, being maybe half-Mexican, looking like a Mexican and definitely of Latin parentage, yet speaking hardly a word of the language. But my mother never thought to send me for Spanish lessons. I think she secretly wanted me to be an English gentleman like Hardy, who was the only real passion in her life. And I've heard this course is good. I think you've met the instructor? A man everyone calls Egg?"

"Yes, at the market with his girlfriend Gillian. He seems like a nice guy."

"I thought so too," Clare says. "And now that you've heard my story, I hope you won't think I'm such a bad guy either, Abby."

He took another gulp of wine and looked quizzically at her.

"Thanks for listening."

His smile was an appeal for forgiveness. But she wasn't sure she wanted to let him off that lightly. Clare was self-absorbed and inconsiderate, and undoubtedly had hurt Tensie's feelings. But then, what was new about that? In her experience, most men thought of themselves first. Her own husband habitually did. And Clare's upbringing must have been strange and contributed to his narcissistic leanings, with that wacky mother of his. Softening towards him, no longer in the mood to censure, she smiled and simply said, "An interesting story."

"I'm glad you think so."

He glanced at her glass, noting that she'd barely touched it.

"I see that you haven't drunk much, Abby," he said, switching on the dazzling smile again. "But I have, and now I need to get some food into my stomach. Shall we ask for menus?"

Although she had no appetite, she said, "Sure."

He called out to the server, who was still leaning against the cash desk, absorbed in his cellphone. The boy looked up, surprised, as if he couldn't believe anyone would eat willingly in this establishment. Two greasy, plastic-covered folders were dropped on their table.

"Hmm. Not promising," said Clare with a chuckle, looking inside one. "I've no idea what the food's like here. I just chose it for the privacy. The place is always practically empty like this. Do you want to go someplace else?"

"No, let's stay. This is fine," Abby said

Having listened to his story, she now ached to tell him hers. Sitting in this awful restaurant, that stunk of stale beer and cooking fat, it would have been wonderful to unburden herself too — to explain that, from the moment she met him, she'd wondered if he was the wife-killer, Pete Gomez. And how she worried for Tensie, getting mixed up with such a dangerous criminal, who might connive to take all her money, destroy her life or even kill her. But this supposition now seemed so far-fetched, so preposterous, so utterly beyond the realm of believability that she felt embarrassed to even think about it. She bit her tongue. And Clare was okay, she decided, but with reservations. He was much too attractive to women and played on the fact that they found him irresistible. It must be hard to fall in love with him and then find yourself abandoned, just as Angel Clare so cruelly abandoned Tess. But underneath all that magnetic charm, he was basically a nice guy too. And a lost soul. He deserved to find what he was looking for.

As they picked at stringy, microwaved chicken, neither of them felt like talking much. They were as quiet as the only other patrons of the restaurant — the old expat couple, sitting in the corner, not saying a word to one another, doggedly chewing through what looked like very tough steak. He paid the bill, and on the way out of the restaurant, sensing that he'd won her over, he took her arm and said, "I confess that I haven't told you everything, Abby. There's another aspect to this story."

"There is?"

A mysterious look came over his face, just as it did so often at the lunch party.

"Yes, but I'm leaving that to Tensie to explain. She says she's going to email you."

"Oh, I see. When?"

"Soon."

Chapter 19
Ajijic, Mexico, 28th April, 2017

Soon? SOON? What exactly did Clare mean by soon?

Abby was on tenterhooks for the next four days waiting to hear from Tensie. So she kept herself busy. She went down to the *Centro Cultural* to register for Egg's course, looking forward to the following Monday, when the course would start. She walked down to the *Malecón* to watch the cormorants and pelicans splashing *i*nto Lake Chapala after the little fish called *charales*, which whooshed in unison to the surface like a million silver coins, flashing in the sunlight. She ambled around Ajijic's downtown, peering in store windows, but buying nothing.

And she gardened.

The red and white amaryllis in the courtyard had finished blooming, so she pruned off their long stems at the base, following her long-time habit back in Darien, where she kept them as indoor plants. She whacked back the *Datura*, which had got too big for its britches, busting out of its elegant urn. She visited a local garden centre whose name she liked — *Vivero Azucena* — and darted about the aisles like a squirrel gathering nuts in fall, feverishly examining the *Heliconia*, the *Calibrachoa* and the dazzling tropical gingers, but wound up disappointing the eager young salesman with a lapel tag saying Eduardo, because she went home empty-handed, unable to decide which of his plants to buy. She wished the Sisters were still here — they could help her choose, except that they'd probably be as bowled over by all the beautiful offerings at the *vivero* as she was and urge her to buy them all. She promised Eduardo that she'd be back.

Yet all the time, she was in a kind of tizzy, unable to settle down to anything, because she couldn't stop wondering when — and what — Tensie would write. And when the email did arrive at last—four mornings after Tensie went home to Colombia, popping into her Inbox with a ping, sandwiched between a missive from Mrs. Nora Dillard Oyeweye in Nigeria who begged permission to send her a million dollars, and an online seed catalogue for shrubs that didn't grow in the tropics — she felt like a student waiting for university entrance examination results to arrive by post. She was on tenterhooks. Her hands even shook on the keyboard. She held her breath, clicked on the message, excited — but also with a sense of foreboding.

And Tensie's email was lengthy. That became obvious right away. It went on and on, down the screen. Her Colombian Sister had clearly invested a lot of time and thought into this missive. No wonder it took her so long to get in touch. So instead of half-sitting on the side of her bed, laptop open on the bedside table — a habit Abby had acquired when checking emails because she could scan and trash them all quickly, then go off and do something vastly more interesting — she shut the lid, carried the laptop out to the courtyard and made herself another coffee.

Then she settled down in a comfy *equipal* at the table before opening the lid again. And what she read there was emotional, dramatic and in so many ways, typical of Tensie.

But it was also not at all what she had expected.

'My dear Sister Abelia,' Tensie wrote.

You are very precious to me, more precious than any of the other Sisters, because you came to my rescue after Juan Diego so cruelly left me. I will never forget how kind and thoughtful — but also how practical — you were. I owe you a huge debt of thanks that I can never fully repay. Because of you, I managed to move on and rebuild my life back in Colombia.

And now I have to reveal something that I have kept secret for many years. I hope you won't be too offended that I have never told you about this before. If learning about it now does make you angry, I beg your forgiveness — but the fact is, I was so determined to bury this shameful part of my life that I almost succeeded. But then it came back to haunt me when I visited you in Mexico. I had a strange premonition before I arrived that this would happen, although the way it unfolded was a total surprise — and I still can't quite believe it.

You've heard Clare's story. Now I must tell you mine, which concerns a time when I was very young.

My grandpapa ran our farm then. He mostly grew shrub roses. And my father was away in the Netherlands for months at a time, learning about horticulture and how to run our kind of business, because they hoped to get bigger and expand into hydrangeas and cut flowers. I lived with my mother and younger sister, Maria Elena, in one of the houses on our land. Juan Diego lived in another, with his mama and his papa (who was cousin to mine) and brother Alejandro and we kids all played together from the time we could walk. Then at eleven, Juan Diego was sent away to boarding school in Bogotá. I, two years younger, was enrolled at convent school, run by nuns, in a nearby town and only came home at weekends. So for several years we didn't see each other much. We were both starting to grow up and perhaps our parents wanted it that way, because they thought we had become too close. But I always knew that I would marry Juan Diego. And that it was all I ever wanted.

Operating the farm was a challenge for Grandpapa — it's always a challenge because profit margins with shrubs and flowers are never high. Yet in some ways, it was less complicated than it is today. Farms like ours are burdened with so many rules and regulations about everything from shipping documentation to the employees we can hire. But back then, bands of itinerant workers moved freely around the Savannah, finding work where they could, and one summer, Grandpapa took on a group of men from Mexico. I don't know why they'd come all the way to Colombia — probably there was no work back home — but they stayed on for months, because Grandpapa liked them. He said they were very good workers and they didn't mind handling the roses which had thorns like needles and made your fingers bleed. He would often drink with them at the end of the day and tend to their wounds himself. He treated them like family.

One of these men brought his son, Paquito, along with him. Paquito was fourteen and worked with the roses too. But he had more free time on his hands than the men and he was too young to sit and drink after work. So on weekends when I was home from the convent, we would meet up under an old tree by our house and talk about what we wanted to do when we grew up. Paquito hoped to have his own farm in Mexico with his papa. But I knew, even back then, that what I wanted

281

was to be a good wife to Juan Diego.

But Juan Diego was away most of the time at school, and on the rare occasions when he did come home, he would torment me by flirting with Maria Elena. Then I'd run off crying to find Paquito, and he'd be kind and gentle and sympathetic. And he was undoubtedly flattered that the granddaughter of the jefe would treat him like a friend. And well, you can guess the rest. I was very naïve, only fifteen when the Mexicans came, but in many ways much younger than that. And I knew nothing about sex, having been raised by nuns. The only boys I had contact with were Juan Diego and Alejandro and they weren't there. Paquito and I started exchanging kisses. Then teenage hormones being what they are, it eventually went further. One evening when the men were off drinking with Grandpapa and the building that the Mexicans slept in was empty, we took off our clothes and lay down together. To this day, I can still remember how the straw mattress underneath us prickled against my back as he entered me.

We did it several more times after that. He was a virgin too and just becoming a man, and it was as much an awakening for him as it was for me. And I discovered after the first time, which hurt a little, that I liked it, the sexual act, even though the nuns had taught us that well-bred girls should never ever allow themselves to be talked into letting a man touch that part of their bodies. But it just seemed such a natural thing to do with Paquito, and it felt good, although I didn't fall in love with him. My heart always belonged to Juan Diego. And I was so innocent, I didn't even realise I'd got pregnant until I started getting morning sickness at about three months. My periods had started later than Maria Elena's, even though she was younger than me. But mine were irregular. When they stopped, I presumed that it was nothing more than that. And at the time our mother was being quite distant towards me and Maria Elena — I learned later that, with my father being away so much, she was having an affair with a man in town — and it wasn't until I was starting to show that I plucked up the courage to tell her.

She hit the roof of course. She flew into a rage with me. But she was even more angry with Grandpapa for becoming too familiar with the Mexican workers. Papa came home from the Netherlands and took over running the farm. Grandpapa was forced to retire and became a bitter old man. He died shortly afterwards. And I was shipped off to an aunt in Barranquilla. But Paquito had long gone by then. I was only about six weeks pregnant when the Mexicans moved on to another farm. He promised to stay in touch but I never heard from him. Communicating by any means in those days wasn't easy. There was barely any mail service between farms out on the Savannah. And I realised afterwards that he was probably illiterate anyway. So he never knew what happened. To this day, I don't even know what Paquito's surname was.

I had the baby, a boy, in a hospital run by nuns in Barranquilla. They took him away from me the day he was born, and I only got to see him once, my little, dark-haired angel, lying in a crib down the hall. In Spanish, we use the expression 'dar la luz' to describe the act of giving birth, which means 'to bring into the light', and I've always hoped that some good light did shine into the life of this poor baby. But I never knew what happened to him. My aunt told me he was being adopted — but by whom and where I was never told.

When I got back to the farm, Mama and Papa refused to

talk about it. Ever. I'd done this shameful thing and disgraced the family but I must never raise the subject again. So I didn't. Then I grew up and so did Juan Diego, and I had a brief period in the limelight when I entered the Miss Colombia pageant at nineteen and was astonished to be chosen as the runner-up. But Juan Diego was indignant. He was so proud of me. He kept saying that I should have won the crown and that he loved me more than anything in the world and couldn't wait to make love to me, but he'd wait until after we were married. And then we did marry, a year later, when he was twenty-two and I was twenty — and on our wedding night, I don't know why, but I told him about Paquito and the baby. I felt it was dishonest to keep what had happened a secret. And he took it very badly. We were on our honeymoon in a grand, old hotel in Cartagena, paid for by our parents, and he'd expected to have a 'pure' bride. Men did back then. Some Latin men still do, even though they get plenty of sexual experience themselves before marriage. I know Juan Diego had girlfriends when he was away from home and he must have slept with them. But he was so disgusted with me, he walked out and didn't come back for several weeks.

So it was fascinating for me to hear Clare's story about how he wound up with his strange name. I've never heard of the book Tess of the D'Urbervilles, or the author Thomas Hardy — I didn't study British classics at my convent school - but the way the poor heroine Tess got abandoned by the man called Angel Clare was kind of what happened to me.

Except that Juan Diego did come back. And, as you know, we were together for years. But it was never a good marriage, when I look back, because there was always this shadow hanging over us. I'd had this baby by another man, and for reasons unknown, I could never conceive again, although we both longed for children. When Cecilia became pregnant, he told me he had to go, because it seemed like fate. And now, I don't really blame him, although I'll miss him forever.

By now, you're no doubt wondering if I think Clare is my son. It would be wonderful if indeed that turned out to be true, but I won't even go there. Not yet. It's certainly possible, but it seems like too much of a coincidence — to me, to him. And I remember standing in that hall, in that dreary Barranquilla hospital, with a stern, spiteful nun in a black habit holding me firmly by the arm, granting me just one look at my baby. He was lying there, on the other side of the glass in the ward for newborns, one in a whole row of little babies swaddled in cribs, all looking the same, all destined to disappear forever from their mothers' lives and be adopted by people they didn't know. And there were so many hospitals like that in Colombia, back when the Catholic church was far more powerful than it is today and getting pregnant when you weren't married was the most terrible thing that could happen to a girl.

But we're going to try to find out. And in the meantime, don't feel too angry with Clare for showing up and ruining our Titan Reunion. He feels very badly about what happened — and so do I. But I'm glad he did come now. Very glad. And I'm looking forward to playing host to all the Sisters in 2020. I will cook Ajiaco for you again. And other exciting Colombian dishes, I promise you!

By the way, how is poor little Eve? Clare says he did in fact find her quite attractive, but he had other things on his mind. I hope she has recovered from being snubbed by him.

With very much love, mi querida Abby,

—Your Sister in plants, Tensie.

Chapter 20

RHODO

Rhodo is disappointed. Deeply disappointed. She wants to hammer with her bare knuckles on the triple-glazed picture window in front of her, to assuage her feelings of rage and frustration. Yet she manages to restrain herself. The window is brand new, just installed yesterday, there's still a sticker glued to the glass, she hasn't even paid for it yet. It would be awfully childish to go and break this window just because she's upset about what has happened — and is continuing to happen — around the world.

She tells herself to calm down, to stop being such a worrier, and admire the view from the window instead. And it is a beautiful view — just as beautiful as the one she had from the hotel balcony near Puerto Vallarta three years ago. Except that it's different. Here, the ocean is a deeper blue, more the colour of pewter, and it's emptier. Much emptier. There are no tour boats full of tourists, no young guys in baggy shorts, parasailing through the air, thrilled and terrified at the same time, screaming like seagulls. No aquamarine swimming pools in evidence. Here, all that's in front of her is an ancient fishing trawler, probably from Iceland, rust down its sides, tied up at the docks, some anonymous grey warehouses, and a lone sailboat, bobbing up and down like a pop bottle on the waves. Then in the distance, rocky hillsides with scrubby trees and boxy, little houses in rainbow colours.

Bay Roberts Harbour. The place where she grew up. The Sisters of the Soil were supposed to take in this view too, during their fifth Titan Reunion, discussed by email ever since four of them met up in Mexico. Although Tensie had badly wanted to host this one, she got too busy at the farm and had to beg off, with profuse apologies, promising to invite them all next time. So Rhodo stepped in. It struck her as kind of like fate because last December, holy moly, to her utter astonishment, she inherited this big, old house from Gramma Mercer's youngest sister, Dorene — and she has room in it for eight guests.

Gramma's house was pulled down years ago, but Dorene's somehow escaped the bulldozers and is in fairly good shape. So she's decided to keep her home base in Toronto, but spend summers on The Rock in future. Then one day, she's promised herself, she'll quit both places and retire to tropical Ajijic, just like Abby did. But in the meantime, a ton of money and effort has gone into giving the draughty saltbox with ill-fitting windows a makeover — for Dorene died at ninety-four, never married, incontinent and afflicted by Alzheimer's. And she left behind urine-soaked mattresses in every bedroom, four folding card tables, a quantity of heavy, dark Victorian furniture and lurid orange shag carpeting from the 1950s laid throughout the house. Rhodo has had to scramble to clean the place up in time for the reunion which was supposed to start next week.

While doing that, she'd pictured how it would be, raising their glasses in front of this view, talking and laughing, discussing plants the way they always do. She had intended to take the Sisters to see the ravishing rhododendrons at the Botanical Gardens in St. Johns, an hour's drive away, the ones that inspired her to take up writing about gardening. Then during their lunch party, she'd planned to introduce them to a fruit that's unique to this rocky outpost of the world: bakeapples. Hannah, she surmised, would get a particular kick out of the mild-tasting treats which have nothing to do apples but are in fact a kind of berry. They'd become yet another candidate for her *Dirty Fingernails* column, which is still going strong in the British newspaper, even though Hannah is coming up to her sixty-eighth birthday and keeps wondering if it's time to retire.

The others are getting older too. Yet they're all still busy and happy and doing interesting stuff with their lives and she was looking forward to catching up with their news. But now the reunion is not happening. Indeed, nothing is happening. Everything is terminated, cancelled, shut down, including Newfoundland itself. People from away are not currently welcome on The Rock. The airport is closed to flights, as airports everywhere are. It's the consequence of Covid 19, the devastating pandemic that originated in China but has rocked the world to its foundations, causing chaos, panic, misery, a frightening number of deaths and a strange vocabulary of new terms to enter people's conversations: lockdown, social distancing, self-isolation and PPE, which everyone quickly learned stands for Personal Protective Equipment.

As frustrated as she feels by the lockdown, Rhodo is glad not to be in her little downtown Toronto house right now. It's safer on this island that's almost as big as France yet so sparsely inhabited. So far, there have been only a handful of

Covid 19 cases confirmed here. She's glad too, that she brought Azalea along for company while the renovations were going on. She wishes Monica were here as well. But she's probably the most glad that there's still email and internet on The Rock. She can stay connected to the world and, as a result, took part in a Zoom call last night with the three Sisters she was with in Mexico. It felt so good to see and talk to them again — if only via a computer screen — instead of being stuck here on her own, staring at the sea, worrying about getting sick.

Abby is still in Ajijic and a property-owner too. She bought the house behind the yellow wall last November after Myra MacDonald died and Bruce decided to move back to Canada because their son John changed his mind about retiring in Ajijic. And the house wasn't cheap, she said, but she treasures her 'little piece of paradise' as she's always called it, and she's keeping it exactly the same, apart from adding still more plants to the courtyard. which is starting to resemble a tropical jungle. The only difference to the street outside is that fat, old Campeon no longer sprawls on her concrete stoop. The dog died last year and she's relieved that Carlos and Santiago, who are growing up fast and no longer play hopscotch, haven't so far found a replacement. But the Mexican chickadees are still around, shrieking 'Kick your rear! Kick your rear' at her from the mango tree, which, now that it's fully mature, is producing great crops of fruit. Rhodo, in fact, pigged out on Abby's chin-staining Ataulfos a year and a half ago when she visited Ajijic again. She was researching a sequel to *Native Rhododendrons of North America*, which has sold beyond expectations. Her new book, *Native Rhododendrons of Central America* is due out next year, all being well, her publisher says.

And it'll appear in both English and Spanish simultaneously, with lots of pictures of the Vireyas at Vallarta Botanical Garden.

And Abby has reconciled with Hollis, who eventually did confirm that Clare was telling the truth about why he dropped by the Titan Reunion. Then Hollis and Jaz visited Ajijic for Christmas, right after she bought the house. They loved the place. Everyone got along just fine. Abby has promised to go and see the girls in New York next. But she hasn't yet — and now travel anywhere, is of course, impossible, due to the crippling consequences of Covid 19.

Yet before the lockdown, she saw quite a bit of Gillian, who's still operating her stall called Zinnia at the organic market. Abby shops there regularly — and hopes the market will reopen soon. She also sometimes visits the farm in Jocotopec, usually in Gillian's old pick-up, but on one occasion riding behind her on the old Norton motorbike that the gringo left behind in the shed where the herbs now hang to dry. She said it was quite an experience, rattling along in the dust, no cushioning at all under her backside, the springs gone. Abby helps with planting and harvesting and cutting bunches of zinnias and also feeds the chickens when she's out there. And it's a pretty spot, peaceful, with views all around, of the valley, but the work is backbreaking and she's relieved afterwards to return to her quiet life in downtown Ajijic. She dated a Canadian widower, a retired high school teacher, for a while and really enjoyed his company. But he started making noises about moving in and she decided that wasn't for her. She truly loves living on her own.

During one of her visits to the farm, Gillian told her that Egg's friend made a mistake about Pete Gomez. It wasn't him at *La Campamocha* after all. Pete is in fact, rumoured to be in Thailand, shacked up with another wealthy American widow, running a coffee shop there, but no one knows for sure. Abby and Gillian often discuss things like this in Spanish now — Abby likes the practice — and she doesn't resort to English either when picking up her morning *bolillos* from Herminio and provisions at Aguacate from Conchita. They're both impressed by how quickly she became comfortable with their language, after her three months with Egg.

Abby sees Eve quite often too. She comes into town every couple of weeks to shop for supplies and has become good friends with Gillian. The wellness retreat in Mazamitla has done remarkably well, guided by Guillermo, who, contrary to what Abby and Hannah thought, has proven to be a smart businessman and a model employer. Named *La Pura Vida*, or The Pure Life, it's attracting young enthusiasts from many countries (Hollis and Jaz were booked to go this year, but had to cancel because of Covid 19) who all love the idea of doing yoga and meditation with Sanjay in the peaceful Mexican mountains, far away from crowded resorts like Puerto Vallarta. And Sanjay still giggles too much, but the guests don't mind. He's such a gentle, caring soul. Yet an equally big draw are the imaginative meals that Eve prepares. Guillermo pays her well, getting a work permit was a breeze thanks to his business connections in Mexico City, and he has given her free rein to do what she likes in the culinary department. So she does. One of her most popular inventions on the vegan menu is a *jicama* and black bean salad. With *epazote*, supplied by Gillian. Abby also reported, during the Zoom call, that Eve, as far as she knows, doesn't chase after men any more. She claims to be 'too busy' to cope with lovers — although Abby did run into

Roberto the other day, cleaning the windshield of his Beetle on Emiliano Zapata and he told her that he was driving over to the other side of the lake to spend the night because Eve had something special to celebrate. And he had an awfully happy smile on his face.

Hannah joined the Zoom call saying apologetically that she didn't have much to report apart from a new grandchild, a girl this time, named Cordelia. But apart from that, life is the same as ever in Dorset, and so she was terribly disappointed that the latest Titan Reunion had to be cancelled. She couldn't wait to come to Newfoundland and meet up with the Sisters again. She also talked a bit about Eve. Eve apparently told her she'd been sick for a while, but declined to say what the problem was, but she is now cured and back to her normal self. As Hannah talked, Rhodo could discern Charles sitting in his armchair in the background, bent over the iPad and the sight made her think — as she always does when she's around friends who are married — that she has no regrets about staying single.

The Sister with the most to say during the Zoom call was Tensie. The others already know that Clare moved to Colombia and has been living at the farm for over two years, in a little house she had built for him near the family home. They also know that DNA testing revealed Tensie is not his mother. Yet the Sisters were also made privy to the mind-blowing soap opera that followed this disappointing discovery. While going through the records of births and deaths at the Civil Registration Office in Bogotá, trying to find out what happened to her baby, Tensie spotted an entry for a boy born to a sixteen-year-old girl named Mariana Estela Pardo, at the same Barranquilla hospital where she gave birth. And at around the same time. This was certainly a surprise. She knew Mariana, a distant cousin who lived in Bogotá. Yet what nearly gave her a heart attack was the next line on the certificate. 'Father's name: Juan Diego Nicolas Hernandez Castro. Age 18.' *Madre de Dios*! It couldn't possibly be, could it? Her own HUSBAND? But indeed, it could. Tensie confronted Juan Diego by phone. Flew to New York. Had it out with him. And he admitted that he'd had a fling with Mariana while away at school in Bogotá, but both sets of parents had — like Tensie's — made them swear never to reveal what happened, to avoid scandal in the family. And this baby — also like Tensie's — was left with the nuns to be adopted.

Yet the extraordinary tale didn't end there. Tensie, always struck by how much Clare resembles Juan Diego, insisted on DNA testing again. He protested but finally gave in. And it confirmed her hunch. Juan Diego is Clare's father.

She wasn't sure of what to make of this bolt from the blue. Nor was Clare. He worried that Tensie wouldn't want him around at the farm any more. But things did settle down — and remarkably quickly. Tensie concluded that although Clare is Juan Diego's biological child, but not hers, what does it matter? She is thrilled to finally have a son in her life. She'll never completely stop loving her rat of a husband either, although his failure to be honest about fathering a child shocked her, because she had, after all, confessed to her own shameful secret. Yet while he's acknowledged paternity, Juan Diego isn't interested in establishing a relationship with Clare. It would cause 'too many problems' with Cecilia and Javier, he claims. (Mariana, they learned, later married happily but died of breast cancer many years ago.) So Tensie and Clare, happy to have discovered each other, both hope that Juan

Diego will never come back to live in Colombia.

And Clare has found his calling on the Savannah, living and working at the farm, with a mother who loves him, and doesn't want to turn him into an English gentleman. He now uses the name Angel — pronouncing it the Spanish way, ANG-hel — and is well on the way to speaking the language like a native. Yesterday, Tensie revealed with a delighted whoop, there's a girlfriend in the picture and it seems to be serious. They might even get married.

But what Tensie was most eager to talk about yesterday was not this tangled tale — by now old news to all the Sisters - but the talent Clare has developed, under Alejandro's expert tutelage, for the tricky science of hybridising. *Flores Rojas Hernandez* will soon introduce a new long-stemmed rose that is a ground-breaking very pale blue, with an iridescent sheen like porcelain — and it was Clare who achieved this magical combination by crossing and re-crossing several hybrids. Advance images of the rose — which they're thinking of calling 'Clare's Angel' — are going up on horticultural websites everywhere and Tensie wanted to know Rhodo's opinion of the name before the rose went into production. Rhodo thought it was catchy, that cut flower lovers in North America would be interested and that it would probably be a hit with wedding planners too. The combination of 'Clare' and 'Angel' evokes appealing thoughts of harmony and love, she said. And Rhodo feels gratified to be involved in the development of this promising new rose, knowing as she does the complicated story behind its creation. She's crossing her fingers that Clare's Angel will be an enormous success.

***

Rhodo stops reflecting on the Zoom call and gets up, delighted about the rose, delighted for Tensie, delighted for Clare. They both sound so happy. She's delighted too, about her new triple-glazed window. It frames the view well and will keep the house warmer when the winds blow, as they regularly do in Newfoundland, all year round. She heads into the kitchen. It's after three in the afternoon and she's suddenly ravenous. Yet the fridge is empty and, in the cupboard above the sink, she knows there's nothing more than the two jars of bottled bakeapples she bought to serve at the Titan Reunion. She feels guilty about her total lack of prowess in the kitchen — she did intend to make a special effort when the Sisters came — but she still dislikes the whole rigmarole of cooking.

A big smelly pizza with pepperoni. That's what she needs right now, she decides, to lift her spirits during the lockdown. And she knows this hole in the wall operation in Bay Roberts that makes far better pizzas than the ones she shares with Monica in Toronto.

She finds her phone, puts in an order. The man who answers says sorry, it'll be at least an hour before we can deliver it, my darlin', we're so busy. She says no problem.

"At least, in this shut-down world, there's still take-out," she yells, after hanging up. "Let's hear it for the joys of take-out!"

Her voice echoes around the room, startling Azalea, who's been snoozing on a window ledge.

While waiting for the pizza to arrive, Rhodo takes a walk along the rocky shoreline. A cool wind is blowing off the Atlantic. She needs a jacket. But it's not really cold, just refreshing. There's a strong, tangy smell of the sea. It feels good to be out of the house.

The pizza shows up exactly when the man said. She opens the flat cardboard box while sitting on the new, grey, L-shaped sofa that she bought because the Sisters were coming. She pulls the cork on a bottle of Merlot, finds a wineglass and tells herself sternly not to drink it all. The only result — if she succumbs to the temptation — will be a cracking headache. Yet how sad it is, being here without her gardening buddies. She'd pictured them all lined up on this sofa, sipping wine and admiring her new summer home and now that won't happen, because of the damn virus. It's shattering, bewildering, she wants to vent her anger on something or somebody, instead of just yelling at an empty room. But then she pictures the other Sisters, one by one, all far away around the world — Abby in Mexico, Tensie in Colombia, Hannah in Dorset, plus Lola in Texas, Mieke in Amsterdam and Nathalie outside Paris (who had intended to come to Newfoundland) and Jing-Jing, so distant in Guangzhou (who'd emailed a while ago, regretting, once again, that she wouldn't be able to make it). And they're all at this moment probably in the same position as her, locked down, isolated, fed up, and as worried and uncertain about the future as she is.

Yet the bond runs deep. Loving plants like they do, they'll never run out of things to talk about. This friendship is going to last forever. She can feel that in her bones. The Sisters of the Soil will meet up again. Of course they will.

She raises her glass in a toast.

"Here's to us, Sisters!" she says, her voice soft this time. "See you all soon!"

And she opens the pizza box.

THE RECIPES

AJIACO
Colombian Chicken, Corn and Potato Soup

INGREDIENTS
For six people:
1 tbsp olive oil
1 large onion, finely chopped
2 cloves of garlic, finely chopped
8 skinless chicken thighs
Two 14 oz (397 g) bags of frozen *papa criolla* potatoes, thawed — or substitute 1 ½ pounds of Russet or a golden-fleshed variety of potatoes, chopped in small pieces.
(Optional) 16 oz. (453 g.) bag of frozen *arracacha* (a starchy root vegetable, also known as cassava) thawed and cut up
1 cup frozen peas and carrots, thawed (or cook fresh ones)
2 cobs corn, cut into thirds
8 cups water or chicken stock.
1 tbsp. dried *guascas* (or substitute 2 tbsp. chopped fresh cilantro)
Salt & pepper

GARNISH (Prepare in advance and serve to taste)
Sour cream
Capers
Thinly sliced or diced avocados
Steamed white rice (optional)

PREPARATION

In a large stockpot over medium-high heat, heat oil. Add onion. Cook, stirring, for 3 minutes to soften. Add garlic in the final minute. Add chicken, potatoes, *arracacha*, water and guascas. Raise heat, bring to boil. Simmer 20 minutes or until chicken is cooked through. In the last few minutes, add the corn cobs. Remove 2 pieces of chicken. Shred meat, discard the bones. Return meat to pot.

TO SERVE

Divide soup among 6 large bowls, making sure everyone gets a piece of chicken and the corn. Add garnish if required.

Author's tip:

Buying *guascas*: Latin-American supermarkets carry guascas, under the Kiska or El Rey brand. You can also sometimes find it online. If tracking down *guascas* is impossible, substitute fresh cilantro or dried oregano. Frozen *papas criollas* and *arracacha* are sold at Colombian foodstores.

Storage: Leftovers can be refrigerated in an airtight container for up to 4 days.

NEWFOUNDLAND COD CAKES

INGREDIENTS
1 ½ pounds of dried, salted cod
¼ cup butter
1 small chopped onion
1 clove chopped garlic (optional)
2 tablespoons dried summer savoury (optional)
½ teaspoon ground black pepper
6 cups mashed potatoes
1 beaten egg
A bit of flour

PREPARATION
Soak the salt cod in cold water for several hours. Repeat with fresh water twice more. A shallow basin is good for this step. You may need to cut the cod into pieces to fit them into the basin.

Simmer the cod in boiling water for about 15 minutes. Drain all the water off the fish and allow it to cool to almost room temperature, then flake it apart with a fork.

In a frying pan, melt the butter over medium heat.

Add onions and cook 'til they go transparent and soft. Throw in the garlic in the last couple of minutes.

Add the flaked fish, along with the mashed potato, egg, pepper and savoury. You do not need to add salt.

Tip this mixture out on to a board. Turn the heat off. Mix everything together until well combined. Form into small cakes with your hands, roll them in flour, then flatten them.

Wipe out the frying pan with a paper towel. Pour a bit of fresh vegetable oil in and heat. Fry the cakes over medium heat, flipping them once, until they are golden brown on both sides.

Serve topped with scrunchions if desired.

Author's tip:

Prep time does not include soaking the salt cod. If you're having guests, do this step the day before. Scrunchions are ½ inch cubes of cured pork fat that are fried till they become crisp, brown and not greasy. Sprinkle them over the fish cakes like croutons.

LUSCIOUS LOVAGE SALAD DRESSING

(Adapted from a recipe that appeared in Beverley
Nichols' memoir: *Down the Kitchen Sink*)

INGREDIENTS

A big handful of lovage

Smaller handfuls of parsley, tarragon (optional) and chives

Yolks of two hardboiled eggs (whites discarded)

2 tablespoons wine vinegar

1 tablespoon lemon juice

4 tablespoons olive oil

Some generous shakes of Worcester Sauce

6 tablespoons single cream

1 teaspoon dry English mustard, mixed with a bit of water

Chop all the herbs finely and put into a bowl. Crush egg yolks
and mix them with the herbs. Add oil slowly, then Worcester
sauce, vinegar, lemon juice and mustard.

Author's tip:

You can also whisk the whole lot in a blender, which is much
easier. But don't overdo it or the cream will curdle.

JICAMA SLICES WITH LIME JUICE AND CHILI POWDER

INGREDIENTS:

1 jicama

Juice of 2 limes

Ground mild chili powder to taste

Salt to taste

Peel the jicama, cut it into quarters, then into slices about ¼ inch thick.

Douse liberally with lime juice. Arrange on a platter. Sprinkle with salt and chili powder just before serving.

Author's tip:

This is a convenient hors d'oeuvres to prepare in advance. Place the slices in a bowl of cold water in the refrigerator so they stay crisp. Be sure to drain all the water off before adding the lime juice and chili and pat the slices dry. They will keep in water for a couple of days.

BLACK BEANS WITH EPAZOTE

INGREDIENTS
3 cups dried black beans, picked over and washed
Water to soak
1 tbsp. canola oil
1 onion, chopped
4 cloves garlic, crushed and chopped
2 or 3 sprigs of epazote, chopped, or a heaping teaspoon of dried epazote
Salt to taste

INSTRUCTIONS
Soak beans overnight. Simmer in lots of water until they start to go soft. This can take several hours, longer than with other dried beans. Heat oil in Dutch oven, add onion, stir 'til transparent, add half the garlic, then beans. Cover with water (save some from the beans) then simmer for about half an hour. Add chopped epazote and the rest of the garlic. Simmer for another half an hour until thick and fragrant, but be careful the beans don't burn on the bottom.

Author's tip:
Mexican supermarkets often sell packets of dried epazote. Yet this herb is easy to grow, even in northern gardens. Planted

seeds will quickly develop into a weedy plant which must be chopped back regularly as smaller leaves are best for use in cooking. If you can't find epazote, substitute cilantro.

CAPITORADA
Mexican Bread Pudding

INGREDIENTS
4 small, soft rolls (called *bolillos* in Mexico) or a loaf of sweet, brioche-type bread
4 ½ cups of water
12 oz. of *piloncillo*, grated or cut up, or 1 ½ cups packed dark brown sugar
4 cinnamon sticks
4 whole cloves
3 cups of a mild grated cheese, like cheddar, Colby, Monterey Jack, or a cheese of your choice.
1 cup raisins
4 tablespoons butter

INSTRUCTIONS
Preheat oven to 350 deg. F

Cut rolls in ½ inch slices and butter both sides, layer on a baking sheet and bake for 3 minutes on each side, until lightly toasted and dry. Remove and cool. Combine water and piloncillo, cinnamon sticks and cloves in a large saucepan. Bring to the boil, reduce heat, creating a syrup. Simmer syrup uncovered for 20 minutes. Remove from heat and let steep, covered for 2 hours. Remove cinnamon sticks and cloves.

Butter an 8 x 10 baking dish, then layer ingredients in the

following order: a third of toasted bread, third of raisins, third of grated cheese, then pour 1 ½ cups syrup evenly over everything. Wait 15 minutes and add more layers. Let the mixture sit again, then use up the remaining bread, raisins and cheese, topped with more syrup. Before baking leave the baking dish for another 15 minutes.

Cover with aluminium foil that has been buttered on the inside and bake for 40 minutes. Remove the foil and bake for another 10 to 15 minutes, until cheese is golden brown. Serve warm.

Author's tip:

You can add pretty much anything to this pudding: try chopped nuts and dates; chopped candied ginger; grated orange peel. But to be authentic, it should include grated cheese.

CAFÉ DE OLLA
Traditional Mexican coffee

INGREDIENTS
4 cups water
About 1/3 cup of *Piloncillo* or dark brown sugar
½ stick of cinnamon
4 tablespoons of ground dark coffee
1 teaspoon unsweetened cocoa

INSTRUCTIONS
Grate or cut up the *piloncillo*. In a heavy-bottomed saucepan, place the water, then add *piloncillo* and the cinnamon stick. Turn on heat and simmer until the *piloncillo* dissolves (about 7 minutes.) When the water starts to boil, add the ground coffee and cocoa, stir, turn the heat off, and leave, covered by a lid, for several more minutes. Pour through a tea strainer into coffee cups.

Author's tip:
Cloves or anise seeds can be added after the sugar dissolves. *Piloncillo* is easier to cut up if you warm it slightly in the microwave first.

CAPRESI CHOCOLATE CAKE
Torta di Mandorle

INGREDIENTS
2 cups good quality dark chocolate, finely grated or ground in a food processor
2 ½ cups blanched almonds, chopped finely, or ground in a blender
2 cups butter
2 cups white sugar
5 eggs (6 if they are small)

INSTRUCTIONS
Soften butter. Beat butter and sugar together until light and creamy. Add egg yolks, one at a time. Whisk egg whites until they are a firm, meringue-like consistency. Fold into the mixture. Add finely ground chocolate. Then add almonds. Mix well.

Grease a round tin, or line it with parchment paper. Spoon the mixture in, spreading it out. Bake in a moderate oven, 180 deg. C. for about an hour (55 to 60 mins). Cool before turning it out on to a plate. Sprinkle with icing sugar. This a flattish cake that should be served in small slices.

Author's notes

This is a work of fiction, inspired by a real live event.

A Corpse Flower did indeed bloom at Brooklyn Botanical Garden, New York, in July 2006 for the first time in seventy years, causing a minor sensation. But things didn't unfold in the way I have described. Go to **bbg.org/news** to read about what happened and watch a video of the flower unfurling. The Sisters of the Soil I have invented as a result of this event don't exist. They are entirely a product of my imagination.

The pretty Mexican town of Ajijic does exist however, and is a popular retirement destination for Americans, Canadians, Brits and other nationalities. The Tianguis market is real too, and currently takes place there on Mondays. The organic market follows on Wednesdays. But most of the other places, locations and incidents that I have worked into this story are fictitious, as are all the characters.

Vallarta Botanical Garden is a reality and I highly recommend it to anyone who loves plants. If you are vacationing in Puerto Vallarta, look for the public bus marked El Tuito, which leaves regularly from downtown, near the public market. It costs only a few pesos and the driver will drop you off right outside the Garden. The half-hour trip weaves along the coast for part of the way and is a whole lot of fun.

All authors, whether they write fiction or non-fiction,

consult a wide range of sources and individuals in the course of putting together a book. For this novel, I am grateful to:

My first readers, Carol Cowan, Kathe Lieber and eagle-eyed Kate Robertson, who came up with some brilliant suggestions to sharpen the flow of the story.

Saara Nafici, for information about the Galinsoga planted at Brooklyn Botanical Garden.

Barbara Sgroi of Ajijic and Carol Merchasin, author of *This is Mexico, Tales of Culture and other Complications,* for insights into life as an expat in a Mexican town.

All the Mexican people — so warm, generous and welcoming — whom I met during my visits to Ajijic.

My gardening buddies, Carol Cowan, Lorraine Flanigan, Carol Gardner, Marjorie Harris, Uli Havermann, Ann Huber, Lorraine Hunter, Sara Katz, Liz Primeau and Aldona Satterthwaite for insights into what older women talk about when they get together for lunch.

Marlene Wynnyk and Robert Finch, author of *The Iambics of Newfoundland. Notes from an Unknown Shore*, for introducing me to Newfoundland and its wonderful traditions and language.

All the proficient cooks who have posted on websites their personal recipes for the dishes featured in this story. They are too numerous to name individually, and as their lists of ingredients all vary slightly, I have experimented with the recipes myself and concocted my own version of each dish.

Archivists at the University of Delaware, keepers of some of Beverley Nichols' papers, for their assistance regarding the recipe for Lady Lilford's salad dressing, which appeared in his memoir, *Down the Kitchen Sink.*

In the tech department: Lisa Thatcher and Harry Buller at

R & R Printing in Fergus, Ontario, Canada, for helping me cope with the ever-changing intricacies of Word; Jenny Rhodenizer, my go-to website person; Barrie Murdock who stepped in when my Mac seized up halfway through writing this book. Couldn't have done it without you, guys.

My sister, Susan Day, also Dave Crean, Josephine Felton, Jessica Ing, Penny Maxwell and Sandra Shatilla for regularly asking 'how's the book going?' thus giving me the courage to keep on writing when my enthusiasm was starting to flag.

Finally, the production team at Olympia Publishing for their professionalism in putting this book together.

Other books by Sonia Day

Non-fiction
Incredible Edibles — 43 fun things to grow in the city
The Untamed Garden — A revealing look at our love affair with plants
The Plant Doctor
The Urban Gardener Indoors
The Urban Gardener
Tulips — Facts and folklore about the world's most planted flower

Memoir
Middle-aged Spread: Moving to the country at 50

Fiction
Deer Eyes

Visit soniaday.com